EARLY PRAISE
OF THE DECEASED SCHOLAR

Historical details were woven into the story, bringing the setting and manners alive in my imagination without slowing the pacing.

— NET GALLEY

My goodness, what a joy to read this book!

— GOODREADS

A masterpiece crafted with scientific precision!

— BARNES AND NOBLE

THE ADVENTURE OF THE DECEASED SCHOLAR

The Early Case Files of Sherlock Holmes
Case Three

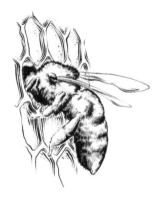

Liese Sherwood-Fabre

978-1-952408-11-3

Little Elm Press, LLC

Copyright © 2020 by Liese Sherwood-Fabre

Library of Congress Control Number: 2020925040

All rights reserved.

No part of this book may be reproduced in any form or by any electronic or mechanical means, including information storage and retrieval systems, without written permission from the author, except for the use of brief quotations in a book review.

Book cover © 2020 by Killion Publishing.

*To Dr. Sally Sugarman, a dedicated scholar, educator, and Sherlockian.
And above of all, my friend.*

CHAPTER ONE

I wrinkled my nose at the Thames' murky waves and shuddered. Anything could be lurking in its fetid waters. Tugging on my collar, I glanced up at the sun's white disk. Despite the day being on the cool side, the crush of people around me blocked any breeze. We'd managed to get spaces right by the stone wall in front of the Old Ship pub. Below us, the incoming tide was rising to cover the river's exposed silt and sand. The Oxford-Cambridge boat race was timed to use the climbing waters to assist the rowers, and those along the route were expecting it to begin at any moment.

The sunlight sparkled off the swells, and, shielding my eyes from the glare, I studied a similar crowd gathered along the opposite bank. No empty space could be seen along that stone wall, either. So many people. All to catch a glimpse of the boat crews as they rowed past.

Rising on my toes, I leaned over the wall, checking

downstream to my left for either boat appearing around the river's bend.

"Quit fidgeting," Mycroft said out of the side of his mouth.

I opened my own to protest, but Mother rebuked him first.

"Really, Mycroft." She fanned herself, although I doubted it did much to cool her. "You can't blame him. If this race doesn't start soon, Sherlock and I are leaving. I'll not have either of us collapsing because of the lack of oxygen in this crowd."

My brother crossed his arms over his chest and gave a little snort. I could almost hear the protests swirling around in his brain. *He* hadn't been the one to decide to come to London for the second part of the season. *Or* suggest we attend the annual Oxford-Cambridge boat race. *Or* insist it was time for him to begin attending some of the season's balls and parties as a country squire's first son. After all, Father had remained at Underbyrne to attend to business affairs for the estate, and we could have too.

Before he could actually express any of these or other sentiments out loud, a far-off shout sent a wave of excited chatter among those surrounding us. Finally, the boat race had begun. Cheers and shouts of encouragement moved up the bank as the boats passed the spectators. Those about us jostled and pushed on all sides, making me feel a little like the flotsam bobbing along in the waters below.

Mycroft bounced on the balls of his feet. While his idea of exercise consisted almost exclusively of strolling between buildings at Oxford—from his rooms to the dining hall, the rented room over a tavern he and some friends used for their Diogenes Society meetings, or to the occasional lecture—I was impressed with both his interest in the race and the exertion he expended in this display of enthusiasm.

"How long before we can see them?" I asked, glancing down the river again.

"The whole race is about twenty minutes," my brother said without taking his eyes from the same spot where I focused. "We're about halfway along the course, so I would estimate eight to ten minutes before they appear."

Ten more minutes of strangers' elbows in my ribs? I wasn't sure anything was worth such torture.

"Excuse me, Mr. Mycroft Holmes?"

The feminine voice made us turn to face a pair of women who had somehow managed to push through the press to our position. They were obviously mother and daughter. Both had the same straight-backed-chin-raised bearing, light brown hair and tipped-up noses. The older woman wore a dark dress that, while fashionable, lacked any flourishes, indicating the final stages of mourning—not yet ready to leave her weeds completely behind. The younger woman, however, wore a pale lavender dress and a jaunty hat on top of a pile of curls.

Mycroft stared at the two, a hesitation broken by my mother's cough. I coughed as well, but to cover my amusement. That these two ladies seemed to know my brother and had shocked him into silence gave me a certain delight. Only the opposite sex ever seemed to ruffle my brother—my mother being, of course, the exception.

At my mother's cue, he appeared to shake himself free of whatever had stunned him and bowed at the waist. "Forgive me," he said when he straightened. "We've only been introduced once, Lady Surminster, Miss Phillips. Allow me to introduce my mother, Violette Holmes, and my brother, Sherlock. This is Lord Surminster's mother and sister."

"Lady Surminster, how wonderful to meet you," Mother said. "You too, Miss Phillips."

The older woman glanced at her daughter before saying, "We recognized you as one of Vernon's classmates and were hoping—"

The younger woman seemed unable to restrain herself. "Vernon is missing." She turned to Mycroft. "Have you seen him?"

My brother pulled back his chin and dropped his mouth open. A second later, he snapped it shut and shook his head vigorously. "I'm afraid I've been here all weekend. With my family."

"But here lies our concern," Lady Surminster said. "He was supposed to meet us here in London as well. We've been in contact with some of his other classmates, and none has reported seeing him since Thursday. We were hoping he might have been staying with a friend."

Mother placed a hand on the other woman's arm. "I'm sure he's simply enjoying the sights of London. He may even be back home by now."

She shook her head and glanced away, as if to avoid us seeing the worry creasing the corners of her eyes. "We would have heard. I insisted a servant find us immediately if he appeared."

Her daughter's mouth drew down, and a line appeared between her eyebrows. "Which is why we came here. We thought he might perhaps be viewing the race. And why we sought you out, Mr. Holmes."

"Mycroft can make some enquiries for you among his classmates. I'm sure we'll have word soon enough."

THE ADVENTURE OF THE DECEASED SCHOLAR

"Our address in town is Saint Abel Lane. Number Seventy-four. Please, if you learn anything, let us know."

"Of course. I would suggest it best to go home and wait. Young men in spring often enjoy kicking up their heels a bit."

Before either could reply, the crowd's shouts had us all turn to watch the first boat pass in front of where we stood.

"That's Oxford. I told you we'd win." Mycroft shifted his gaze in the direction they'd just come. "Cambridge is just now passing the bend."

A bit of pride for Oxford swelled within me. Because my father's plan involved me attending the same university as Mycroft, I already felt a certain affinity for the school. While I still hadn't completed my first year at Eton and, at fourteen, had five years before I would enter university, I couldn't suppress a smug grin at the much-less-enthusiastic cheers flowing through the crowd as the "Light Blues" of Cambridge rowed by.

Another shout downstream followed after the second boat moved on. My breath caught in my throat when I realized the crowd's emotion was different. Instead of cheers, screams punctuated the rumbling. Some rushed in the direction of the noise while others appeared to be moving just as quickly away. One young man wearing Oxford colors ran from the bank, caught sight of Mycroft and waved him over to his side.

My brother actually *jogged* to his classmate and even faster back to us. A rock formed in my stomach. The lack of expression in his face indicated this was no ordinary event, and most likely involved Oxford in some manner.

"Lady Surminster. Miss Phillips," my brother wheezed out upon his return. "There has been an incident. An accident, from what I was told. It has been recommended those of a delicate nature leave the area. I assure you I'll make enquiries and get back to you about Lord Surminster."

The younger woman glanced toward the river and the melee of people. Almost all of the women and children were heading toward the street. She turned to her mother. "Perhaps it would be best," she said. "Come. Let's leave before the crush of people makes it impossible to return home."

After Mycroft's reassurance one more time he would seek out any knowledge of the whereabouts of Lord Surminster, they took their leave.

Once they were gone, Mother turned to Mycroft. "Should I go down to the accident? I know there are most likely doctors in the crowd, but perhaps I can be of assistance."

Mother had participated in medical classes in France, and she tended to most of the family illnesses and injuries. As a result, I trusted her more than those who formally practiced in our village.

She took a few steps in the direction where people were still fleeing or converging, but Mycroft stopped her.

"There's no need, Mother." She arched her eyebrows when she faced him. "The person was drowned. The police have been summoned."

"But Lord Surminster? We might spot him in the crowd."

"Again, not necessary." The flatness in his voice warned of the dire news about to come. The rock in my stomach grew heavier. "The drowning victim was wearing Lord Surminster's suit. The man who waved me over recognized it."

THE ADVENTURE OF THE DECEASED SCHOLAR

"Oh, dear," Mother whispered.

She glanced at the spot where the crowd had gathered and then toward the street where his family had headed. Her fan flew in her hand. With the crowd now dispersed, the air had cooled, but the flush in her cheeks suggested she wasn't experiencing it. My mother wasn't a fainting woman. I'd watched her sew wounds and fight off a murderer. But this news had somehow affected her differently.

The rock in my stomach was now a boulder threatening to pull me down. I checked my brother. The composure he'd displayed with Lord Surminster's family had dissolved, and he now chewed on his lower lip as he studied my mother's pale face.

Without waiting for any direction from either of them, I reached out and cupped her elbow. My movement spurred my brother to do the same on her other side. Together we led her to a small bench nearby. The sight of boot marks on the wooden slats made me grimace, but I decided Mother would forgive us if we soiled the back of her skirt—and it would be preferable to her swooning face-down onto the ground.

Once seated, she continued fanning herself, and her color slowly returned to normal. Mycroft and I simply stood there, shifting on our feet and watching her like a pair of oafs. I didn't know what affected me more, the weakness she displayed, or my inability to provide any words of comfort.

After a few minutes, she gazed up at us, and a small smile graced her lips. "Please, close your mouths and quit staring at me as if I were some sort of newly discovered specimen for your father's insect collection."

She twisted about on the bench, checking around her,

and then popped up. "We must get to Surminster's house immediately. Before the police arrive."

Mycroft's teeth recaptured his lower lip. "Mother, we barely know them. Why do you want—"

"I'll explain in the carriage."

She was off in the direction of our hired transport, and all we could do was keep up the frantic pace she now exhibited. My concern over Mother's state of mind grew as we continued to the street. We had just met the two women. Calling on them at this time seemed to overstep the bounds of social protocol.

Only when we'd settled into the landau's seats did any of us have the breath to speak, and Mycroft gave words to my worries. "Surely you can't be serious about calling on Surminster's family now? What compels you to think they would welcome us?"

"I know we were just introduced, but when I learned the drowned man might be Lord Surminster, I had—I can't call it a premonition as I don't believe in such things—but an overwhelming fear—as if it were one of you who was injured. You saw how deeply the mere thought affected me. Imagine if it were true. How much more shattering it would be. The news they are about to receive requires both a sympathetic ear and possibly someone who knows how to mix a sedative."

She steadied her gaze upon Mycroft, a tool more effective than words. I recognized that stare—a simple survey from feet to head carrying as much a dressing down as any verbal rebuke. I felt for my brother. The unease it created made him run his hand through his hair.

In the end, he made a simple concession. "Glad they gave us the address."

THE ADVENTURE OF THE DECEASED SCHOLAR

With most spectators now leaving at the same time, the trip to Surminster's home crawled along. Several police wagons raced between the carriages toward the river. The presence of more than one surprised me. How many were needed for a single body?

Before I had a chance to speculate, another thought occurred to me. I turned to my brother. "How well did you know Lord Surminster?"

He raised and lowered his shoulders. "I'm not sure what you mean by 'know.' We are—were—in the same college. Have—had—the same tutor. But I would hardly call him more than an acquaintance."

My experience suggested Mycroft truly had only acquaintances. Growing up in the country, we weren't around many others our own age. And at Eton, Mycroft had gravitated toward a select group of boys who spent their time studying and reading—his Diogenes Society. Social discourse was not his forte, and it showed in his reluctance to attend the dances and other gatherings Mother insisted were part of his duties as a squire's eldest son.

This gave rise to another question.

"Wasn't Lord Surminster a member of your Diogenes Society?"

The glare he gave me suggested he wasn't pleased with my mentioning the group. I understood why in the next moment.

"What's this society?" Mother asked.

He shifted in his seat. While I hardly considered it a secret—after all, most of the boys at Eton were aware of it, and I'd even been invited to join—he must have viewed it as something not to be shared with women—or perhaps mothers.

"Merely a fellowship of like-minded students who prefer strict quiet to pursue their studies or reading. I started it with another five students because we found the noise and horseplay of most of the fellows at Eton less than conducive to serious study. Over time, it grew. Still exists, according to Sherlock. When some of us went on to Oxford, we kept it up. I understand others started one at Cambridge as well."

"So, nothing untoward?"

I snorted. "Only if boring is 'untoward.' Seriously, the whole atmosphere is absolutely stifling. You can be dismissed by simply shuffling papers too loudly."

"Gets on some people's nerves, you know." Mycroft snapped his sleeves over his cuffs. "Studying and reading. That's all it is."

"And Lord Surminster was a member?"

"Yes. But I hadn't seen him in the last week."

"But he'd been to tutoring?"

"Can't say."

"I wonder if we could determine where he was seen last," she said, mostly to herself.

My brother faced her. "Mother, this is not our concern. He is—was—nobility. Father has no legal standing here. And no county constable like Gibbons has come to investigate."

"I suppose you're right," she said with a sigh.

While I had observed this exchange in silence, I supported her interest. We'd successfully solved more than one murder at Underbyrne, our family estate, and I was certain she was as eager as I to apply the logical approach we'd used on yet another case. All the same, Mycroft was right as well. We were talking about a late earl. In London. Far outside our social circles.

Simply driving to Surminster's home was enough to show how much above us they were. We left the cramped quarters of the buildings near the river for much broader avenues with houses set back from the road, fenced-in and secure. Lawns, only just beginning to turn green, stretched toward the three-to-four-story buildings, all with wings sprawling out from a central entrance. Trees lined the pathway to the front entrance and blocked from sight the movements of those inside, despite tall windows spaced evenly across each floor.

And Surminster's was no different.

When the carriage slowed and turned toward one particular structure, I leaned out to get a better glimpse of it. At first, I thought the ladies had arrived only moments before us because the gate stood open. Perhaps a servant simply had not yet arrived to close it? Then I noticed a small carriage standing near the portico over the front entrance.

I sat back inside. "I'm afraid we may be too late. The police are already here."

"All the more reason they may need a familiar face—even if it's not a well-known one," she said.

The butler who received us took Mother's calling card and then stepped back to allow us to stand just inside the foyer. While the Devonys' manor back in our village was larger, Lord Surminster's London home far surpassed it in opulence.

The ceiling where we stood reached all the way to the third floor. A grand staircase hugged the wall to our left, then curved along the back wall to open on the right side, creating a gallery in front of the rooms on the second floor. Landscape and portrait paintings covered the walls along the staircase. Despite the cavernous space, a plush blue carpet covered the first floor as well as the stairs and muffled any footsteps.

The butler returned almost immediately and asked us to follow him. A police officer stood with his back to us while he studied a portrait of a much younger Lady Surminster over the mantel.

Mother cleared her throat, and the man turned to face her. He held his helmet over his chest as if to put some barrier between him and the rest of the world.

"Lady Surminster?"

"No, I'm sorry. Mrs. Holmes. And my sons, Mycroft and Sherlock. We're…family friends of Lady Surminster."

Before the man could ask more, the two women entered the room, their faces marked by the strain of Lord Surminster's disappearance. Creases outlined their down-turned mouths. Miss Phillips assisted the older woman to a settee near the fireplace.

"You have news of my son, Officer…?"

"Johnson, ma'am." He shifted on his feet, and I had the distinct impression he hoped to make a hasty retreat once he delivered his message. "Beggin' your pardon, your ladyship, but I have some bad news."

Both women blinked at the man as their faces paled. Miss Phillips grasped her mother's hand.

He pulled on his collar as if it had blocked the words in his throat. "He was found a little while ago. On the shore of the Thames. Appears to have washed up there when the boats passed."

"You mean…the noise during the race…?" Miss Phillips turned to Mycroft. "You knew? You sent us away?"

The venom dripping from the young woman's question made me want to defend his action. Our father had

THE ADVENTURE OF THE DECEASED SCHOLAR

impressed upon us the need to protect the fairer sex because of their more delicate nature. Now, he was being condemned for having done so. Only social convention kept me from responding to her accusation. Nothing, however, constrained my mother from doing so.

"He had only been told of an unfortunate accident. We didn't learn of the identity until later. We had no idea the police would have known where to go until we got here."

The officer found his voice again, and with head lowered, as if unable to meet their gaze, said, "We found some of his calling cards in the breast pocket of his jacket. That's how we knew where he lived. Of course, we'll need someone to come down and identify the—identify him."

"To the police station? I'm not sure…"

"Actually, ma'am, he's at a hospital. They took him there in case he—they took him there."

"I…we…can't," Lady Surminster said, shaking her head.

"We'll go," Mother said, drawing stares from all the others, including Mycroft and me. She raised her chin. "We are more than familiar with such proceedings. My husband is a justice of the peace. My son was a classmate of Lord Surminster."

Lady Surminster's features relaxed, the lines on her face fading. "Would you? I-I'm not sure I could—"

Mother raised her hand. "I understand. If you will permit, perhaps someone from your staff who also knows Lord Surminster could confirm our identification?"

"Yes. Yes. A good idea." Lady Surminster focused on the butler standing behind Mother. "Hamilton, would you mind accompanying them?"

If the request seemed odd, his response gave no indication. He merely bowed and said, "Yes. Of course, Your Ladyship," as if someone asking him to identify a dead man was a matter of routine.

"I'll give you the address," the bobby said to Hamilton and followed him from the room.

"Vernon? Gone?" Lady Surminster whispered in a harsh voice to no one in particular. Her lips quivered, and tears spilled down her cheeks. Her daughter put a steadying arm about her mother's shoulder, and the woman leaned into her.

Mother stepped to their side. "Lady Surminster, Miss Phillips, please let me express our deepest sympathies and let us know if there is anything you need."

After a stony glance from our mother, Mycroft spoke up as well. "Lord Surminster was a good man. Studious. Conscientious. He will be missed."

Lady Surminster seemed unable to respond, but the younger woman glanced up and said, "Thank you."

"We'll find Hamilton and be on our way," Mother said.

As I turned to leave, I considered Mother's reaction when she learned of Lord Surminster's death. The brief display of a raw pain for someone she barely knew gave me an insight into the anguish Lady Surminster was experiencing at the moment. I imagined the sort of grief I would feel if it were my brother…or mother. Unfortunately, I wasn't sure how to express what I was feeling. After all, their social position limited any intimate interaction with them.

In the end, at the drawing room's doorway, I turned and said, "Sorry for your loss."

Wholly inadequate, but the only words I could find.

THE ADVENTURE OF THE DECEASED SCHOLAR

AT THE HOSPITAL, we were led down a flight of stairs to a brick-lined basement where the sun's light and warmth never reached. Given the coolness of the day, this area proved chilly and damp. Pushing open one door, the officer indicated we should enter into a rather large room lit by oil lamps hanging from the soot-covered ceiling. Before us stretched a row of ten wheeled tables, a sheet-draped form on each. A cold shiver ran down my spine as I considered that only the day—or perhaps hours—before these had been breathing persons, now left to be viewed, examined, and, at some point soon, interred.

Despite those on the tables most likely being recently deceased, the room still held the stench of decaying flesh mixed with moldy dampness. The odor forced the other three men and me to cover our noses as we entered, but Mother seemed unaffected. Then again, she'd observed more than one autopsy when she had audited medical classes in France. I wondered if this brought back memories for her.

The police officer whispered to an attendant in the room and then led us to the third table. Once we were assembled, the attendant glanced at us before lifting the sheet to uncover the face. With several murders having occurred on or about our home, I'd seen several dead or injured persons, but I drew in my breath at the sight of this particular corpse. Mud plastered his hair to the scalp. The mouth gaped open, revealing some missing teeth. The silt on his neck had dried in rivulets, accentuating a much older, wrinkled skin—not the smooth neck of a young man.

While I'd never actually met my brother's classmate, even I could tell this wasn't the missing earl. I checked my mother's expression to confirm my own observations. She caught my eye over the man's chest and gave a little shake of her head.

Before either of us could voice our opinion, Hamilton spoke up. "That's not his lordship."

The officer dropped the sheet and stared at the butler. "Are you certain?"

"I believe I'd know someone I've been around since he was a boy."

"He's right," Mycroft said. The officer turned his attention to my brother. "Definitely not Lord Surminster. I don't know who this is, but I've never seen him before."

"A thief, most likely," Mother said, lifting up the sheet to uncover more of the man and his muddy clothes. "Do you recognize the suit, Hamilton?"

The man took half a step forward and gave a quick glance at the man's well-cut trousers and waistcoat.

"Yes, I believe those do belong to his lordship."

"I'm surprised, Officer, you didn't notice this yourself. The clothes are well-made, but do not fit the individual as they should." She grabbed the man's pant waist and tugged. "These were made for a heavier man. And the shoes," she pointed at his feet, "are worn—not at all what would accompany a man of wealth."

"If he's not Lord Surminster, who is he?" the officer asked.

Mother dropped the sheet back over the corpse. "I haven't a clue. Have you checked his pockets—beyond the calling cards you said you found? Perhaps there's a clue there? Or contact the hospitals in case someone's been enquiring for a missing relative? You asked us here to identify this person. And I think we can all agree this man is not his lordship."

THE ADVENTURE OF THE DECEASED SCHOLAR

Before the officer could express any frustrations with my mother's attitude, a group of well-dressed men followed another man, top hat in hand, to a corpse three tables down from where we stood. A chill, unrelated to the room, went through me. I recognized a coroner's jury from my mother's own experience with having been accused of murder. These men were viewing the body—the first step in an inquest to determine the cause of death.

"A most interesting case," the leader said, directing the others to gather around while he uncovered the face. "More than one effort to kill himself. Identity as yet unknown."

Beside me, the butler sucked in his breath.

My brother turned to see the origin of Hamilton's shock. "Good God," he whispered. "Lord Surminster."

The coroner pointed to a noose still encircling the man's neck. "As you can see, he most likely had some difficulty with the rope. It apparently broke, but rather than try again, he decided to drown himself. Rocks were found in the pockets of his jacket and pants—sufficient to hold him just under the water's surface and drown him, but not enough to keep him from floating to the surface. In the case of a murder, better effort would have been made to sink the victim completely. And most incriminating is this." He pulled something from the man's pocket. "While the woman in the picture has yet to be identified, her pose and, er, dress, hardly suggest a virtuous lady. That her face is scratched with an 'X' suggests some falling out between the two, leading to his decision to take his life—one way or another."

The men in the jury frowned and murmured among themselves, their disapproval of Lord Surminster's demise clearly colored in the hard tones they uttered under their breath.

The butler's shout echoed through the chamber. "No!"

In a flash, Hamilton rushed to the table where the men were gathered. His outburst took us by surprise, and by the time my brother, the officer, and I reached him, he was nose-to-nose with the coroner. The butler's cheeks were now a deep scarlet, and he puffed onto the other man's face, reminding me of a bull about to charge.

"I have known this man since he was a boy in leading strings. He had no reason to-to…do this to himself."

The members of the jury stared slack-jawed at the confrontation playing out in front of them. I supposed even in London, such a spectacle was rare for this portion of an inquest.

Mycroft pulled on Hamilton's arm to make some room between the two men. "Please excuse us, sir. It was a shock to discover the deceased in such a manner."

"You know him?" The coroner's gaze shifted between my brother and Hamilton.

Before either my brother or I could answer, the butler spoke up again. "Didn't I just say so? From the time he was a babe still in Lady Surminster's arms."

"Lady Surminster?"

"Yes," Mycroft said before Hamilton. "This is her son, Lord Surminster."

The coroner pulled back his chin at this statement but recovered a moment later. "I had—I mean—there was no identity—"

"You have his identity now," Hamilton said, straightening his spine. "I'll make arrangements for retrieving the… Lord Surminster."

During this discussion, I realized Mother hadn't joined us. I glanced over my shoulder and noticed she'd slipped back the sheet on the other man and was riffling through his pockets. To keep her subterfuge a secret, I turned my back to her and observed the confrontation before me.

"Now just a moment," the coroner said, puffing out his chest and addressing the butler. "As coroner, only I can say when he may be removed. Following this viewing by the jury, there will be an inquest—"

"But there's no need to keep the…Lord Surminster for the inquest," Mother said, stepping up behind me.

Somehow, the coroner managed to pull himself even straighter. "Who are you?"

"A family friend. My husband is a justice of the peace, and I've attended more than my share of inquests. Surely you'll be able to allow the family to bury him shortly?"

"There are some…extenuating circumstances in this particular case." He glanced at the jurymen who were observing the discussion more than they were the corpse. "Gentlemen, any questions or observations you wish to share at the moment?"

Twelve stony faces moved back and forth in response.

"I believe you can all agree with my preliminary conclusion of death by suicide."

"What? No," the butler shouted again.

Mycroft and I tightened our grip on the older man's forearms. I feared he might actually take a swing at the Crown's man, bringing even more problems to the family.

"We will be hearing from witnesses. Perhaps you can share your views then, but an outburst like this doesn't support a reversal of my preliminary assessment."

Mother stepped between the two and faced the butler. "Please, Hamilton, I will speak to her ladyship and Miss

Phillips. I'm sure we can show this decision is misplaced in this case."

The coroner snorted. "And what makes you think you know this?"

Mother spun about to face the man. "Being familiar with the means of death and the victim." She pointed to the corpse's neck. "You say the rope broke. Look at the end. It was cut. My guess is that it was fashioned into a knot and placed around his neck to make it appear as if he tried to hang himself. As for the stones in the pockets, that is not his jacket. He attended Oxford. Those are Cambridge colors. He would never put on such an item. Even in jest. Someone else dressed him and put the stones in the pocket. And the owner of the jacket is most likely the one who can identify the woman in the photo."

Several jurymen stepped closer to confirm my mother's statement. A few pointed at the rope and nodded. I took a deep breath as they recognized my mother's careful study was correct.

The coroner, on the other hand, lifted one side of his mouth in a sneer, and his gaze traveled from the top of her hat to her shoes. A sudden impulse to release Hamilton and let him have a go at the man swept over me. "Well, Mrs. Justice of the Peace, I appreciate your observation. It will be entered into the record."

"Lord Surminster's clothes, identified by this man who has been in his service for years, are on the man over there." She pointed to the other body. "You may wish to record the following. While water in the lungs is a common occurrence in drownings, he might have been drugged and then dumped into the water. This can be confirmed by checking the stomach contents. Also, there appears to be some strange residue in his ear."

As she spoke, the coroner's face deepened to a dull burgundy—from anger or embarrassment, I wasn't sure—but before he could get past sputtering a few words such as "impudent," and "of all the—" she turned back to us and said, "I believe we need to return to Lady Surminster now."

During her speech, Hamilton had relaxed in our grip, and my brother and I released him. He now bowed to her and said, "Yes, ma'am. Of course, ma'am."

She turned one last time to the men gathered around the remains of poor Lord Surminster and dipped her head. "Gentlemen. I bid you good day."

Several of them bent at the waist. Others touched their heads as if they were tipping an invisible hat, and we all followed my mother from the room.

In the hallway, Mother whispered harshly to my brother and me, "I had hoped this would be the end of our duties, but I'm afraid we must get involved."

"Mother," Mycroft whispered back, frustration sharpening his words into a hiss. "It isn't our place."

Hamilton turned around and asked, "Excuse me, madam. Is there a problem?"

She straightened her spine and composed her face. "No. No problem. We were discussing whether we might dine out tonight."

She quick-stepped toward the exit, we three men in tow. But my stomach remained uneasy, and not from the stench of death still lodged in my nostrils. I agreed with my brother that our involvement might not be appreciated. So, what had convinced Mother such interference in the investigation of Lord Surminster's death was necessary?

CHAPTER TWO

The carriage ride back from the hospital was oppressive. I felt for Hamilton. How was he ever to explain to Lady Surminster about the coroner's preliminary decision? As devastating as his death was to his mother, being considered to have taken his own life would prove to be a much greater shock. Perhaps more than she could handle.

Of course, Hamilton had fought with the coroner over his conclusion. During my brief time at Eton, one student had died following a mishap that some rumored wasn't accidental. According to what others whispered in the halls, toward the end of his final year, the young man had received word of two crushing events. Oxford had refused his admission, and Cambridge—not interested in Oxford's rejects—had also denied him. Beyond that, a girl many assumed he would marry when he came of age announced her betrothal to his older brother. During a visit to town, a carriage ran him over. Witnesses didn't agree on whether he

THE ADVENTURE OF THE DECEASED SCHOLAR

fell or stepped in front of the carriage intentionally. Not knowing the student, I withheld judgment, but did attend the memorial at the school's chapel.

Glancing at Mycroft, I wondered if he knew of any similar events in Lord Surminster's recent past that might have led to such a decision.

Mother broke into my thoughts by addressing the family butler, giving voice to some of what had been swirling around in my head. "Excuse me, Hamilton, I know what you said to the coroner at the hospital. But I wondered if you were aware of any events that might have caused him to become despondent?"

The butler jerked as if awakened and shook his head violently. "No. Of course, his father's death a few years ago was difficult for him. Hard for the whole family, actually, but he bounced back. Returned to his studies. Appeared to be looking forward to his future."

"No idea of the young woman in the photo? One who might have caused him heartache?" When he responded negatively, she asked, "And the man wearing his clothes? Did you know him?"

Another shake of his head. "He hardly appeared to be someone who would associate with his lordship."

She shifted her gaze to my brother. "And you? Anything about Lord Surminster or the man wearing his clothes you could share?"

Mycroft frowned and, after a pause, shook his head as well. "Other than he was reading for the law, same as I."

The manservant winced and spoke up again. "You seem to know about these things. Could you tell what he...died of? I'm certain Lady Surminster will be asking."

"Unfortunately, I was not able to examine him closely.

Perhaps the inquest will shed some light. He'd been in the water. He might have drowned."

"How am I going to tell Her Ladyship?" Hamilton asked with a shake of his head. "She'll have so many questions I have no answer to."

"If you wish, we can report back to her. Does she have any family? A sister or brother? She and Miss Phillips should have family with them at a time like this."

"I'll talk to the housekeeper about sending for someone. I believe there's an old family friend in town. Thank you for the suggestion." He checked out the window. "As for telling her, I'd appreciate it if you could be nearby."

"My mother has a great deal of knowledge regarding teas and other herbs to help calm her," I said.

They all turned to me. I shifted in my seat under their attention. My place as the youngest and still underage was to "be seen and not heard," or preferably "not seen or heard," but I felt compelled to ensure Lady Surminster and her daughter were cared for. From Hamilton's reference to the previous Lord Surminster, he hadn't been gone all that long ago either. Two blows so close together would make the loss even deeper.

The butler dipped his head. "Thank you for the information. I'll have the housekeeper send for the family physician. I'm sure he'll be able to suggest something."

Mother said nothing, but the way her lips formed a straight line messaged her disdain for most physicians—even one in London. She had many times recited their vices of the overuse of laudanum and bleeding and failure to clean properly—customs, I was certain, of even some of the best physicians available.

When we arrived at the Surminster manor, Hamilton

directed us to the drawing room and then went in search of the housekeeper. We arranged ourselves by the seats but remained standing. I glanced about the room, marveling at the opulence. The fireplace was large enough for me to stand in with my arms outstretched. The oriental carpets were a deep blue and matched the draperies on the windows overlooking the street. The furniture was also a brocaded blue. Several small tables were scattered about the room, each with its own item—a lamp, a statue, or other decoration. Despite the elegance and wealth on display, the room lacked the warmth and coziness of our own parlor at Underbyrne. Or was it because it was not my own home?

A sigh slipped through my lips. I glanced about, but no one appeared to have heard it. Perhaps they were too buried in their own thoughts. I hadn't been home since I left for Eton after Christmas. The longing for familiar surroundings I had been able to suppress while at school rushed over me. Had I been alone or had Lady Surminster and Miss Phillips not entered at precisely that moment, I might have been overcome by melancholy.

The ladies barely stepped into the room, leaving just enough space for Hamilton to close the door behind them. The widow straightened her back. "Well? Was it…Vernon?"

"I'm afraid I have bad news," Mother said. The older woman whimpered, and her daughter placed an arm around her shoulder. "Lord Surminster was found on the shore of the Thames. The coroner had just arrived to view the—to begin his inquest. I'm sure he'll share his decision with you as soon as he has one."

Lady Surminster sobbed into her daughter's shoulder. Despite her own tears, the younger woman managed to choke out her thanks. "I appreciate you taking on this burden. Your kindness will not be forgotten."

"Of course. If you have need of us, please don't hesitate to call. I believe your physician and a family friend have been summoned, Lady Surminster. If you wish, we can stay until someone arrives."

The woman shook her head without lifting it from the girl's shoulder.

The butler must have been standing by the door because he opened it to let us out and the doctor in.

The carriage ride back to our London house was as silent as it had been from the hospital. My brother closed his eyes and rested his head against the seatback. My own thoughts spun around in my mind, preventing me from doing likewise. While a part of me was glad we'd left without further obligations, I was also frustrated that so many questions remained unanswered.

My turmoil increased when I glanced out the window and realized we were not heading home.

"Where are we going?" I asked.

Mycroft opened his eyes and sat up to check out the window. "What are we doing in Bloomsbury?"

"We're going to the British Museum," Mother said in the same tone of voice as if she'd announced we were having beef for dinner. "The Reading Room, actually."

My heart skipped a beat as I understood what was happening. I faced her, knowing she had more to share.

"You found something, didn't you?" I asked. "When Hamilton was making all that fuss with the coroner, you searched the other man's suit pockets."

"The police, coroner, *and* jury obviously weren't interested in what had truly happened to Lord Surminster. So, I

THE ADVENTURE OF THE DECEASED SCHOLAR

didn't see the harm in checking for any indication of where he'd been before he died. His murder is completely apparent—as plain as the nose on your face. Just because a woman pointed it out, they are all going to dismiss it and with dire consequences for his family."

While I considered the shame and scandal associated with someone taking his own life, I didn't see these as dire as she was suggesting. "I know he can't be buried in the churchyard, but—"

"She's referring to their finances, you fool. When someone commits suicide, their assets are returned to the Crown. Supposed to keep them from considering it because they would leave their family penniless."

I stared at my brother. "You mean Lady Surminster and Miss Phillips would—"

"Keep nothing," Mother said with a shake of her head. "Unless Lady Surminster has some funds or property of her own, she'll need a relative to take her in. And the girl's marriage chances...."

She let her voice trail off, and I sat back as I considered the prospects awaiting Lord Surminster's family. Grim, indeed. Between losing their fortune and the stigma of suicide on the family name, any marriage prospects the younger woman might have attracted could be scared away.

Mycroft broke into my thoughts with a question to my mother. "So, what did you find?"

Whether out of a sense of duty for his friend's family, or more likely his own curiosity, I didn't know, but he was as intrigued as I.

She opened her reticule and pulled out a damp paper. "This is a request slip from the Reading Room. It certainly didn't belong to the man who was wearing the suit."

He took the paper and studied it for a moment before handing it back. "Definitely from the Reading Room, but how did you know?"

"Because I'm a member."

While that bit of information made me stare a little slack-jawed at her, my brother remained at least outwardly unimpressed. Instead, he raised one eyebrow and asked, "You found more, didn't you?"

"And I thought you weren't looking."

She pulled two more pieces of paper from her bag and placed them on the seat between the two of them. I reached across and picked up one. Although as damp as the one from the Reading Room, the writing was still legible. "A ticket to the opera in Covent Garden. For"—I studied the smeared printing—"the night he died. But he wasn't dressed for the opera."

"It wasn't until later in the evening. Plenty of time after the library closes for him to go home and change," Mother said. "More importantly, a man with a ticket to the opera certainly doesn't seem to be suicidal."

Mycroft studied the other paper on the seat. "I'm not sure what to make of this."

Unlike the ticket, the paper wasn't complete. Rather, it appeared to be the torn-off corner of another document and contained a hand-drawn image—an elongated circle with a sort of crown on top.

"I'm not certain either," she said. "Possibly some sort of symbol. It could be a thistle, which would point to Scotland, but I have no inkling of how it relates to Lord Surminster."

While I turned over the image from the torn corner in my head, I glanced out the window for a better view of our destination—a structure that never failed to impress me.

THE ADVENTURE OF THE DECEASED SCHOLAR

The British Museum's central entrance resembled the drawings I'd seen of ancient Greek temples with a figure-filled pediment supported by Corinthian columns. Two wings, also with Corinthian columns, came forward from the central building to create a squared "U." A tall wrought-iron fence stretched along the street, allowing limited entrance onto the grounds.

Mycroft helped our mother step from the carriage, then she faced us. "The trick is to act as if you know exactly what you're doing. Mycroft, I know you've been here. Sherlock, hold yourself tall. Children aren't permitted in the Reading Room, but I'm certain I can have them make an exception for you. We must hurry. It closes at four."

We stepped through the front gate and up the steps to the main entrance. We all nodded and smiled at the guard at the door, who asked, "Readers?"

Continuing on past the glass exhibit cases with indifference, Mother marched through the cavernous facility with total familiarity. Her assured confidence reminded me I still had much to learn of her life prior to marrying my father.

A man blocked our progress at the door to the museum's library. "Children are not permitted."

"He is my son. I know he appears young, but he just hasn't gotten his growth spurt yet. I will vouch for his behavior." The man raised one eyebrow but didn't move. "Let me share two letters from my uncle and grandfather I used as part of my original application."

She passed two yellowed parchments to the guard. While my French relations' paintings adorned both our townhouse and Underbyrne, Mother's ancestry was not something my parents ever used for self-aggrandizement. Father would have considered it unseemly to flaunt one's pedigree. Mother cared more about her own accomplishments than any accident of birth. All the same, it was nice to know my ancestors' well-known reputation could open doors—even at the British Museum.

The man took the papers, raising one side of his mouth in disdain. It dropped back into place, and then his whole mouth fell open as the impact of the authors hit him. After a moment, he stepped aside and pushed the door open for her. "Enjoy your time here."

"Yes. Thank you."

Once inside, I just barely caught Mycroft's whisper. "Do you always carry those letters?"

"Of course not," she said, as she continued toward a huge circular table at the center of the room. "After the race, I had hoped to visit the library to review the most recent medical journals and thought they might come in handy to gain entrance. It appears I was correct."

My brother's *harrumph* was directed at her back because she had picked up her pace toward the central desk, where readers consulted heavy volumes lining its perimeter. After reviewing these bound catalogues, patrons then wrote on a slip of paper, not unlike the one Mother had found in the dead man's pocket, and handed it to one of the librarians behind the desk. Radiating from this central point were reading desks assembled like spokes on a wheel. Men pushing carts of books moved among them, stopping to provide patrons with their requests. All the activity going on about me reminded me of our beehives at Underbyrne.

Despite Mother's haste, I couldn't help but pause to take in the room, which was not easy, given its dimensions. The ceiling was formed by a tremendous dome reaching several stories into the air. Bookshelves covered the walls of the round room, and I glanced with envy at those who were perusing the spines, taking one or another book out to study the pages. I longed to join them in such a pursuit but knew now was not the time to do so.

By the time I reached her side, Mother had copied the information from the slip she'd retrieved from the dead man's pocket. The new request in hand, she studied the assistants scurrying to and fro. After several moments, her eyes rounded, and a smile spread across her face. She rushed toward one.

"Mr. Donaldson, how good to see you again," Mother said when she reached him with us just a few steps behind her.

The man, shuffling through a stack of slips, raised his gaze to her, and a smile similar to her own graced his mustachioed face. "Miss Parker, how long has it been?"

She had taken a breath to say something but paused before responding. "Oh, my, it's been so long since I was referred to as 'Miss' or 'Parker.' More than twenty years. Mr. Donaldson, you make me feel like a young girl again. It's Mrs. Holmes now."

"And these are your sons?" When I nodded, he winked at me. "Ask her about the anatomy room. She was very much the scholar back then."

I tucked that question away for later because her current interest lay in another line of enquiry, which I supported wholeheartedly.

"You dear man. You always knew how to flatter me," she said with a laugh. For a moment, I could hear the younger version of my mother and saw how she must have charmed the man back then. "I need to see this item as soon as possible. Closing time is approaching and—"

He held out his hand. "I'll get it straight away. Just have a seat."

When Mr. Donaldson approached the two desks we'd taken during our wait, his expression made me glance at Mother and Mycroft as creases appeared on their foreheads. Whatever he was about to share was not good news.

"Mrs. Holmes," he said, speaking at a rapid clip. "This is terrible. Just terrible. I located the requested folio and opened it to check it was the correct item. And…oh, dear."

We all stood, and she waved her hand at Mycroft, instructing him to force the man into a seat. He had paled, and I wasn't certain he wouldn't swoon if left standing.

"What did you find, Mr. Donaldson?" Her voice was soothing and without any of the anxiety I was certain she felt.

"Ripped. It was ripped," he answered in a wheezy voice.

"You mean a corner?" Mycroft asked.

I glanced at him. Was he thinking about the small piece Mother had found with the strange symbol?

"No. Almost the complete page. Gone. We're supposed to check when the item is returned, but somehow…. Such destruction. The last requester will have his membership revoked. And the assistant who received it will most certainly lose his position. Thank goodness, it wasn't me."

My throat tightened at the mention of punishing Lord Surminster for his destruction of the manuscript. I could see him once again, lying on the table, the rope around his neck, and the jurymen studying him as if he were some sort of oddity at a fair. If given the choice, I was certain the man would have preferred banishment to his current condition.

Mother spoke, bringing us all back to the issue at hand.

"Might we see the actual folio? There still might be something we can glean from the document."

The man pulled his face from his hands to stare at her. His chin quivered, making his words come out in a slight stutter. "I-I suppose it's possible. I was so stunned. State of shock, I guess. I put it back on the shelf. I don't know why."

"We'll follow you," she said, pulling the man to his feet. "So you don't have to bring it here. We might even have an idea of what happened to it."

"Yes. Yes. I suppose you can take a peek at it. Of course, I'll have to report this to my superiors afterward. We'll have to hurry. The room will be closing shortly."

I checked the time as we trailed after Mr. Donaldson. Already half-past three. When my brother glanced at the clock over the central desk, I heard his stomach rumble. Without a doubt, he would insist on seeking a café or other place to eat as soon as we left. He adhered to a rather strict meal schedule, and our trips to visit Lady Surminster, the hospital, and now here had certainly side-railed his timetable.

The librarian brought out a flat, leather case and placed it on the nearest empty desk. After checking over his shoulder, he opened it. The case contained a number of very old parchments. All maps. The one on top had been folded—not flat like all the others. He turned it over and spread out the part underneath. A jagged edge marked where the rest of the map should have been.

She ran her finger along the broken border. "It must have been done in a hurry. All the desks here have a penknife. Using one would have been more efficient and might not have been as obvious to the staff as this type of destruction."

"What can you tell us about this particular item?" my brother asked.

The man stared at Mycroft as if unable to comprehend the question. Only when he repeated it did the librarian nod his head. He pointed to the brown volumes by the central desk.

"With the number of the item, you will be able to find the description provided when it was entered into the folio and library." He slapped the case shut and tucked it under his arm. "Now, I must share this with my supervisor."

She held out her hand. "Thank you, Mr. Donaldson. You have been most helpful. I hope to see you again soon."

"Soon. Yes. Soon," the man said.

Following a bow and mumbled "good-bye," he left us to search for the appropriate record ourselves.

Mother seemed to have practice in searching for such information because after a quick scan of the volumes by the center desk, she pulled one from a shelf and flipped through the pages until she found the one desired.

Mycroft and I followed her finger as it traveled down the lines, finally stopping about three-quarters down the page.

"Historical maps of Wrightminster," I read aloud. "But he was the Earl of Surminster, correct?"

Mycroft gave a noncommittal grunt. He was focused on the listing of the contents. After a moment, he said slowly, "I didn't see all the maps, but I do recall what was written on the torn one. In particular, "Wright—"

At times, my brother's eidetic memory had proved useful, the present instant being one.

"Minster?" I asked.

He rolled his eyes toward the ceiling. "No, 'Wrightmoor.'"

"Wrightmoor," I read the line he indicated with his finger. "'Boundaries of St. Indre convent. 1534.'"

Mother tapped her finger against her lips. "After the reign of Henry VIII. You don't suppose—?"

"That the Crown claimed the convent after 1534? And gave it to some nobleman? Highly probable," Mycroft said. "But why would Lord Surminster be interested in the map of another's estate?"

"Why don't we ask Lord Surminster's family?" I asked.

The other two stared at me so intently, I felt the heat rise to my cheeks. Before either could respond to the suggestion, the librarians signaled the close of the collection for the day and directed us—along with all the others—toward the exit.

Once outside the Reading Room, Mother faced us. "Sherry dear, I believe you're right. We must return to see Lady Surminster."

"Now?" Mycroft asked.

Tilting her head, she mulled over his one-word accusation. With a nod, she said, "You're right as well, dear. We can't go there now."

I covered my mouth to hide the smile appearing by itself as my brother's shoulders slumped with relief. A moment later, however, we both tensed when she announced our next destination.

"We need to go back to the hospital."

With her intention made clear, she strode toward the museum's main entrance without glancing back to ensure we were in step.

Once in the carriage, Mycroft plopped onto the seat with such force, the whole assemblage rocked. "What's stopping us from at least having tea beforehand?"

"Really, son, you've been there. An empty stomach serves you much better than a full one."

He crossed his arms and stared out the window with an expression of longing so obvious, I had to check what he'd seen. We were passing a tavern, and my stomach rumbled at the mere sight of the establishment. All the same, my mother had the more important point. A full stomach would have made a much greater protest where we were going.

As we approached the hospital, Mycroft spoke for the first time. "I should go in alone." When she opened her mouth to speak, he raised his hand. "At least at first. Last time, the police officer accompanied us. The attendant might not feel the need to allow us the same liberties this time."

Another head tilt before a nod. "Please try and get us in to examine both men."

While we waited for my brother to return, her stomach gave a loud grumble. I stared at her, and we both laughed.

"Don't tell your brother," she said when she had calmed. "I'll never hear the end of it."

A moment later, we heard footsteps and glanced out to see my brother returning. He spoke to the driver and then climbed back into the carriage.

"Where are we going?" I asked.

He met my gaze. "Home."

"Oh, dear." Mother pursed her lips. "They wouldn't allow us back in?"

"I suppose they might have. But there was no use. Neither Lord Surminster nor the man in his suit is there anymore."

CHAPTER THREE

We bounced along the city street in silence. Mother and I rode forward while Mycroft took the seat opposite. Upon making his pronouncement, he'd leaned back, closed his eyes, and crossed his arms. I couldn't be sure he was asleep, but he made it clear he wasn't interested in any more delay in returning home for a late tea.

Mother stared out the window, but her steady, vacant gaze made clear her thoughts were not on the scenes passing by.

She finally turned her attention back to my brother. "Did the attendant tell you what happened to the bodies? Perhaps they took Lord Surminster to his home? I need to examine—"

He squinted at her. "You are not going to examine anything. We have done what we agreed to do—identify the body. I even followed along as we sought out information regarding what you had collected from his pockets. We may have even identified him as a thief who purloined a map of some family's estate. But given the man's death, I hardly consider it an issue we need to pursue. It is over, Mother. Father's not here, but I do know how he would respond to your statement about needing to examine the body. No, you do not *need*, you *want*, which, in this case, are two entirely different concepts."

After this pronouncement, he shut his eyes again, as if signaling the conversation was closed.

Both of us stared at him—out of shock, but for different reasons. In my experience, my brother, while possessing a deep, analytical mind, had never given such a long speech in his life—and most assuredly not to our mother. The most surprising consideration was that he had not saved his remaining energy (having missed lunch) and had chosen instead to pull on his reserves to scold her.

And a scolding from her son did not sit well with Violette Angelique Parker Holmes.

"Of all the insolent—"

Without even opening one eye, he said, "Perhaps I was rather abrupt, but I'm only speaking for Father. He's not here, leaving me as the head of the household."

"Mycroft, I'm still your mother, and—"

"Please. I don't want to argue anymore. I want to go home, have some tea, rest, and think of anything besides the odd assortment of places we've been to since breakfast." He turned to her. "Besides, isn't there some event or other you planned to drag me to tonight?"

"Yes. Of course. I'd entirely forgotten. The Evans' recital. A soprano, I believe. Should be an interesting evening, and Francine Evans is a delightful young lady."

"There," he said and adjusted himself into the seat cushions. "Can't possibly view the body at Surminster's manor if we're at the Evans' recital."

"They took the body to their home?" I asked.

He opened his eyes wide and stared at me. I glared back at him. I hadn't exactly shared a secret. Mother most certainly had picked up on his slip as well.

"I suppose it would be the most logical place." She settled back against her own seat.

A smile graced her face as she relished this small victory over my brother.

Logical, indeed, that the family would lay him out at home. Burials were usually the first Sunday after the death, but one day would hardly be enough time to make arrangements for an earl.

"I suppose you might be able to examine him at their home," I said. Another scowl from my brother, and a returning glower from me. I couldn't help it. I wanted to determine what actually happened to Lord Surminster as much as Mother did. Not to mention, possibly saving Lady Surminster and Miss Phillips from the streets. But I did shift in my seat, not relishing the scrutiny he was giving me. "Of course, not today."

"No," Mother echoed as she once again directed her attention to the streets passing by the window. "Not today."

Another rebuke might have been forthcoming—except the carriage turned onto our street and pulled to a stop at our townhome. Mrs. Simpson opened the front door before we could step from the carriage. She must have been listening for our return. We were expected hours ago, and I was certain she worried something had befallen us.

Having alighted, Mother sent the carriage on, and we

ascended the steps to the four-story structure of the Parker family's London residence. As the eldest male in the Parker family, my mother's brother Ernest owned the house—although he rarely visited London. He preferred to remain in the country where he could work on his inventions. Mother had not been able to induce him to join us on this trip, despite the opportunity to meet up with Colonel Williams, an old acquaintance from his time in the military.

My great-great-grandmother had been a Parker and had married into the Vernet family. My British ancestors had continued to visit their French relatives, and one such distant cousin (also a Parker) had met my grandmother on a visit and married her. As a result, my mother and Uncle Ernest spent time in both France and Britain. While Grosvenor Square was a step down from Surminster's London address, it was still a well-appointed area.

Of course, the home was practically a gallery with all the paintings displayed in the rooms. Three generations of Vernets provided a variety of talent on display—landscapes, battle scenes (my great-grandfather was known for his exceptional depictions of horses), and portraits—primarily family members, but there were some other well-known personages interspersed. One of my favorites, of course, was of my mother. While she scorned most of the social conventions attached to young women, she had been presented to the Queen due to a distant relative's connections to the court. Her uncle had done her portrait in her white presentation gown. He managed to capture not only her high, intellectual forehead and bright, inquisitive eyes, but also her defiant carriage. A straightness of spine and tilt of her chin warned all not to overlook or dismiss her.

"I expected you home hours ago," Mrs. Simpson said as we entered. "There's tea in the drawing room for you. I'll have the girl bring some hot water."

"Thank you, Mrs. Simpson. I think we shall change first." Mycroft and I paused in our path to the parlor. "We have no idea to which illnesses the visit to the hospital might have exposed us."

Mrs. Simpson certainly took in Mother's casual announcement about our whereabouts for the last few hours, but her face remained unreadable. She'd been with the Holmes family long enough not to be shocked by anything my mother said or did. Her unconventionality was well known back in our father's district.

My brother and I glanced at each other, a silent debate between us about the desire to eat and the necessity to avoid some disease. After a moment, we both turned to follow her up the stairs. I gave one last glance over my shoulder at the tray visible across the hall and exhaled.

"It will be there," she said without glancing back at me. "Mrs. Simpson, please have Constance meet me in my room."

Somehow, I was the first to change and return downstairs. To my surprise, I found Constance there as well. I'd met her almost a year ago when my mother had been accused of murder. She had helped us find crucial information in that incident as well as in a second series of murders over Christmas.

She had an excellent singing voice, which Mother was helping her to develop. And to assist in cultivating her manners, she had brought her to London as her personal maid. As part of the household staff, Constance's duties occupied most of her time, and we hadn't the same opportunities to spend time together as we had at Underbyrne.

Her back was to me while she studied my mother's portrait. When I called her name, she faced me. "She looks so young."

"She was," I said. "About sixteen."

"Just a year older than me. She said you'd be down here and sent me down to make sure the tea was ready. I've sent a maid to fetch the hot water." She glanced at the portrait again, her eyes shining. "So elegant. I'm learnin,' but I gots—er, have—a lot to study. I'm going to be like her someday. Just you wait."

I glanced out the window and sought another topic for our conversation. She was progressing in her reading and writing—her letters were more erudite than when she had first corresponded with me—her speech had improved—although I'd notice she'd slip back whenever she was angry—and with my mother's repurposed dresses, her appearance had also put her in a higher class. All the same, she was still a servant with limited prospects.

Before she could ask my opinion of her prediction, I changed the subject. "Oxford won." She stared at me. "The boat race this morning. Oxford won."

My effort served better than I would have expected, with some information I had never anticipated.

"I knew that. Someone came to the house lookin' for you. Said he saw you at the boat races, and Oxford had won."

"Looking for me?"

"Well, for your mother. But you'd been with her."

"Who was it?"

"Some gent."

I considered checking to see if the person had left a calling card, but before I could move, someone knocked on the door.

"Maybe it's 'im, comin' back."

We headed to the door leading to the hallway and listened to the voices drifting down the hallway from the front entrance. I could pick out Mrs. Simpson's voice and a woman's voice in reply.

"Unless he brought someone with 'im, that ain't—isn't —'im," Constance whispered.

A swish of skirts indicated the visitor was coming toward the drawing room to wait while the butler informed my mother of her arrival.

I peeked at Constance. While Mother accepted our friendship, we'd been warned to be careful about letting those outside the family view us as too familiar. Constance signaled me to be silent and slipped out of the room through the doorway in the back leading to the dining room.

She had just slid the door shut when Miss Phillips stepped into the room.

While I had never been particularly attentive to our presentation to the world, I knew our home didn't display the opulence of her social sphere. I swallowed and found my collar suddenly tight when I observed her gaze sweep over our serviceable, but less elegant furnishings. Of course, her gaze lingered on the oil paintings hanging on the walls. I somehow knew she recognized them as originals.

Drawing upon the etiquette lessons my father had instilled in me, I said, "My mother will be down in a moment. Would you like some tea?"

She drew her lips together and shook her head. After

seeking out the nearest chair, she pulled out a handkerchief and twisted it in her hands. Before I could offer any words of comfort, footsteps sounded outside the parlor door and pulled us to our feet.

The girl fairly flew toward Mother when she entered. "Oh, Mrs. Holmes, I must ask you for your help for the second time this day. Only this time, on a much graver issue."

Once the two women were seated, Miss Phillips glanced at me and then my mother. "Could we speak…in private?"

Mother's glance told me not to argue. I stood and took my leave. As I closed the door, she called after me, "Please check on the tea."

When I stepped into the hallway, Constance appeared from the shadow of a large plant by the staircase. "Who's that visitin'?"

"The sister of an…acquaintance of Mycroft."

While I wasn't sure why I didn't explain to her about Lord Surminster, I found it didn't matter. Her interest lay elsewhere.

"Lord, she's a fancy one. Did you see the carriage she came in? It's got a crest on it. Just like Lord Devony's back home. How does Mycroft know someone like her?"

"He and her brother were at Oxford together."

"Were?"

"Her brother…died."

"No wonder she's upset."

I shifted on my feet and glanced at the door. While the two ladies' murmurs could be heard, I couldn't make out any words. What had Miss Phillips come to ask my mother? Turning my attention back to Constance, I said, "I'm supposed to remind Mrs. Simpson about the tea."

"But you want to hear what's goin' on in there. I can read it in your eyes. I'll show you where you can listen to them, then go tell Mrs. Simpson."

I followed her to the entrance between the dining room and parlor. I'd learned from Constance that servants had their ways of listening in on their employers and guests, and now as part of the house staff, she probably knew even more tricks.

With a finger to her lips, she stepped to the sliding door she'd used earlier when Miss Phillips had arrived. After pointing to a thin opening where the door hadn't closed completely, she tiptoed out.

I took a position beside the opening in case my shadow could be seen through the slit.

"I understand your brother has been removed to your house—"

"Not yet. He's been taken…elsewhere. Until a more proper appearance can be arranged. Our solicitor assisted in making the arrangements after Hamilton told me about"—she took a deep breath—"about his…condition."

"There were some discrepancies in his appearance, and I'd tried to point it out to the coroner. Unfortunately, he wasn't interested in hearing what I had to say. You see, it's obvious he hadn't dressed himself, and then there was—"

"Didn't dress himself? Are you suggesting someone changed his clothing? After he-he…"

The rest of her thought was cut off with a whimper.

A rustle of skirts suggested Mother had moved closer to the girl, perhaps to better comfort her. "I believe that's how the other gentleman was found in Lord Surminster's suit. Someone had discarded—or given—your brother's clothing to the other man."

"Hamilton shared with our solicitor that you argued with the coroner and had a theory about the true cause of his death. Because of the circumstances, our solicitor was able to get the inquest postponed until Saturday, the day before Easter. We have a week to collect more information to be presented."

"His state suggests someone else had a hand in his death. Of course, further examination of the—of Lord Surminster would be required for any additional information."

"And it would rule out a suicide?"

"Such a decision would be up to the coroner and the jury, but if presented in court, it might provide the jury with the evidence needed to declare another cause of death."

A door opened, and I could hear a maid bring in the hot water. Their conversation paused as cups were filled and served. During this brief intermission, I pondered why Mother had yet to share the information we had just gleaned at the Reading Room. While Miss Phillips had focused on the suicide, it didn't preclude my mother from asking about his interest in the Wrightmoor convent. A part of me wanted to signal her to shift the conversation in that direction, but I forced myself to focus on what was unfolding in the other room. Mother always had her reasons for her actions, and I had to trust her.

Finally, the maid's footsteps retreated, and the door closed again. A rattle of teacups reminded me I had yet to have tea. My stomach growled once again at the thought, and I froze, fearing I'd been heard in the other room. Miss Phillips continued conversing, and I breathed normally again.

"Hamilton said it was suggested"—she dropped her

voice—"my brother had made more than one attempt." A whimper cut her off, and, after pausing, she continued. Her voice took on a sharp, bitter tone. "Do you have any idea of what sort of *ruin* this would bring upon us? Suicide?"

"My dear girl. This must be an awful shock to you and your mother. I can only imagine the pain. I'm truly sorry for your predicament but am at a loss to know how I could help you. I have no standing to provide any information at the inquest. While I can share my observations with someone who can, I have no means to—"

"Mycroft does. He can speak at the inquest. Say he knew Vernon had no desire to end his life. Otherwise, we could be stripped of everything."

The younger woman's voice hit an octave higher on this last word. While her grief had cracked through her reserve before, this was the first time her desperation had truly appeared.

Mother's own calm contrasted with Miss Phillips' emotional state. "I'm afraid my son told me he barely knew your brother."

"But they knew each other better than those making these statements against Vernon." Here, she paused before adding in a most level, but all the same menacing tone. "And I have heard some of their classmates are suggesting your son has some unusual behaviors of his own. Perhaps you should ask him about the woman in the photo?"

Rarely was my mother at a loss for words. Her responses tended to be quick and on-point. For this revelation, however, she had no ready rejoinder. I could almost picture her, frozen, perhaps with a teacup halfway to her lips, gaze fixed on our guest.

In the ensuing silence, the younger woman pushed on.

"That Diogenes Society he helped form. I've been told it's... it's...well, I'm afraid I can't be so indelicate."

This comment was enough to help Mother find her tongue. "I have it on good authority the Diogenes Society is nothing more than a place where young men—students—gather in total silence. To study. I don't believe anything untoward can occur in total silence."

Our guest sniffed, and a brief shuffle indicated she handed a paper to my mother. "Then perhaps you need to read this."

A moment passed while she allowed my mother to read whatever she had shared.

During this interval, I sensed a presence enter the room. My heart, already racing from the accusation Miss Phillips had just thrown out, skipped a beat. Had I been found eavesdropping? I glanced behind me, and Constance's lips tipped upward. My breathing returned to normal, but my cheeks still burned with both rage and fear. How had my brother gotten mixed up in this? And what would it mean for his future? Not to mention for our family?

My friend made it to my side but said nothing. I appreciated her silence, but at the moment, not her company. She had no need to know what this woman was saying about my brother. After all, she and my brother barely tolerated each other. Mycroft failed to understand my friendship with a girl below my social level, and she found him pompous. While their critiques of each other were not entirely baseless, I still appreciated and enjoyed the company of both. All the same, I hadn't been able to get them to see the other's merits as I did.

Mother's next remark cut into my growing alarm.

THE ADVENTURE OF THE DECEASED SCHOLAR

"The note is addressed to a 'Rose' and signed by 'Albert.' While the sentiments expressed are not within social bounds, I fail to see how this implicates Mycroft—"

"What is your son's middle name?"

"It's not so uncommon there wouldn't be another young man at Oxford named Albert. And while the French is adequate, it is quite below the level of my son's grasp of the language."

"True. But my interest is not in releasing the letter or seeking to dispute the writer or receiver. I have another purpose in sharing this letter. To have Mycroft speak at the inquest. If he doesn't, I will release this letter. Your position in society has always been tenuous. The Holmes lands are not so big or prosperous that a scandal wouldn't affect Squire Holmes' standing in his community. And his brothers-in-law…well, I would suggest they could find it difficult to conduct any business if the whole community were to shun them thanks to the common knowledge of your son's involvement with a-a—I'm afraid I cannot bring myself to even say the word."

My hands formed fists at my sides. I couldn't help but wonder what color my mother's complexion had become. I forced myself to take more deep, meditative breaths, recalling the lesson about how a still mind and body permit concentration amidst chaos. Perhaps my mother was remembering the same because her response was both calm and measured.

"We have no proof—at least none acceptable at the inquest. We also have no standing. And I cannot ask my son to perjure himself. I understand your plight—"

"I'm not so concerned about me. I will still be able to

find a good—if not great—match. My mother's situation is what concerns me. She is devastated by the circumstances of my brother's death. We have managed to keep from her how he was found. But the ruling of suicide would be a blow from which she would not recover. There is also my younger brother to keep in mind. He would lose his inheritance. I cannot let that happen. And I will do whatever it takes to ensure my family is safe." Here she paused, and I'm certain held my mother in her gaze. "Including blackmail."

A rustle told me Mother had stood. She was ending the young lady's visit. A second rustle from Miss Phillips followed.

Mother's icy tone sent a chill down my spine, even from this distance. "I believe you have made yourself clear. Let me consult with my son to determine how we might approach this. You have to understand—"

"Mrs. Holmes, you are the one who must understand. I have managed to have my brother removed from that dreadful place to be cleaned and properly dressed before my mother sees him. And to set the inquest a week from today—thanks to our solicitor and my brother's rank. If at the inquest he is found to have taken his own life, I will make certain our family is not the only one destroyed by scandal."

Footsteps signaled her departure.

Once I heard the front door open and close, I faced Constance.

"What do you think your mother and brother will do?" she whispered.

Before I could answer, Mother spoke from the doorway. "Mycroft will have to agree we must be involved in resolving Lord Surminster's death."

I dropped my gaze, unable to meet my mother's. She'd

caught me eavesdropping in the past, but this time, I'd involved another in my trespass. Mother might be angry with me, but Constance could be sent back to Underbyrne —or even dismissed.

Hoping a chagrined expression might mitigate any consequences, I asked, "How did you know we were here?"

When she didn't answer immediately, I glanced up at her and saw the corners of her lips twitched as if she were trying to suppress a smile. "Because this is where I would have hidden to listen to something happening in the other room." Her gaze strayed to the drawing room on the other side of the door, and she asked, "What did you think of Miss Phillips' threat?"

"I've already told you the Diogenes Society is nothing like what she described."

"I believe you. Just as I'm certain 'Albert' is not Mycroft."

"Are you going to do what she demanded?"

The corners of her mouth turned down. "I can assure you I'm not pleased to be forced into solving this murder for her. But I'm also somewhat sympathetic."

"She's truly vicious," Constance said.

I nodded. "And she seemed so polite and reserved earlier today."

"You will learn women have been taught to hide their feelings and thoughts from the time they are young. I would guess she learned her lessons well. But you've been on enough hunts to know a cornered animal is often more dangerous than one able to flee. And at the moment, her whole way of life is threatened, boxed in."

"But she plans to ruin Mycroft. Doesn't she realize she has done the same to us? Can't we be dangerous as well?"

Mother met my gaze and cocked her head to one side as she considered me and my observation. "While I think she recognizes we may be of some use to her, I don't think she fully understands our potential in uncovering her brother's death. We're not truly trapped."

CHAPTER FOUR

Mother paused before saying, "We need someplace to think. Work things out. I do miss our classroom. I could certainly use the blackboard to gather our thoughts. I've found it helpful to write it large."

"Perhaps there's something in the attic? Some old school equipment?"

She widened her eyes. "I think you're right."

Exiting the dining room, she moved to the stairs, signaling for Constance and me to follow. The fourth floor had been the children's area for previous generations but hadn't been used by Mother and Ernest because they'd been grown when they returned to London. After his return from India, Ernest spent time upstairs to enjoy peace and quiet and tinker with small inventions. The area had been turned into a small suite with a bedroom and its own stairway to the street. Mother called it a *garçonnière* or bachelor's quarters. The toys and school items had been removed from all but one room and shoved into a corner room previously housing the nursery.

Because the *garçonnière* was still for family use, the maids maintained it as they did the rest of the house, but not the room with all the children's items. Simply entering the area set off a small cloud of dust that made the three of us sneeze.

Mother waved her hand in front of her face as if to chase away the small cloud stirred up by her skirts. "Why don't you see what you can find? I'm going to seek out Mycroft and share with him what Miss Phillips has threatened. If you find some slates and chalk, bring them down to my sitting room."

Constance stepped into the room and glanced around. "Did this used to be a school?"

"It's a classroom like the one we have in Underbyrne."

She stepped farther into the room, picking up different items and examining them. "You could get a few quid for some of these."

"I suppose." I studied an old lead soldier, its paint worn off in most places. "But most are broken or so old, they wouldn't be worth much. Besides, it's not ours."

She turned to face me, an old, broken fan in her hand. "Isn't this your house?"

"It belongs to my mother's family. The Parkers. So, my uncle owns it. But he doesn't like the city and never uses it. Father's not fond of London either."

"Oh, I thinks London's grand."

She waved the fan in front of her, mimicking the women I'd seen sitting on park benches or strolling along the road. "I do say, sir, it is rah-ther warm today, wouldn't you agree?"

She peered at me over the fan's blades. Little lines crinkled at the corners of her eyes. I wanted to return her smile and merriment but couldn't. As much as I enjoyed her company, I feared she would never be the lady she was pretending—or wanted—to be.

Before she pushed her impersonation further, I changed the subject. "I think I see the slates she wants over there in the corner."

She turned to see where I was pointing, and I moved toward a desk shoved against a wall. Several trunks were piled between us and it, but a stack of slate tablets was just visible above them. We had to pull some of the boxes and furniture this way and that to make it to the wall.

I handed them to her one at a time until we had four.

"These are heavy," she said.

"They're old. Why don't you put them down on the trunk while I check inside this desk for some chalk?"

She helped me pull out the desk enough to get to the other side. In the middle drawer of the left-hand side, some chalk rolled and rattled when I opened it. In addition, I found another fan as well as a hat with a feather. Both were old fashioned, but in better shape than the one she'd found earlier. Somewhat plain, I assumed they had belonged to a governess or nanny during my grandparents' time. While I feared encouraging her fancies, I still retrieved them along with the chalk. I had no right to condemn her dreams—any more than anyone should squash mine.

"Did you find the chalk?" she asked.

"Yes." I held up the fan and hat. "And these. We can ask, but I'm sure Mother will let you have them. Let's go back to the sitting room."

After we pushed the desk back into place, we maneuvered through the trunks to the hallway. Once there,

Constance set the hat on her head, opened the fan, and fluttered it in front of her face. "How do I look?"

"Very elegant."

"Why, thank you, sir," she said with a curtsy.

"You can't very well wear them while you're in your uniform. Let's leave them here and you can get them later if Mother says you can have them."

When we returned downstairs, however, we completely forgot about the fan and hat. Mycroft was pacing in front of Mother, and he spun about and glared at the two of us as we entered.

Before he could speak, Mother said, "Constance, would you please ask Mrs. Simpson to arrange for our dinner to be brought up here? You can then join the rest of the staff for their dinner."

"Yes, ma'am," she said, dropping a brief curtsy.

She said nothing, but Mother's dismissal certainly stung. I blamed myself. I forgot sometimes she was part of the staff now. Mother had sent the message without a rebuke, which was her way.

Once Constance had shut the door behind her, Mycroft faced Mother and pointed at me. "How much does he know?"

"Enough," Mother said in her most calming voice. "I asked him and Constance for the slates in order to determine how best to respond to Miss Phillips' request to investigate her brother's death."

"Request." Mycroft sneered as he pronounced the word. "I say we just ignore the woman. She's distraught. She'd never carry through with the threat."

Mother's mouth formed a straight line. "I'm afraid you underestimate her as well as women in general. Females have been trained to appear weak and simple, but they are often more clever than they let on. Didn't your experience with Miss Meredith show you that?"

My brother's involvement with the niece of one of our uncle's friends had led to some rather surprising conclusions. I had to agree with Mother. Miss Meredith certainly exemplified some women's devious nature.

He gave a snort, but at least sat down. "I still say this is a matter for the police. This is London, for God's sake. Not our village."

"Really," Mother said, annoyance tinging her voice. "There's no need for such language. If you don't want to be involved—"

"No," I said, stepping forward, gripping the slates to keep them from sliding from my grasp. "He has to be involved. He's the one whose reputation is being threatened. And through him our whole family." I faced him. "If you don't care, I do. We have to save the family name. We've already had one scandal when they arrested Mother. We can't have another."

Mycroft's face flushed, and his jaw worked as he seemed to force his emotions under control. A glance at Mother and a long, slow exhalation released most of the tension in his face. In the end, he threw up his hands. "Fine. I suppose we can collect information to share with the authorities. I'm only helping to make sure you don't muck it up completely."

Mother waved her hand to the small table by her chair. "Why don't you put the slates there, and then we'll review what I found in Lord Surminster's suit pocket."

Mother had the windows open, and the evening breeze sent the drapes fluttering. At Underbyrne, or even Eton, the air carried the scents of green grass and perhaps early flowers. In the townhouse, I caught only the smells of city dust and smoke. For the first time, I understood my father's preference for the country.

Before we could assemble about the table or even lift a slate, someone knocked on the sitting-room door.

At Mother's direction, Constance entered the room and handed her a card. "Excuse me, ma'am. There's a man waitin' to see you in the drawing room."

"A detective?" Mother said after studying the card my friend handed her. "Tell him I'll be down shortly."

After Constance retreated, Mother glanced at my brother and me. "Really, boys, do close your mouths."

"What do you suppose he wants to talk to you about?" I asked.

"What do you think, you twit?" Mycroft scoffed in my direction. "We just identified a lord who drowned."

"I know. I mean, do you think it's about Lord Surminster, or the man in his suit, or—"

"Why don't we find out?" she asked, rising from her seat. "Please come with me. I think observing a true detective at work might be enlightening."

Constance was waiting outside the drawing room door and beckoned to me as I followed my mother and brother into the room. She whispered to me, "He's the gent I was telling you about. What was here earlier."

I nodded and entered the room, pulling the door closed behind me.

Given all the accounts I'd read by Mr. Dickens concerning London's police detectives in his *Household Words*, I found my illusions shattered in the face of reality. The person in the rather common suit did not resemble at all the Inspector Fields whom the novelist had described in so many of his articles. He was neither middle-aged nor portly. The slim young man stood ramrod straight in the center of the room and gave off more the appearance of a soldier or one of the guards at Buckingham Palace. I could almost feel him suppressing a salute as Mother addressed him.

"Inspector Roggens, I'm Mrs. Siger Holmes, and these are my sons, Mycroft and Sherlock."

After exchanging a few more pleasantries, the man said, "I want to thank you, Mrs. Holmes, for seeing me on short notice."

"Always ready to assist those in law enforcement. You see, my husband is—"

"A magistrate. I understand you shared this information with the coroner this afternoon."

"Precisely. Why don't we sit? Shall I ask for tea?"

"Thank you, but not necessary at this time."

Once seated, the man pulled out a small notebook and pencil. After flipping through the pages, he found what he was looking for and paused to study his notes. While he was distracted, I checked the door to the dining room and caught what I thought was a shadow. Constance had to be listening in. I settled back, knowing we'd be able to share impressions later.

We proceeded to answer the most basic questions such as how we happened upon Lady Surminster and Miss Phillips, and why they asked us about Lord Surminster. I found myself growing bored with these rather innocuous questions too mundane for the likes of a Scotland Yard detective.

When he reached some point in his notes, his posture shifted. He straightened and cleared his throat. My attention sharpened when he set his gaze upon my brother.

"You say you weren't Lord Surminster's friend, but you went to the hospital to identify him. How did that come to pass?"

"I knew him well enough to identify him," Mycroft said in a voice conveying more than a little annoyance—most likely as much at the pace of the questioning as the impugnation of his integrity.

"If you please, Inspector Roggens," Mother said. The detective gave her a steady study. She continued without hesitation. "I was the one who volunteered us to go with the police officer to the hospital. His mother and sister were too upset to have done such a task. We simply accompanied their butler Hamilton as secondaries. I believe we proved useful, given his outburst."

The man shifted in his seat. "Of course, his outburst. But you made an impression as well, I understand, Mrs. Holmes. Telling the coroner his business."

"I merely pointed out—"

"I know what you told him."

She leaned forward as if eager to hear his response to her next question. "And was I right? About the man in Lord Surminster's clothes?"

"Name was...." He flipped through his notebook. "No clue as yet. Probably not from the area. No one reported missing. Appears to have drunk too much and fallen in. While it might not look it, the river is dangerous—what with the currents and all. Always pulling one or another out after too much gin."

"Interesting." She tapped her finger to her lips. "Have you found the tavern where he became inebriated? They might remember him if he was drunk enough to fall into the

Thames. And can you explain whatever the residue was in his ear?"

Roggens puffed out his cheeks. "Now see here. I came to find out about Lord Surminster. Not some drowned wharf monkey. I know all about you. You were in the papers not more than nine months ago. Accused of murder. And I'm sure your constable will provide me even more details."

I could feel all of us stiffen at that pronouncement. The following silence apprised the inspector he had hit a nerve. The scandal of my mother's arrest had cast a shadow over our family and caused both my brother and me to be pulled from school. Try as we might to put the incident behind us, the events somehow had yet to leave us in peace.

Mother swallowed and said in a calm voice, "I'm sure Constable Gibbons will provide his own description of how the murder was solved, but I can assure you, he wouldn't have succeeded if we hadn't contributed to the investigation."

"I can see how you might harbor ill feelings about your village constabulary, but this is London, home to Scotland Yard. You'll find our methods much more advanced. We won't need your help."

"And yet you are here." Mycroft leveled his gaze at the man.

"Only to get a clearer picture of the de—Lord Surminster. His family doesn't know about his life at Oxford. Mr. Holmes and his mates can fill that in."

"As I told the police officer earlier, we were in the same college, but not so close."

"Would you say he was closer to…" Roggens consulted his notebook. "A Mr. Maurice Edmonds?"

Mycroft paused—whether to think or to compose his

answer, I wasn't sure. "He was also in the same college, as I'm sure you know. But I don't recall seeing them together all too often."

"Just who did you see him with, then?"

This time, Mycroft seemed prepared. "I'm afraid he was a bit of a loner. Like me. Neither of us go—er, went—for all the...*imbibing* some do. You won't find me at a tavern or public house. I find intellectual stimulation—reading, mostly—much more to my taste. I would say Lord Surminster had a similar disposition."

"So, you wouldn't know how the man got out of"—he glanced at my mother and me and then shifted his weight in the chair as if a lump had suddenly formed in its cushions—"the clothes they found on the other man?"

Before Mycroft could respond, Mother spoke up. "As I mentioned to the coroner, *someone else* had to change his clothes."

"The coroner told me what you said. The family lawyer who claimed the body agrees. But it doesn't tell me what I want to know." He stared unblinkingly at my brother.

"No. I have no idea."

Mother stood, forcing all of us to rise. My breath caught in my throat. She was ending the interview? Now? There was so much more I wanted to hear. My fingers itched to see what he had penned in his little notebook. But Mother seemed to have other ideas.

"I believe this is all we have time for at present. We have a recital to attend tonight, and we must get ready."

"A recital. Right," Inspector Roggens said with a draw as if he didn't accept her explanation. "I suppose I've got enough at this time. You've been most...helpful."

"Always ready to support those in law enforcement," Mycroft said, extending his hand.

Roggens pumped it and then bowed at my mother. "Thank you, Mrs. Holmes."

We escorted him to the door, and as Mother opened it, she said, "I would suggest you consider examining the garments Lord Surminster was wearing for an indication of their origin. Especially among those currently attending Cambridge. According to my son, no Oxford man would voluntarily wear a jacket from the school—even in jest."

"Already done so," he said and stepped into the hall. "I'll show myself out."

After the door closed, Mother said, "We must take a look at those clothes. Both sets."

"And the recital?" Mycroft asked.

"We should be able to learn about this family lawyer who took Lord Surminster's body. Inspector Roggens all but told us the lawyer is in possession of his remains—and possibly the clothes as well." She tapped her finger to her lips. "Of course, I suppose Scotland Yard could have taken the clothes. Either way, we'll have to go to the house to at least get one more review of the body."

THE NEXT FEW hours involved Mother's and Mycroft's preparations for the recital: a hasty dinner, bathing, dressing, and a recitation of my brother's complaints about the whole affair. Constance helped my mother, and I spent the time keeping out of everyone's way. In some manners, I was more than a little grateful I was too young to attend, but in others, sorry I couldn't be there to hear first-hand any information gleaned about Lord Surminster, his lawyer, or opinions concerning his mother or sister.

Shortly after they left, someone knocked on my bedroom door. Assuming it was the maid bringing the tea I requested, I called out my permission to enter and returned to the book I was reading.

"Are you disappointed?" I heard Constance ask. I must have startled because she giggled when I turned to her. "About not going to the recital, I mean?"

I considered her question before responding. "Not necessarily to the recital, but not being there to learn if they are able to get any information about Lord Surminster, yes."

"Ooh, I'd so love to hear the singing," she said, stepping up to where I sat. She dropped her voice as if sharing a secret. "Your mother told me all about it. How the woman singing also sings on the stage."

I put my book on the table. "I didn't know that. Who's singing?"

"She said Ila Augustin. Have you heard of her?"

My mouth fell open for a second when I realized my brother and mother were in the presence of perhaps the most famous soprano in the world. For the first time since Mother had mentioned the recital, I regretted not being included at the event for a reason other than ferreting out the name of Surminster's lawyer.

I glanced at Constance.

"What?" she asked. "Do I have a smudge on my face?"

"Come with me," I said.

After descending the stairs, I led her to the library and sought out a stack of London papers on a desk toward the rear of the room. After shuffling through them, I came across the one I'd read a few days ago about the soprano. I placed the paper with her likeness flat on the desk. Pointing at the image of a woman with her hair in a large bun on the back of her round head. "This is Ila Augustin."

"Lors, she's in the papers." She peered closely at the sketch and then raised her head to glance at me. "But she's not at all as I'd imagined. Her nose is too broad. And flat."

"People don't come to study her nose. They come to hear her voice."

"Papa always says the sugar on top makes the cake. A beautiful voice should come from a beautiful woman."

She studied the paper again, running her finger over the headline and the first few lines of type. "Ni-ni—t—"

I bit my lip to keep from helping her work out the nickname for Miss Augustin. Just as my mother forced me to make the effort to work out a problem or translate some text, so I did with her.

"Nightingale," she said, triumphant in her achievement.

"Right. It's her nickname. 'The French Nightingale.'"

"She must have a special voice. Do you think I might sound like her?"

I paused to consider the question. "I don't know. I've never heard her. Mother might be able to tell you after tonight."

"I wish I could have heard her," she said, running her finger over the woman's photo. "When do you think they'll be home? I'll have to help her undress, and maybe I'll ask her then."

"Mother said the recital was to begin at eight. Then there will be refreshments. If they're good, Mycroft will insist they stay to enjoy them. If he doesn't care for them, or if Mother pushes him too hard to meet people, they'll be home earlier. I would say not to expect them until at least after eleven."

She glanced down at the paper. "I'll take this to read in the meantime."

"If you like, we can go to the drawing room and read together. I'll get my book. That way, I can help you with any words."

Once seated in separate chairs near the fire, we were soon each absorbed in our own perusing. A calm fell over the room, punctuated by an occasional crackling in the grate and Constance's efforts to sound out and confirm certain words. At one point, I glanced up from the page to check on my friend. Her creased forehead and silently moving lips revealed her concentration and determination. I recognized a serenity—a contentment—I rarely experienced. The book, the fire, and my friend had formed a sort of oasis of peace I rarely found at school where I was surrounded by other boys who often competed to be the center of attention. I also realized this was what I had observed between my parents at times. Mother, with some treatise she was studying, and Father, with his own materials, seated in our parlor at Underbyrne. Was this what some married couples were blessed with? A companionship transcending the need to speak, based simply on being in the presence of the other?

Did Mycroft feel similarly when surrounded with those in his Diogenes Society? A companionship of like-minded fellows who simply reveled in their camaraderie—no talking needed?

I'd always considered my brother's life a rather solitary one and condemned his Society's requirement of complete silence during their gatherings. Now, however, I would have to reassess both. He wasn't as solitary as I thought—just with a different idea of fellowship than those who accompanied others to the pubs or cricket fields.

At some point, my eyelids drooped, and I had to re-read the same page about three times, still without comprehending. I let the book fall into my lap and my head rest on the settee's back.

After what seemed only a few minutes later, I jerked awake when I heard the front door open and voices echo down the hall.

"Really, Mycroft," Mother said, "I find your objections more than a little exaggerated."

"All I said was the reception fare could have been better."

The voices and footsteps drifted toward the drawing room, and I glanced at Constance. She was awake and upright in her seat, but a smudge of newsprint on her cheek implied I wasn't the only one who had fallen asleep while reading.

"Sherry dear. Constance," Mother said when she entered.

Both of us stood, with my friend giving a bobbing curtsy when addressed.

"How was the recital?" I asked. "Did you—?"

"Let's discuss the evening later," she said with a tired shake of her head. "Constance, can you help me out of this dress? I do say, I can't wait to return to Underbyrne where I'm not forced into such confining outfits."

"We could return tomorrow," Mycroft said.

While the remark made my thoughts fly back to my own room at our home with a wish it could be so, no one needed to point out the sarcasm in his voice.

"If only," Mother said. "In between making the proper acquaintances for you and resolving this issue with Lord Surminster, I'm afraid we're here for the holiday's duration. Shall we all go to bed?"

About halfway up the stairs, Mother turned to speak to me. "Sherry dear, you'll need to be up by nine for breakfast. We'll be calling on Lord Surminster's lawyer tomorrow."

"You have his name, then?" I asked. "And you made an appointment?"

"The name, yes. The appointment, no." She proceeded up the stairs. "But I think he'll see us all the same."

Upon reaching the top, she turned and spoke again, although not to anyone in particular. "I can't believe this morning our only concern was whether Oxford would triumph over Cambridge. Now we have been blackmailed into proving a murder, which it most definitely is, and must find a way to examine a corpse without anyone being the wiser."

By the time I reached the second-floor landing, Mother and Mycroft had parted, each to their rooms. I did the same, knowing her announcement was a plan as much as an observation. Unfortunately, learning what she'd determined to do would have to wait and possibly make it difficult to sleep.

CHAPTER FIVE

A few blocks from St. Paul's Cathedral, the carriage pulled to a stop beside an impressive three-story building. Mother checked the paper in her hand. "Yes, this is the address."

Mycroft glimpsed out the window and frowned. "Please tell me his office is not on the third floor?"

"I can't tell from the office number," she said. "Besides, a bit of exercise wouldn't harm you."

A chuckle rose to my lips but died when my brother directed a withering scowl at me.

"*You*," he said, as if reading my thoughts, "didn't have to spend an evening sitting on a spindly chair, your muscles braced to keep your weight from collapsing the reeds impersonating its legs."

Mother rolled her gaze to the carriage's roof. "Really, Mycroft, you *sat* for two hours listening to perhaps the most famous soprano of our time. I had a similar chair and know it was more than sufficiently substantial."

Any additional complaints were interrupted by the driver opening the carriage and assisting us all to the ground.

"Have the driver wait for us," Mother told Mycroft as she stepped toward the building.

As my brother feared, the office of *Nathan Edmonds, Proctor,* was on the third floor. His wheezing as he pulled himself up the last flight suggested Mother's admonishment for additional exercise was not out of place—especially when you considered Mother had more than twenty years on him and her corset most likely restricted her lungs to some degree. I observed she wasn't breathing any harder than when she'd stepped from the carriage. Despite my lack of sympathy for his labored efforts, I did turn to confirm he was not in any immediate danger of collapsing or falling backward down the steps. While his face was a light pink, I determined he was most likely exaggerating for our benefit.

Outside the office door, we all paused to study the gold lettering on the varnished wood.

"The man's a proctor?" Mycroft asked. "No wonder his office is so high. Probably all he can afford. A dying breed, if ever there was one."

"Apparently, the family has been consulting with this firm for a number of years. I believe it has to do with the administration of some land belonging to Lady Surminster's mother."

"In Surminster?" Mycroft asked.

"Or Wrightminster?" I asked.

"The ladies around the lemonade bowl weren't certain, and I couldn't press too hard without raising suspicions."

With a jeer, Mycroft opened the door, and we all stepped inside.

THE ADVENTURE OF THE DECEASED SCHOLAR

A gentleman in a suit sat behind a desk between the front door and another leading to an inner office. He glanced up from the document he was preparing, put his pen in its holder, and stood. "May I help you?"

"We are seeking Mr. Edmonds. Is he available?" Mother asked.

"I…I'll see," he said and wiped his hands on his thighs. "Who may I say is calling?"

"Mrs. Siger Holmes and her sons Mycroft and Sherlock," she said, handing him her calling card. "Please let him know we are here on behalf of Lord Surminster."

"Lord Surminster, yes." He took a step and faced us again. "Lord Surminster? He's—that is to say, I'm afraid—"

"We are aware of his demise," Mycroft said before Mother could reply. "It is in reference to his death we are here."

"His death. Of course."

The man literally *scurried* into the inner office after the scantest of knocks.

Nathan Edmonds was a tall man. I've noticed some men are tall because of long legs, but in this case, his height was more due to his torso. It seemed stretched out in some way, and I couldn't help but speculate he must have to have his clothes specially tailored to fit him.

After introductions, Mr. Edmonds rubbed his hands together and said, "I understand this relates to Lord Surminster?"

Immediately after the question, he glanced at a clock ticking on the wall to one side. Was he considering how long he would have to wait before we took our leave? Or if he would need to have us removed?

Mother followed my gaze when the attorney checked the

time and most likely had the same thought as I. He needed to be drawn onto our side, or we would leave without any new information and one alienated proctor. To help the man's decision along, I said, "My brother attended Oxford with Lord Surminster."

The others stared at me, but I straightened my spine in response. I'd spoken out of turn, but at least Edmonds was no longer counting the seconds until he could dispense with us.

"Oxford?" the man asked Mycroft. "I have a brother there as well. The same college as Lord Surminster. Maurice?"

My breath caught in my throat for a second, and I swallowed to cover any hint of surprise. Inspector Roggens had asked about the man as well. What connection existed between him and Surminster?

Mycroft studied the ceiling as if reviewing his acquaintances to see if he could identify the student, effectively covering any similar shock from the name. "Maurice Edmonds?" he asked when he dropped his gaze. "Tall. Prefers red, double-breasted waistcoats."

The proctor stared at him before nodding. I was certain he had not met many with my brother's powers of observation for minutiae. I smiled to myself. He was definitely more attentive to us—rather than the clock—now.

"Actually, Miss Phillips shared you were assisting them with some of Lady Surminster's business matters, including Wrightmoor," Mother said in a casual matter as a statement, and once again, I admired her ability to lie so coolly. Having been privy to their conversation, I knew Miss Phillips hadn't mentioned Wrightmoor. The ladies around the lemonade must have been more forthcoming than she had let on.

THE ADVENTURE OF THE DECEASED SCHOLAR

"Were you aware Lord Surminster stole a map from the British museum the day he died? One of Wrightmoor? Showing the convent?"

"I still don't understand—"

"We don't either. Which is why we're here. To learn if Lord Surminster shared any concerns with you about Wrightmoor, the convent, or…perhaps something else?" She gazed at him, her eyes wide.

With a great deal of will, I forced myself not to stare at her. She'd pulled different bits from what we'd gleaned at the library as well as whatever the ladies at the recital had provided into a series of questions for guiding this current interchange. My current regret was not having been there to observe how she had solicited the gossip.

"Surely you don't think his death is related to a…a map?"

She blinked at him in a way I would have interpreted as guileless, had I not known my mother. "Again, we don't know. But it seems odd for his death to follow so shortly after the theft."

"I'm not sure of any connection," the man said, glancing at the clock again.

My stomach squeezed. The man was becoming increasingly uncomfortable, and again, we risked losing our chance to gain the information collected. I glanced at my bro*'* He seemed to share my concern because, in *'* moment, he changed the approach.

"Would you mind sharing some of the Mycroft asked. "I'm reading for the useful for me to hear about the cas heard in civil court."

The man paused as if to consider

before speaking. "Wrightmoor belonged to Lady Surminster's mother, Edwina Kemper. It was put into a trust to be administered by the Chancery Court for Edwina and her future children. Something about her being the only surviving child, and her father—Lord Frampton—not trusting the man to whom she was betrothed. When she died, the property passed to Lady Surminster—before she was married. There may have been something to Lord Frampton's concerns. Edwina's husband—Lord Thanbury—did seek to break the trust, and the case has been in the court now for more than thirty years."

"Thirty years?" Mycroft gasped and shook his head. "And the court has been administering it that long? Has the property been maintained?"

"Prior to his death, Lady Surminster and her husband spent a great deal of time there. As the name implies, it is part of the moorland south of Bristol. After his death a few years ago, she found it too hard to visit, and the trustee put it up to let. Lord Thanbury's suit has not affected it or the income passing to Lady Surminster."

"So, in addition to the court, a trustee runs the estate for her?" Mycroft asked. "Are you familiar with the man?"

"Why are you asking about him?"

More than a drop of suspicion tinged the man's voice, making my stomach squeeze again. He would be escorting us from the office soon if we continued to ask such questions.

"As I said, I am reading for the law and was considering how convoluted this whole structure is. Perhaps it's not out of line that Parliament has sought to reform the whole process."

The lawyer's mouth turned down. "I'm afraid I don't

agree with you there. The Chancery Court has been able to decide these matters for centuries. What does a civil court know about equity or the need to protect the wife from an unscrupulous husband?"

"Do you think Lord Thanbury will be able to break the trust?" Mother asked. "I would hate to think of Lady Surminster being stripped of her inheritance."

"I can assure you. The trust is safe. Both real and personal property."

"Personal property?" Mother asked. "Are you referring to the furnishings and buildings?"

The man hesitated as if considering what he wanted to share. He must have come to some conclusion because he said, "Some rather peculiar references appear in the original documents about 'a nun's chest.' I'm afraid I don't know the entire story. Perhaps Lady Surminster or Miss Phillips will be able to tell you more. Not that it matters. This mythical chest has never appeared."

"Fascinating," my brother said. "I might seek out more on these aspects of the law. I had no idea there was so much to it."

The lawyer chuckled. "Which is why all this reform will not be the result Parliament wanted. The Chancery Court has been in existence for hundreds of years. Those not steeped in their understanding will create more delays and poor judgments. Mark my word."

"We won't keep you from your efforts, then," Mother said. "Perhaps my son can visit again sometime and learn more?"

"I'd be delighted."

My brother thrust his hand forward. "Excellent. Most pleased to have made your acquaintance."

A while later, we were back in the carriage and returning to the townhouse. No one spoke. I was certain all three of us were analyzing what Edmonds had shared.

Mother finally broke the silence. "We must visit Lady Surminster again."

Mycroft's frown suggested some annoyance with her. She'd already ruined his morning routine by having to visit the proctor, but I considered these extraordinary times. We were, after all, seeking to save Mycroft's reputation. While I thought his attitude out of place, I was less bothered by it than by my curiosity about Mother's sudden announcement.

"I know you want to examine Lord Surminster, but—" Mycroft said.

"There's more. Edmonds didn't share everything with us. Whatever Lord Surminster was researching, it had to do with Wrightmoor—or the personal property on it."

"But a map would indicate his interest lay in the real property, wouldn't it?" I asked.

"Unless…" Mother tapped her finger against her lips. "What if it showed where some part of the personal property was hidden?"

"And it's hidden because…?" Mycroft asked.

"I know," I said, fairly jumping on the seat. "If it weren't, they would be fighting about it in court as well."

Mother grinned at me. "Exactly. Let's return home and change. We must pay our respects to Lady Surminster and her family. At the recital last evening, I learned he would be laid out today."

Mycroft rolled his eyes. If he'd objected to attending the recital, he was even more disinclined to visit the bereaved family, but his reaction indicated he'd come to the same conclusion as I. Viewing the corpse was important, even if

THE ADVENTURE OF THE DECEASED SCHOLAR

the prospect wasn't appealing. Also, better to do it at the beginning of the week, rather than the end. The anatomy classes Mother had arranged with a medical student before I began my studies at Eton had taught me decomposition initiated as soon as the body ceased to function. By the third day, the body would bloat and give off the odor of decay. When Lord Surminster's family finally buried him, a whole garden of flowers wouldn't be able to fully mask the stench.

When we stepped into the house, Mrs. Simpson met us at the door.

"Squire Holmes is here," she said as she took Mother's parasol. She spoke in a low voice as if she didn't want to be overheard. "He asked for you three to meet him in the drawing room."

Her quiet demeanor and tone warned us my father might not be in the best of moods. While I steeled my spine before entering, Mother breezed past me with all the casualness of someone returning from making social calls. Father, who had been sitting near the fireplace at the far end, stood as we stepped into the room.

Without any hesitation, she moved to him, her hands outstretched. "Mr. Holmes, *quelle surprise*. We hadn't expected you in town until after the boys were out for the summer holiday. I do hope this doesn't indicate something has happened."

"Something *has* happened," Father stopped his thought to absent-mindedly give a kiss to each of Mother's cheeks. He continued in a brusque tone. "I received a rather disturbing visit from Constable Gibbons."

"Oh, dear. I did fear that might occur after the man from Scotland Yard mentioned his name. You see—"

Before she could complete the sentence, Father pulled

himself straight and barked at us. "Sit. The three of you. And tell me how you came to be involved in yet another murder."

We all instantly obeyed, Mycroft and I sinking into a settee and Mother into an armchair near Father and the fireplace. I shoved my hands under my thighs to keep the others from seeing them tremble. While I didn't fear any physical harm from my father's current state—he'd never given me any reason to be concerned on that account—I feared being the object—or at least one of them—of his wrath. The possible consequences could range from being sent back to Eton (not all boys were able to return home for the holiday and so there were lodgings available) to returning to Underbyrne. As I reviewed all the options, I calmed, recognizing neither was too distasteful a punishment. Unfortunately, my reflection on my father's emotional state and possible future reactions caused me to fail to notice a particularly important bit of information in his short tirade.

Mother, however, had not. If she was distressed about his mood, she didn't demonstrate it. On the contrary, she raised her chin and smiled. "You said 'murder,' not 'death.' Did Inspector Roggens use the term? Because we've said all along—"

Father rocked back and forth on his heels, his hands clenched behind his back. I'd seen this stance before. Usually when he was listening to someone brought into his court just before he pronounced his decision regarding the person's guilt. "An inspector—from Scotland Yard—doesn't need your opinion. Whether he calls it 'murder' or 'plum pudding' is irrelevant."

"I'm afraid it means a great deal to the family, and we

THE ADVENTURE OF THE DECEASED SCHOLAR

have already been helpful to them in this matter." Two spots appeared on Mother's cheeks. The same sympathy I'd felt when we'd identified the body reappeared as I watched her struggle with both her anger and the humiliation from Father's rebuke. "The coroner wouldn't even have known who the man was if we hadn't been there."

Mycroft cleared his throat. "If I may interject here, Father, you need to know more of the facts. I'm afraid whatever Gibbons may have shared with you is only part of what we have learned."

"And you know Gibbons doesn't like Mother," I said.

The moment I spoke, I regretted speaking out of turn. Mycroft's and Father's glares told me not to say another word. Only Mother's soft gaze suggested some sympathy for my comment. I leaned on that sentiment to retain my calm. After all, Mycroft was correct: our father was making conclusions with limited information—above all, Miss Phillips' threat against my brother. *That* explanation, however, needed to be left to my mother.

"There's more you need to understand," Mother said, and quickly summarized the events leading to us identifying the body, the subsequent information we'd shared during the coroner's examination, and the call today by Inspector Roggens. As she continued, I could see Father's jaw muscles relax. He seemed to comprehend we had not interjected ourselves, but rather simply been present when the situations appeared. Until…

"And we have now been tasked by the family to collect information to be presented at the inquest. The coroner is saying it's suicide. You do realize the family will be destitute if the inquest comes to the same conclusion? I'm afraid his sister has threatened to implicate poor Mycroft if we don't help her before the inquest at the end of the week."

She quickly reviewed the meeting with Miss Phillips and what we had learned to date. Father's color shifted from red to white to red again, as he took in the unfounded lie Lord Surminster's sister had concocted and its implications for our family. When she finished, he blew out through his lips and muttered several oaths to himself.

"Of all the unmitigated…. How could she…?" He raised his gaze to the ceiling and said, perhaps to the Almighty, "Will our family ever be rid of such scandals? What has brought such wrath upon us?"

I pulled my hands from under my thighs and let my shoulders drop. Father might still be angry, but no longer at us.

Mother's voice also lost the strain tinging her words when she had begun her tale. "I believe you will see, once again, we have no course at the moment but to proceed in our efforts to clear Lord Surminster of any accusations that he took his own life. We're convinced it's murder, but to collect something to be shared at the inquest requires further investigation."

Before Father could ask what we had learned to date, she said, "The body has been laid out for visitors, and it is imperative we have a chance to view him again. We were about to change and visit the Phillips' home. Perhaps you would care to join us?"

Father rubbed his chin, his fingernails raking his beard. "I suppose it would be best for the whole family to be there for the show."

"We'll have tea and then go. I have good news. We have tickets for the opera tonight. I read last week how a French opera company would be performing and recognized the manager as an old family friend. I wrote to him before I left, and he sent me tickets for a box with an excellent view. They arrived early this morning."

She moved toward the hallway, but Mycroft remained rooted where he stood.

"A recital last night and the opera tonight?" He fairly spit out his words. "I refuse. I have had as much singing as I can take for the week."

Mother turned to face us. "Miss Ila Augustin will be singing again. Sherlock and your father haven't had the pleasure yet. I suppose you can be forgiven if you prefer to stay at home."

"Thank you," he said with relief.

That pronouncement was enough to get us all moving toward the dining room for a light meal. With great effort, I managed to keep my expression blank, but inside, I was rejoicing at the opportunity to hear the French Nightingale. With Mycroft crying off, I wanted to put in a word for Constance's attendance. A night at the opera would mean more to her than any of us. I only hoped Mother agreed.

WHILE I'D ATTENDED other funerals and visitations, they'd never been along the scale of Lord Surminster's. The elaborate black wreath hanging on the front door announced both the family's wealth as well as their sorrow. Once we entered, I discerned various other mourning traditions had been carefully observed, as required by their rank. Not a single clock was ticking. All had been stopped. With the man's time of death open to speculation, I assumed they were stopped when his death had been confirmed: a quarter past one.

Black crepe covered all the pictures and mirrors, and everyone moved in subdued paces and spoke in low tones. Hamilton opened the door for us, and Father passed his calling card to the man. The butler indicated we were to pass into the drawing room and left us to find our way.

Lord Surminster lay in his coffin in a very different state than last we saw him. He had been cleaned and groomed and dressed in a suit that fit him. Two women dressed in black were seated at each end of the flower-filled coffin. Both were older women, their grey hair pulled into buns at the base of their necks. I had seen such mourners at other funerals, although Lord Surminster did not require them for the usual reason. Such persons were there to render aid should the person not be truly deceased and suddenly awaken from some sort of deep unconsciousness. This vigil would continue until he was buried. In the case of this man, I was certain no sudden resurrection would occur.

The scent of burning candles and flowers filled the space, making both my head and stomach ache. With all windows shuttered and draped in black, the stifling atmosphere fostered a strong desire to tug at the high collar I wore for the visit. One glance at my father's down-turned mouth told me to resist the urge. He had agreed to accompany us but made it clear he wasn't fully supportive of the endeavor.

Mother approached the woman at the coffin's head and murmured some appropriate words of condolences. She then leaned closer to the dead man's head and clucked her tongue.

"So young," she said. "And healthy looking."

"Yes." The woman nodded. "Lord Surminster was very athletic."

"Really? Did you know him well?"

"I'm Emily Simms, a friend of the family. I grew up on the estate next to Lady Surminster and visited Wrightmoor often as a child. Of course, back then, Lady Surminster was Miss Lillian Canton."

"I'm sure she appreciates having such a good friend about her at a time like this. So good you've kept in touch."

"Oh, more than that," she said, raising her chin, "My father was her mother's trustee. After my father's passing, my husband continued as trustee—now for Lady Surminster after her mother died."

"Did you come up from Wrightminster? That is where Wrightmoor is located?"

"Oh my, no. I'm here for the season. My youngest, Cora, was presented this year. She's already made a very favorable impression on several young men." A smile spread across her face, and she chuckled. "I wouldn't doubt we'll be announcing an engagement before long."

"Congratulations. I do hope a good match is found." Mother glanced over her shoulder at my brother. "My son Mycroft has attended a few events as well. Perhaps we'll see you at some function in the future? He was in the same college as Lord Surminster."

Mother turned her attention to deceased again. "Just look at his cheeks. So rosy." She leaned over the young man's still face as if studying his complexion. "No rouge, then?"

She received a scoff in response. "Certainly not. It's his own color."

"My mistake."

She straightened, and Father appeared at her elbow.

"I think, Mrs. Holmes, there may be others who wish to also pay their respects."

"Yes, of course, Mr. Holmes." She turned to the lady and passed a card to her. "Please share our respects with the family. And please feel free to call on us. I would love to meet Cora."

On the carriage ride back home, Father sat next to Mother and kept shifting his weight about as if unable to find a comfortable position. Mother remained quiet, almost reflective with her eyes half-closed, seemingly oblivious to his agitation. The contrast between the two raised my own discomfort, and unable to restrain myself further, I finally pulled on my collar, responding to a desire I'd suppressed for almost an hour.

"Will you stop fidgeting." Father snapped his mouth shut.

Mother opened her eyes and turned to him. "I know the enquiry from Scotland Yard has disturbed you, but I feel there is more to your distress than what you have shared."

He adjusted himself in his seat to face her more directly. "First was your scrutiny and possible insult concerning Lord Surminster and his complexion. And after that, your efforts to push Mycroft into some matrimonial arrangement."

"Hear, hear," my brother said and slapped his hand upon his thigh.

Mother shot her gaze in his direction, and he dropped his own. While the dialog was clearly about him, her glance told him he had no claim in the discourse. She turned to Father and brushed her skirt.

"I suppose you're referring to my discussion with Mrs. Simms and the invitation to her and her daughter." She shifted in her seat to address Father more directly. "I needed to examine the young man's face closely. I couldn't very well say, 'Do you mind if I study Lord Surminster's right ear?' I had to come up with some other observation. By the way, he *was* wearing rouge. No man's cheeks are that pink two days after death."

Unable to resist my curiosity, I asked, "What did you find?"

"Unfortunately, not what I'd hoped. They had done something to the ear. Actor's putty, if I'm not mistaken. Just as they had with the overall makeup. Any damage has been disguised."

"Whoever prepared him must have noticed the wound then," Father said. Up until now, he'd not voiced any interest in what had happened to Lord Surminster other than he'd prefer we weren't involved. This turn in attitudes caused us all to stare. He spoke, but more to himself. "There was a case I read of…Thomas…Bowerman. Something about an awl."

Mother tilted her head. "An awl. Or something like it. Long. Sharp. Thin. Yes, that would do it." Her gaze was directed between Mycroft and me, but her attention was far from the carriage. I could see her imagining the entrance of the object through the aural cavity. "If it entered there, it would enter the brain and…" She turned to Father. "I do believe you've identified it, Mr. Holmes."

Father smiled at the praise his wife had just showered on him. "You're not the only one who reads."

"Such an attack would have hurt like the devil, though," Mycroft said. "Had a master at Eton who used to box your ears. Made more than one boy scream. And he only hit the outside of the ear."

"No one would simply allow someone to stab something in their ear," Mother said with a nod.

I leaned forward, eager to be included in the conversation. "You noted gin on the old man, what about Lord Surminster? Could he have been drunk as well?"

"He wasn't much of a drinker," Mycroft said.

"Maybe he didn't know what he was drinking? Or he was given a sleeping draught?" I said.

"There. You can report this all to his family and suggest they present it at the inquest." Father pulled on his waistcoat as if tidying the argument away. "Then we can go back to our lives. Such as attending the opera tonight. I have to say, you showed much forethought in requesting the tickets before you left."

"Yes. It was good fortune a French company owned by an old family friend is touring here. George Pelletier. He arranged for the box—as a gift. Are you sure you don't wish to attend tonight, Mycroft?" He whipped his head back and forth, leaving no misinterpretation of his sentiments. "You'll be missing something special. Oh, and don't worry about my invitation to Mrs. Simms and Miss Cora. It wasn't meant for you. You can do much better than the youngest daughter of a barrister."

I hadn't missed Mother's effort to deflect any further discussion about the opera. I suspected she had an ulterior motive for attending. Someone there might have missed Lord Surminster's presence, given the ticket she'd found in his pocket. Father, however, had focused on this new topic.

"How did you know so much about Cora?" he asked.

"I inferred it from her mother's clothes, my dear. The woman may have been born into the upper classes, which I assume given her proximity to Lady Surminster when they were youngsters, but her dress doesn't reflect such rank now. The style was at least two seasons old—although I have to admit I might not have the most fashionable mourning dress if I only were to use it on a few occasions. And the fabric was not of the best quality. Her husband has some rank, if they are here for the season, but not at the same level as Lord Surminster's family. He could be a physician who has come down some in the world. I would venture, however, he's most likely a barrister what with him serving as Lady Surminster's trustee."

Father paused as he considered her observations and then asked, "If you have no interest in the daughter, why the invitation?"

"Because I want to speak at greater length to the mother. If she knew Lady Surminster as a girl, and they grew up together near each other—"

"She might know about the nun's chest," I said.

Father telegraphed another scowl in my direction, but Mother gave me a smile. "Exactly."

"You might be a great help to us, Mr. Holmes, on this matter as well," she said, turning to him again. "We learned a particularly odd bit of information with respect to Lady Surminster's trust. Her grandfather had stipulated both real and personal property were part of the trust, including 'the nun's chest.' While Lady Surminster might be able to shed some light on the situation, I'm afraid we can't visit with her at this time, given her seclusion during the mourning period. It may be something or nothing, but the only way to know is by learning what it is."

"And how might I be of help? I know very little about nuns. Or their chests."

"But you know the law. Why would this particular personal property be so ordered in the trust?"

"Without seeing the full documents, it's hard to say. I would guess it has some particular meaning to the settlor who created it. Regardless, it will be of no concern to us once you have shared the information regarding Lord Surminster's death and extricate Mycroft from testifying at the inquest."

Mother tapped her finger against her lips as if contemplating this bit of news. After a moment more, she shrugged. "True. I am curious, however, about this chest. Let's hope Mrs. Simms will take it upon herself to come for a visit and share her knowledge. In the meantime, I have arranged for a quick early supper before we change for the opera."

When we arrived home, I pulled Mother aside. "I was wondering…" I glanced about and dropped my voice. "You see, with Mycroft not attending…"

"You want to include Constance, do you not?"

My chin bobbed up and down. Her intuitive understanding of my hesitation to broach the subject relieved my fears.

"She would so enjoy the performance," I said. "But Father—"

If Mycroft had problems with Constance and her place in our home, Father's attitude toward my friend was definitive. Constance was, after all, in our employ, and I wasn't certain he would agree to her attending the opera with us tonight.

Mother placed her hand against my cheek. "Sherry dear, it is not uncommon for a lady to attend such an event with her maidservant. What if she needs an item? Who would get it for her? For your father, this would be appropriate protocol. Now, please find Constance and have her come to my sitting room. We will need to ensure she is appropriately attired for the event tonight."

She left me to seek my friend out and share the news with her.

CHAPTER SIX

The Covent Garden Theater was a massive building. Located on Bow Street, it had been rebuilt only ten years earlier. The edifice sported Corinthian columns with statues and bas-relief in the portico above the entrances and the triangular roof's facade. Inside was just as resplendent with wide staircases leading to four levels of balconies. And once inside the theater itself, its crystal chandelier and gilded white-and-blue bas-relief took one's breath away—especially Constance's.

Stepping inside our box, she let out a little cry of surprise. "Lors. Ain't—I mean, isn't—it elegant?" To which I agreed.

Thanks to Mother's friend, we had a box near the stage, but not at such an angle that it created any difficulty in viewing the performance. Arriving at the box had been an adventure in itself. The press of people had propelled us up the stairs to the entrance, through it, and up more stairs to our box. Along the way, Constance seemed not to know where to focus. Her head swiveled about as she took in the women in their colorful evening dresses and the hall's opulent surroundings.

Given her position as ladies' maid, Constance wore one of Mother's older, muted brown dresses which had been altered to fit her. It was rather plain—no bright trimmings—but it set off her red hair. Instead of her usual long braid, my friend had pulled her hair from her face and shaped it into a tight bun at the back of her neck.

Once in the box, Mother and Father arranged themselves in the front, and Constance and I took seats behind them. A muted roar came from all sides of us as the attendees spoke to one another. From high above in the gallery, occupied by those with few funds, shouts and shuffling provided an overtone to the rest of the buzz. I found it difficult to hear Constance, who was seated next to me.

Craning forward, she said, "I'd wager there's more people here than in the whole village."

I didn't argue with her, although I thought our village's population was larger. Cramming so many into one building, however, certainly made it feel overpopulated.

Mother pulled out her opera glasses and examined those taking their seats on the benches in front of the stage. She then scanned the boxes of the four tiers in front of us.

"What are you seeking, Mrs. Holmes?" my father asked.

"Nothing in particular," she said without taking the glasses from her face. "Just observing who's here. It's not often one has a chance to hear Miss Augustin sing, and I wondered who has chosen this opportunity."

"Would you like to see?" I asked Constance and offered her my glasses.

Following my mother's example, she held them up to her

eyes and turned to me. She gave a little yelp. Father turned in our direction—his signal that we were making too much noise. Two bright spots appeared on her cheeks, and she lowered the glasses to speak to me.

"You're bigger," she whispered.

"That's their purpose. So you can see the singers on the stage better."

She trained them onto the still-curtained platform, studied the image for a moment, and then turned to me again. "I could see a boot mark on one of the boards. They need to clean the floor better."

She then turned her attention to those on the benches and boxes, as my mother continued to do. With her attention elsewhere, I allowed myself a smile. As much as she knew of worlds I'd never encountered—prison life, for example—she still had a naiveté about her I found refreshing. Things I took for granted, she was enjoying for the first time, and I experienced them anew through her.

The gaslights dimmed in the auditorium and brightened on the stage. A murmur passed through the crowd.

Constance leaned toward me and whispered, "Is it starting?"

When I saw my father swivel his head in my direction, I knew better than to answer her with anything other than a nod. With that assurance, we both settled back into our seats for what I was certain would be a treat.

The conductor took up his baton, and the orchestra hit their first chord. Constance craned her neck, held the glasses to her face, and remained as still as a statue. I hoped she remembered to breathe. It wouldn't do at all to have to revive my friend.

The production of Verdi's *Don Carlos* was as dramatic

THE ADVENTURE OF THE DECEASED SCHOLAR

and engaging as I hoped it would be. And Ila Augustin didn't disappoint. When she appeared in the first act, she was dressed as a sixteenth-century royal, with a stiff ruff around her neck and a heavy, dark-velvet gown. For each of her solos, she would walk to the center of the stage and sing in a strong, high voice, reaching top notes without a single screech.

As the first act ended, Constance whispered to me, "Who was that woman?"

"Ila Augustin," I said, rather surprised at the question.

She blew through her lips and glared at me. "I know she's Ila Augustin, but who *is* she?"

Understanding her question now, I regretted not having explained the libretto to her earlier. In short sentences before the second act began, I quickly explained she was Elizabeth, sent to marry the prince Don Carlos to create peace between France and Spain. Only she learned she was to marry his father. In the next act, Elizabeth would marry the king, and Don Carlos would decide to leave the country because he couldn't bear to see his love married to another.

"How sad," she said.

I decided not to mention how much worse it would become between the two, with Don Carlos being condemned to death. She'd learn it soon enough.

During the first intermission, I stood and stretched. When I turned to her, I noticed she now bore a pout, marking a storm brewing inside her.

"Is it over?" she asked.

I thought she was disappointed it had ended, so I quickly explained to her there was still more to come.

"No, this is the intermission. There are still three more acts. We can get a lemonade or stroll around if you wish."

She nodded and stood, but she didn't smile in response to my news. What had come over her?

I followed her out into the hallway behind the box. The atmosphere there was actually closer than where we were sitting. Patrons milled about, some sending for lemonade, others simply clustered about talking. Instead of stopping a waiter for a drink, Constance marched ahead to what appeared to be a line at a refreshment stand, and I could only follow. I considered briefly noting to her that as the man, I should truly be in the lead, or at least, at her side, but I quickly vetoed the notion. Any such statement at the moment would not rearrange our positions and would bring the brunt of her mood upon my head.

Once in line, I hoped to distract her by saying, "Miss Augustin has a beautiful voice, don't you agree?"

Staring at the man's coat in front of us, she said, "I suppose so."

"She's one of the most highly paid sopranos in the world. I heard she demands eight thousand pounds to sing."

At that bit of information, she turned to me. "And what do you think of my voice?"

I froze. While Constance had a lovely voice and with the training Mother had provided, it had been strengthened, in no way could I compare the two. While exercises can enhance a voice, I was of the mind a base talent had to exist for them to be effective. One could teach another the basics of logic, but a certain mental agility is required to be able to make a strong argument. Constance was not at the level of Ila Augustin, but I wasn't familiar with another soprano who was. I stated as much.

I wasn't sure what my friend expected to hear, but she didn't receive what I said with detached emotion. She only

THE ADVENTURE OF THE DECEASED SCHOLAR

made a thin "oh," when her hand flew to her mouth. Tears welled in her eyes, and she pushed through the crowd down the stairs and toward the entrance. I followed, in part because I felt my remark had forced her to flee, but also because of my fear of where she'd run once on the ground floor. Surely she wouldn't dash into the road?

I'd heard enough tales to know a London street wasn't safe for an unescorted young girl after dark. In the back of my mind, I planned to arrange for a cab to take her home should she refuse to return to the theater. I had the coins Mother had passed to me to purchase lemonade.

Calling her name, I pushed through the milling crowd, trying to catch a glimpse of brown among the colorful gowns and black coats. Halfway to the entrance, I saw her red hair passing through the doors to the street.

Once outside, I ran down the steps, searching up and down for her. Unable to catch sight of her, I turned around and studied those idling about the columns. I noticed a patch of red and brown by the far-right corner, and I rushed back toward the entrance stairs, cutting in front of two men and a woman walking down the street, and tripping the first gentleman.

"So sorry," I said, stepping back and taking a moment to survey the man I ran into. A second later, I added, "Mr. Edmonds. How surprising to see you here. Sorry to dash away, but I'm on an urgent errand."

As I rushed off, I heard the man speak to someone. "Rose. Maurice. I'll be just a minute."

The woman's name didn't register with me until I was halfway up the stairs. A part of me wanted to turn around and return to Edmonds and possibly the mysterious "Rose" from the note used to blackmail Mycroft, but the part reminding me my friend was hurting and needed me pushed me to complete my ascent.

Reaching her, I puffed out my apology. "Constance, I'm sorry if I hurt your feelings."

Her back was to me, but her shoulders moved up and down with a deep sigh. She turned about and swiped at the tears on her cheeks. I handed her a handkerchief from my pocket.

"It's just...." She gave another shudder and brushed her cheeks with the linen square. "I just always thought I could do that. Be like Ila Augustin. Only tonight..."

She couldn't complete the thought, but I understood. I'd known for some time how important singing was to her. I was beginning to grasp the impact of class upon the ambitions of those seeking to better themselves, especially women. While a woman might be able to find employment above her station, she would be in competition with those already in possession of the skills and breeding she was trying to acquire. More than once, my friend had said her singing offered a way out. Observing Miss Augustin's talent tonight made her aware of how stiff the competition might be.

"Do you know how old Miss Augustin is? Because I do. I read it in the paper not long ago. She's thirty. She's been on the stage since she was thirteen. Before that, she was training, learning the songs she sang tonight—and scores more. She even had to quit for a few years to rest her voice because she hadn't been properly trained. You have time to develop your talent, but you have to do it correctly."

"Do you think I could be like her when I'm thirty?"

"All I know is she trained to be on the stage. Something anyone can do. Vocal lessons, learning the songs. I know you can do that part. And then you'd need to get the attention of one of the proprietors. You probably wouldn't begin as a soloist, but if you continue to—"

She gave me a wide-eyed stare. "How do you meet a proprietor?"

I swallowed. I had no idea how one accomplished such an introduction. My knowledge of the stage and the business of opera and other entertainments came from what Mother had shared of the artists who had been her French relations' friends.

"Mother knows at least one. He procured her tickets for tonight. Maybe not here at the Royal Opera House, but she knows those who are involved in entertainment. I suppose I can request she provide an introduction—at the proper time. After you've studied more."

She reached out and grabbed my hands, squeezing so hard I thought my bones would break. "Thank you, Sherlock."

"Shall we go back inside?"

We turned to re-enter the opera house. Someone called my name from behind. I recognized Mr. Edmonds from the street. I sucked in my breath, having completely forgotten about the proctor. When I completed my turn, I discovered he was two steps below me and almost eye level with Constance and me.

Following a brief study of my friend, he gave me a wink. "I see your urgent matter."

The familiarity he shared made me drop my friend's hand and shift my weight on my feet. His gaze drifted back to her and let it rest longer than was polite. Constance lifted her chin as her cheeks reddened, a signal of both defiance and unease.

"May I be of service?" I asked to draw his attention away.

Edmonds gave a little smile I somehow felt was not genuine. "I may have spoken out of turn earlier to your mother. I believe I may have some information on the … matter discussed in my office. Please, let her know I'll stop by tomorrow to see her."

"I'll let her know. Can you name an hour? To ensure she's home?"

"About two tomorrow afternoon, if that's all right?"

"Certainly."

As he turned to go, the lady I had seen with him on the street appeared next to him. She was very fetching with blonde curls piled high and a classic Grecian face. "Come, Nathan, they're waiting for us at *La Lampe et le Chien*."

Her pronunciation of "The Lamp and Dog" had an accent similar to my mother's, which made me take a second study of her. Her clothes appeared fashionable and fit her well. I considered her a tourist or foreign friend of Mr. Edmonds.

"Of course, Rose." He bowed to me and dipped his head to Constance. "Master Holmes and Miss…?"

"Constance," my friend said without hesitation.

Edmonds' lips thinned at her impropriety. Social convention required me to make the introduction, but I would explain it to her later.

His gaze took her in again from head to foot before saying, "Miss Constance."

With a swish of her skirt, Rose turned him about, and the two descended the steps to join their companion. She linked her arm through the third man's, and his red satin waistcoat caught a streetlamp's light with a glint. Based on my brother's earlier description, I knew him to be Maurice, Edmonds' cousin.

Constance stared at the backs of the retreating trio before we returned to our box for the evening. The crowd was thinning quickly as the production began for the next act. To my surprise, my friend didn't rush back as I had anticipated. Instead, she made slow progress up the stairs as if in deep thought.

Halfway up, she whispered to me, "Lors, she was a rather peculiar one, don't you think?"

"How do you mean?"

"I know speakin' French makes her different, and maybe they do things differently over there. But I've learned from your mother her dress was all wrong for the time of day. She had on a *day* dress at night."

"She seemed quite fashionable to me."

For some reason, I felt the need to defend my lack of knowledge of women's wear. I made a vow to make a study of women's clothing—although not where Constance or my classmates at Eton would see. I didn't need mocking from either audience.

"You saw the ladies in there. Their shoulders are showin' and it's all satin and 'broidery. She's not goin' to the opera, but still. It's all wrong."

Pausing on the steps, I considered this information. Nathan Edmonds and his cousin Maurice had been in the company of a French woman who didn't have the funds or knowledge to dress appropriately. She, then, wasn't either a wife, or even someone from their social status, which left...

"Do you think she's a-a—?" I couldn't pronounce the word in the presence of a female, especially my friend Constance.

She, on the other hand, had no problem completing the thought. "A dollymop?"

I could only nod, impressed with her ease at referring to those young shopgirls or workers who offer other services on the side to well-to-do gentlemen. Given that Rose was from France certainly put a different lens on both the Edmonds. If Miss Phillips could threaten ruin on my brother, what would it mean for either or both of them?

"Maybe that's why he wants to speak to Mother. He's afraid I'll say something about him and his cousin with a d—woman like her."

With a glance up and down the near-empty stair, she said, "We'd best be goin' in."

"I think we've missed some of the next act."

"Is that Miss Augustin goin' to sing some more?"

"I believe she has at least one more aria."

She took a few steps along the hallway, then turned to me. "I knows you were bein' honest with me about my singing. And I even thought it myself. It still hurts, though, when you hear it out loud."

I nodded, unsure what else to say. While I could have lied, it wouldn't have been fair to her. Meeting her gaze, I said, "I'm not saying you don't sing well. You do. Exceptionally well. But a soprano like Miss Augustin, she comes along maybe once in a lifetime. I'd say you are a much better singer than all the others on the stage tonight."

"Really?" she said, letting a small smile grace her lips.

"Honest."

By the time we returned to our balcony seats, a good portion of the act's first scene had already passed. When I took my seat, Mother asked, "Where have you been?"

I glanced at Father and whispered back, "I'll tell you

later, but Mr. Edmonds will be visiting you tomorrow at two."

Her eyebrows drew together into the question she couldn't ask at present, and she turned her attention to the stage. How I came to see Edmonds—or the mysterious "Rose"—would have to wait.

Even after the opera ended and the performers had taken their last bows, I didn't have a chance to share my experience with Mother. We were turning to leave the box when a gentleman stepped inside. He was dressed in the traditional black evening wear, with a small stick pin in his lapel.

"Violette, *ma chérie*," he said, extending his arms.

Mother took his hands and smiled at him, responding to him in French. "George. Thank you so much for the tickets."

"And you must be Monsieur Holmes," George said in English, beaming at Father. "You are a very lucky man. Violette is a gem." He turned to Constance and me. "Are these your children?"

"My son, Sherlock," Mother said, "and a family… friend, Constance."

I bowed to the man. "*C'est un plaisir.*"

Constance gave a little curtsy. When he turned away, however, I caught her studying the man, her eyes round. The man's uncommon flamboyance and energy amazed me and seemed to have a similar effect on her.

"A marvelous performance, especially by Mademoiselle Augustin," Father said in French.

"Would you care to meet her?" he asked in his native tongue. Before we could answer, he beckoned us to follow him. "Come. Come. I will introduce you."

I hung back with Constance to allow the adults to exit first. As we stepped toward the back of the building, skirting the patrons now leaving their boxes and the theater, Constance whispered to me, "Is he a proprietor? The one who hires the singers? Where are we going?"

"He's Mother's friend and is going to introduce us to Miss Augustin," I whispered back, realizing she hadn't been able to follow the discussion in French.

While I had made a vague promise to introduce her to a proprietor only an hour ago, I hadn't expected such an opportunity to present itself so soon. I stared at the backs of the adults, wishing I had time to explain the need to tread cautiously. She didn't know Mother had introduced her as a family friend—a convenient side-step to explaining her presence in the box—but Father wouldn't tolerate her imposing herself on George or Miss Augustin—a serious breach of etiquette in his eyes.

The backstage area bustled with rough-looking men moving scenery and props about, performers—some in stage makeup and others now in street clothes—rushing in different directions, and some women in maid uniforms carrying pitchers of water or clothes toward a row of doors. George greeted different performers as we made our way to a door bearing a sign with Miss Augustin's name.

George knocked, and a maid answered. After he returned the greeting, a woman's voice called to him. "Please come in, *mon cheri*."

"I am not alone," he said as we stepped in. "This is a very old friend, Violette P—Holmes. Monsieur Holmes. Her son, Sherlock, and a friend, Constance."

Miss Augustin had removed her wig and wore a wrapper but was still in her makeup. She rose from a settee and

THE ADVENTURE OF THE DECEASED SCHOLAR

stepped toward us. "Any friends of George's are, of course, welcome. I am so pleased to meet you all."

"The pleasure is all ours," Father said. "An incredible performance."

She sat again and studied Mother for a moment. "You were at the recital last night. But there was a younger man with you." She glanced at Father. "He resembles you. Another son, perhaps?"

"Mycroft," Mother said with a nod. "He was unable to make it tonight. We both enjoyed it immensely. Particularly your rendition of Rosina from *Il barbiere di Siviglia*. I'm sorry we didn't get to experience the entire work. But the performance here was by another company, I believe."

"Yes," said George. "Also from France. But they have already returned to the continent."

Once again, I was able to observe my mother's ability to interrogate without arousing suspicions. I was the only other person in the room who knew Lord Surminster had a ticket to that performance. What was she seeking from these two?

"A pity," Mother said. "We had been invited by my son's friend, but we were unable to make it. Lord Surminster. Are you familiar with him?"

Both George and Miss Augustin responded immediately they didn't know him, and given their quick answers, I held no suspicions they were hiding information. If Mother was disappointed, her face didn't betray her.

Miss Augustin stood. "If you don't mind, I would like to change to leave the theater. These performances tire me, and I need to rest."

After thanking her again, George escorted us to an exit. He chatted amiably about upcoming performances and those who would be part of the productions. At one point, he turned to Mother. "Do you still sing?"

She shook her head and laughed. "Not really."

"She has a beautiful voice," he said to my father. "So natural. Don't you agree?"

Father glanced at Mother as if checking to see how he should answer. I, myself, had rarely heard her sing and couldn't recall anything remotely similar to the talent displayed by Ila Augustin.

In the end, Father said, "There is nothing more beautiful than my wife. Including her voice."

George gave a hearty laugh and slapped Father on the back. "Well said. Well said."

"The one who has a beautiful voice is Constance," Mother said.

Father's mood had lightened, but I noticed his face muscles tighten at the mention of our assistant groundskeeper's daughter.

"*Vraiment?*" George asked, his gaze settling on Constance. A wide smile adorned her face, along with two bright red spots on her cheeks, giving her a coloring more natural and endearing than Miss Augustin's rouge. "If her voice is half as attractive as her face—"

"Truly," Mother said. "She has been training. Developing a repertoire. Another year or so, and her voice will be professional quality."

At my mother's assessment, Constance's smile faded. I suspected she had hoped the man would have her sing for him right then and there—not to mention possibly hire her on the spot. Two less-than-stellar appraisals in one evening had to be a harsh reality for her. All the same, I was relieved when George didn't insist on hearing her. As much as I

THE ADVENTURE OF THE DECEASED SCHOLAR

wanted Constance to succeed, I wasn't ready to see her leave Underbyrne. I found comfort in knowing she remained at the estate, along with my family—part of the continuity that abided despite my absence.

The carriage ride back to the townhouse seemed filled with a suppressed tension. When the light passed through the window onto Father's face, I could make out the chords in his neck. Constance spent the entire trip staring out the window. I considered offering up some inoffensive observation about the performance or the weather but couldn't determine any remark that might not lead to tripping some snare. In the end, I followed Constance's example and simply watched London's streets slip by in the gloom.

After breakfast, I met with Mother in her sitting room to share my encounter with Mr. Edmonds and Rose. After summarizing the brief meeting, I asked, "Should we tell Father about possibly meeting the Rose from the note?"

Mother tilted her head to one side as if weighing the options before she spoke. "I don't think Rose will have any bearing on the information Mr. Edmonds plans to share. If she does, then we can reevaluate this decision. At the moment, I think we should respect her privacy as well as Mr. Edmonds'."

"But you are going to have him meet with you and Mr. Edmonds?"

"I will share the appointment with both Mr. Holmes and Mycroft, telling them you happened upon Mr. Edmonds and his companions, and he said he thought of something to share with us. I'm afraid, once again, your father wouldn't consider it your place to be in such a meeting. Your father also wishes to meet Inspector Roggens."

I stared at her, seeking to understand her statement. She returned a half-smile, signaling she found my confusion amusing.

"Your father is concerned about our involvement with Scotland Yard—or rather what he considers interference. He told me last night he intended to speak with the inspector to ensure our interactions with the Yard have been completed. Because we have already shared what we have observed about Lord Surminster's death, he plans to confirm the inspector will convey these findings at the inquest, and thus remove Miss Phillips' threat."

My own half-smile crept across my lips. "But you're not through yet, are you?"

"While Inspector Roggens appears thorough and above average in his efforts, I don't believe he can obtain the same information we can. Lord Surminster was murdered for a reason, and I don't think he will be able to discover it. Wrong social circles, you know."

"But aren't we in the wrong circles as well? I mean, Father is simply a squire, hardly a lord."

"True, but we do have some access to the family and its history, thanks to Mrs. Simms. Which reminds me, I must send a card now, letting her know we will be available today. You told Mr. Edmonds two in the afternoon. I think I shall tell her a quarter past."

I studied her one more time, my admiration for my mother's strategy growing during the conversation. "You want them to see each other. Where did you learn such tactics?"

"You have to understand, Sherry dear," she said, as she

rose from her chair to seek out a card from her writing desk, "you cannot underestimate females and their abilities to maneuver social situations or exploit men's misperceptions of such skills. While I doubt any of them have read *The Art of War*, women certainly understand the strategy of playing one interested party off another. For most, it relates to seeking the most favorable match for their offspring, particularly daughters, by considering the competition."

The reference to marriage sent a frisson of fear down my back as I contemplated my brother's own venture into marriageable age. Unable to restrain myself, I spoke aloud part of my fear. "Where is love in all this?"

She faced me, and our gazes met. "You asked me about learning such social strategies. I answered with respect to my own observations about such efforts. For my part, love was the basis for my decision to accept your father's proposal. And I wouldn't want anything different for either you or Mycroft." She turned to pen a short note on a card. "In this case, we are using it to address another matter altogether. Just because Mr. Edmonds appears willing to share some information, his knowing we have also been in touch with Mrs. Simms and have additional information regarding Wrightmoor might make him more forthcoming with his own knowledge."

While Mother thought Edmonds might share information, the same couldn't be said for Inspector Roggens. He arrived shortly after I spoke with Mother. Because both Mycroft and I had viewed the body at the hospital and in repose, he insisted we also attend the interview. He'd pulled out his little notebook and pencil, prepared to write down Mother's observations. When she noted the effort to disguise the wound inside the ear, he glanced at her over his pad, shut it, and put it back into his pocket.

"That's all the information you have?" he asked. "We aren't so dense as to not notice something so obvious."

Father cleared his throat and sat back, obviously assured this matter was now settled. "Then you'll be testifying at the inquest that the death was a homicide?"

"I will be presenting our findings. As you know, it's up to the coroner's jury to determine whether his death was perpetrated by another."

"Surely it is in this case?" Mother asked. I observed a tightness in her voice as if she was restraining a frustration at his statement. "I know the coroner's first opinion was suicide, but it is now obvious the man was murdered. No man would dress himself in a rival university's colors, stab himself in the ear, and throw himself into the Thames. It's physically impossible to accomplish. One or two, yes, but not all three. Other parties were involved, leading to a determination of homicide."

The man shrugged—actually *shrugged*—triggering my own incredulity at the man's response. My respect for Scotland Yard dropped precipitously with that small gesture.

"Can you tell us anything indicating otherwise?" she asked.

Roggens grunted, shifted in his chair, and studied the room about him as if to confirm no one else was listening. Leaning forward, he said in a low voice. "The man had been drinking gin."

Mother glanced at Father. When he didn't respond, she did. "I would guess that might be rather evident." The inspector stared at her, and she continued. "As I mentioned, no one would voluntarily stab an instrument into his ear.

THE ADVENTURE OF THE DECEASED SCHOLAR

Even if he were to perpetrate it himself, upon entering the brain, he would be unable to remove it, and the object would remain there. The most effective way to complete the murder would be for the man to be unconscious—either drunk, drugged, or both. Given the man who was dressed in Lord Surminster's clothes carried the odor of gin, I would guess Lord Surminster might also have been pressed to drink as well."

Roggens stared at her as if taking in what she had shared and debating on how to respond. He opened his mouth but shut it when his gaze shifted to my father. Whatever he considered saying, he seemed to decide against it in my father's presence.

Instead, he simply said, "Thank you for your time. I must be going."

We all stood with the inspector but, before he could take a step, Mother asked, "What time is the inquest on Saturday? I would like to hear the decision."

Again, another review of Father before responding. "I have to check but will let you know."

When the man had been shown out, Father turned to Mother. "Are you truly planning to attend the inquest?"

"I would prefer not to, but you heard the inspector. My fear is the decision will continue to be suicide. The coroner seemed intransigent at the hospital."

"You know you can't testify. You have no standing."

"But Mycroft does. We have only to convince Mr. Edmonds to have us brought in as witnesses. Luckily, he will be visiting us in a few hours. I must make certain Mycroft understands the import of this visit."

CHAPTER SEVEN

Three hours later, when Edmonds entered, I was ascending the stairs. I turned, and our gazes met for an instant. A chill passed through me. Rather than glancing away, he gave me a studied stare, as if to warn me to keep my distance. Almost as fast as the unspoken threat had been telegraphed, he turned his head and followed Mrs. Simpson into the drawing room where my parents and brother were waiting.

Constance met me when I reached the top of the stairs. "Lors, he was menacin', weren't he?"

I checked over my shoulder. The drawing room door had shut. Still, I whispered my response. "I think he's worried about us seeing him with Rose. I only told Mother. That my father and brother are also receiving him should put him more at ease."

"They didn't invite you, too?" she asked.

"I had to make the pretense of going to my room," I said with a shrug. "Shall we take our usual spot?"

THE ADVENTURE OF THE DECEASED SCHOLAR

Once again, I found myself next to Constance and listening through the crack in the door. I was almost certain Mother was aware of our presence because she arranged for all three men to sit with their backs to us.

After introductions and passing the teacups around, Mother opened the conversation. "My son Sherlock said you wished to speak to us today. Before you present your information, will you indulge me in sharing a bit of news as well? You may already know, but Miss Phillips visited and asked me to look into Lord Surminster's death. She was concerned the coroner was suggesting a suicide. When we accompanied the butler, I observed the circumstances didn't indicate the man took his own life. I had an opportunity to consider him yesterday while he was lying in state. As a family friend and attorney, I would request you pass on the information to the family that he was murdered."

While I couldn't see his reaction, the shock—or perhaps anger—was apparent in his response's tone. "Are you certain?"

"Positive." She paused. A rattle of a teacup suggested she took a sip before continuing. "If you examine the right ear, you will notice a wound from the exterior into the interior. It is obvious because whoever prepared him for the viewing covered it up with actor's putty. Someone stabbed a sharp object through his ear and into the brain."

"Such a cause of death has been observed before," Father said almost before she concluded. Edmonds' reaction must have suggested more than a modicum of disbelief because my father continued in a rather defensive tone. "As you know, I'm a magistrate and familiar with crimes across the country. There is a documented case. In that one, an awl was used."

"Penetrating the brain," Mother said, as if to conclude the argument, "causes almost instantaneous death."

"Do you—?" The man's gulp was audible through the door's crack. "Who would do such a thing?"

Father's tone took on a grimmer aura. "Scotland Yard would have to determine that, I suppose. We shared the information with an Inspector Roggens only a few hours ago."

"Scotland Yard?" The man cleared his throat and spoke in a calmer voice afterward. "Please excuse me. All this is news to me. I assisted Miss Phillips in arranging for her brother's removal and dressing, but I knew nothing about any irregularity with his ears. If there was putty in it, I suppose those who laid him out noticed it. At the time, I told her the trust created by her great-grandfather would protect them from losing that property. Sad as it is that he was murdered, this is very good news that the full estate will remain with them."

"You will pass on the information to Lord Surminster's family then?" she asked. He must have assented because she then asked, "I believe you mentioned having other news for us as well?"

This time, a chair squeak accompanied a teacup rattle. Edmonds must have shifted in his seat. I shallowed my breathing, afraid I might miss a word.

"I shared how the suit has been in the courts for more than thirty years, and I have been defending Lady Surminster against her father. What I didn't mention was the trustee. Mr. Simms, a long-time family friend, inherited the responsibility from his father-in-law."

"We met a Mrs. Emily Simms yesterday when we visited

THE ADVENTURE OF THE DECEASED SCHOLAR

for the viewing," Mother said, a thoughtful note in her voice. "His wife?"

"Correct. Her father was the original trustee, and her husband has now taken that mantle."

"And the suit?" Father asked.

"Lord Thanbury sued to gain his late wife's property following her death, claiming he had a right as the husband. The trust, however, clearly states both the real and personal property remain in the hands of her children, er, child— Lady Surminster. Given Lady Surminster's circumstances, she has not had a need for most of the personal property. The estate is as it was when it originally passed to her mother."

"So, the trust is still flush?" Mycroft asked. "Who will inherit Lord Surminster's assets if the inquest agrees his death was not a suicide?"

"Lord Surminster's younger brother is attending Harrow and will receive the title when he reaches majority. His brother's death has upset him terribly. I don't know whether he will return to school to complete this year's term."

The man's assessment of the future Lord Surminster's prospects sent a chill down my spine. It had not been so long ago I had been called home from Eton because of Mother's arrest for the murder of the village midwife. The ordeal had been unsettling for the whole family despite successfully proving my mother's innocence. I tried to imagine the boy's loss of his older brother and now the mantle of responsibility he would hold as the new Earl of Surminster. The same would happen to me, on a smaller scale, should both my father and Mycroft pass. I would inherit Underbyrne and the role of country squire. The prospect of such possible events struck me with a reality I'd never experienced previously.

Footsteps in the hallway drew my attention away from the drawing room. I had been so intent on the conversation in the other room and my own musings, I'd failed to hear the activity at the front door until Mrs. Simpson announced the arrival of another visitor. She must have passed a card to my parents because Mother said to Mr. Edmonds, "It appears Mrs. Simms is at the door. I'll have her and her daughter join us for tea."

Several sets of footsteps echoed in the hall, and I took more than a little delight knowing Mycroft was now trapped in the drawing room with Cora Simms, who was on an intense search of a husband. My only regret was not being able to see his reaction or following discomfiture with their arrival.

Once more tea was served, and the conversation shifted to topics considered appropriate for those of a more delicate nature. I contemplated leaving but knew Mother had a way of soliciting information without others being aware, and she might possibly draw out something useful from the Simms women.

Mother began with an inoffensive question, "I believe you know Mr. Edmonds?"

"Oh my, yes," Mrs. Simms said. "He's been in touch with Mr. Simms over the years concerning that pesky lawsuit Lord Thanbury has been pursuing."

"I'm surprised he hasn't simply dropped it after all this time," Father said.

Without hesitating, Mrs. Simms jumped on this observation. "He'd never do such a thing. The man was and is a spendthrift. Gambling, you know. Has owed everyone in the

THE ADVENTURE OF THE DECEASED SCHOLAR

county at some point. Lady Thanbury and her daughter both kept him from being sent to debtor's prison, but nothing beyond. First, my father, and then, my husband managed the payments to his debtors. Enough to keep the wolves at bay, but no more."

"I'm glad to hear your husband has been a well-reasoning trustee," Mother said. "I understand Wrightmoor is very beautiful."

"It is," Mrs. Simms said with a vigorous head bob. "The lands came to the family when church property was seized in the 1500s. It was once a convent."

Cora Simms spoke up for the first time. Her voice was soft and not unpleasant. "That's where the legend of the nun's chest comes from."

Mother prodded very gently. "Legend?"

"The story goes that one of Catherine of Aragon's ladies in waiting entered the convent following the queen's death. She brought with her a chest said to hold her most precious possessions. Of course, it was turned over to the convent when she took the veil."

"You know how villagers gossip," Mrs. Simms said with a laugh. "They make up a story and it grows over time. An old housekeeper at Wrightmoor once told Lillian and me flat out the chest never existed. When the family took over the land, the abbess told them no one from the Court ever entered the convent. The family was convinced they had buried the chest and were lying about its existence. They went so far as to tear down the buildings to seek the treasure, but nothing was ever found, and they used the stones to build the manor house."

"They didn't simply convert the convent?" Mycroft asked.

"I suppose they hoped to find the chest on the grounds and didn't want to cover it over by accident," Mrs. Simms said. "Of course, it's not the only legend. There's another one about how the nuns who had been buried in the convent would come back and sing masses where the chapel had been. One night, Lillian and I slipped out of the house to see if we could spy them. The only thing we caught was a chill from walking over the lands to reach it. Lillian spent over a week in bed with a fever. We never tried it again."

"Was it a long way? Between the manor and the ruins?" Mother asked.

"It seemed to us to take all night," Mrs. Simms said. "We were young and not certain of the way in the dark."

"I believe I can help," Mr. Edmonds said. "After you left, I sought out a copy of a map of the Wrightmoor estate. This may give you an idea of the distance between the manor and the ruins."

A bit of shuffling and teacup rattling ensued. With my limited view, I observed Edmonds rise and step out of my sight. His receding footsteps indicated movement toward a table set by the window overlooking the street. The others followed.

I almost let a sigh escape my lips. How I longed to be there, among the seven studying the map. Was it similar to the one Lord Surminster had stolen from the library? What had he seen or needed from the other map? And what did the current copy reveal? I'd have to rely on my mother's and brother's recall abilities. Mycroft, of course, had an eidetic memory (and mine was almost as keen), so I had no doubt he would be able to reconstruct it later, but still, it grieved me to be excluded from a first-hand view of this important piece of information.

THE ADVENTURE OF THE DECEASED SCHOLAR

The change in location also limited my ability to hear. The voices of those facing me carried better across the room, but unfortunately, almost all had their backs to me now. As much as I wanted to press my ear against the crack, I feared a shadow might give my presence away. I stilled myself and shallowed my breathing to catch what I could of the discussion around the map.

Edmonds mumbled something like "manor."

Mrs. Simms must have been on the other side because I could hear her say, "It doesn't appear so far on the map, but here everything is drawn flat. A hill actually exists between the two. The walk is much longer when you consider that piece."

"What is this mark?" Mother asked. Through the crack, I could see her leaning over the table and the drawing.

Edmonds' response was again a jumble of sounds, and Mother's response was a non-committal, "Oh, I see."

I added the mark to the items I would ask about after I was alone with her and Mycroft.

Another paper shuffle let me know he'd now folded the map and put it under his arm. They all moved to the door, and I could again make out his remarks.

"It was nice to see you again, Mrs. Simms. Miss Simms. Also, pleasant to meet you, Squire Holmes. I do hope this information assists you in your efforts, Mrs. Holmes."

"What efforts are those?" Mrs. Simms asked.

All sounds on the other side of the door ceased for a breath, and I stilled as well. Mother gave a light-hearted chuckle. "'Efforts' is probably not the right word. 'Curiosity' would be better, I think. My son Mycroft is reading for the law at Oxford—at the same college as Lord Surminster had been. He once shared with Mycroft about his mother's own trust and the ongoing legal battle. We were curious to learn more about the estate. A very interesting case—from a legal perspective—don't you think?"

"Yes," said Mrs. Simms, drawing out the vowel as if to suggest she wasn't certain whether to accept the explanation or not.

Mycroft spoke up, as if to reinforce Mother's explanation. "We went so far as to visit Mr. Edmonds at his office—just to learn more about the case. I do find the Chancery courts fascinating. As a magistrate, Father is involved in the law as well, but this provides a different perspective."

"You're reading for the law, then?" asked Mrs. Simms. "Cora is most familiar with the life of a lawyer—her father being a barrister, you know."

Father seemed to catch the bait Mrs. Simms threw toward my brother and said to the group, "Speaking of which, I do have some paperwork needing attention, and I require Mycroft's assistance. If you ladies will excuse us, we'll see Mr. Edmonds to the door."

Additional leave-taking and assurances of help followed, and the men departed, allowing Mother her privacy with the two ladies. I started at the sound of footsteps in the hallway—my father's and Mycroft's—and turned to find Constance had disappeared.

Her voice drifted from the hallway. "I fetched your coat, sir."

With the women now alone, I turned my attention back to the parlor to see what Mother was able to ferret from her guests.

"Have you been enjoying your season, Miss Simms?" Mother asked once they were settled.

"Oh my, yes," Cora said enthusiastically. "It seems I

THE ADVENTURE OF THE DECEASED SCHOLAR

have a party almost every night." She paused and said in a more demure voice. "Of course, I've been declining events this week, out of respect for Lord Surminster's family."

Mrs. Simms spoke up immediately. "With the family in mourning, we've been assisting them with certain arrangements. Cora's been a great help to Sophronia—Miss Phillips—this week."

"It's important to have close friends during such times," Mother said. "What about Lord Surminster's friends? Have they been in contact with the family?"

"A number of them have been by to pay their respects. Many from his college in Oxford, and some who studied with him at Harrow—where his brother is now."

"And how is the young man doing?"

"Devastated. As is the rest of the family. But Mr. Edmonds has proved a great support to them all these past few days."

"Odd he didn't mention being with the family during our conversations."

"Not this Mr. Edmonds," Cora said before her mother could answer. "A cousin of his. Lord Jared Edmonds. His father is the Earl of Wittdam."

"I think there may be a match soon for the future earl," Mrs. Simms said with a singsong tone.

"Congratulations, Miss Simms."

"Oh no, not me." Cora giggled. "Miss Phillips and Lord Edmonds. Of course, any announcement has been postponed for the present."

"I had no idea the Edmonds and Surminster families were so close."

"The late Lord Surminster, the father, and the current Lord Wittdam were friends. It was Wittdam who suggested his nephew to my husband when the original attorney defending the trust passed on."

"Do the Edmonds own land near Wrightmoor?"

"Why, my dear, they are Wrightmoor's tenants."

AFTER THE SIMMS ladies took their leave, Mother stepped into the dining room.

"Sherry dear, please seek out your brother and have him join me in my sitting room. I believe we need to review what we have learned this afternoon. Also, ask Mrs. Simpson to bring fresh tea for us."

I stopped Mother before we left the room. "Did you see anything interesting about the map?"

"That's why I want you and Mycroft to join me in my sitting room. To compare my impressions with those of Mycroft and examine this relationship between the Edmonds, Wittdam, and Surminster," she said.

I nodded. "It does sound rather…incestuous, doesn't it? Or are such arrangements always the case with the upper classes?"

"My observations have been from the edges—both here and in France—but the circles appear rather tight. Secrets are difficult to keep among them. For example, if Lord Surminster did have some thoughts of harming himself, I doubt someone around him wouldn't have known it."

"All the more reason to think someone else was involved."

"What we have yet to learn, however, is who and why. And those answers might be important for the inquest."

A short time later, the three of us were assembled in her

THE ADVENTURE OF THE DECEASED SCHOLAR

sitting room. Mother had one of the classroom slates at the ready on a nearby table, and after Adeline brought the tea and closed the door, she turned to my brother.

"It's a pity you didn't remain with me during the rest of the Simms ladies' visit." She held up her hand when Mycroft made a movement to protest—probably about his lack of interest in Cora Simms. "While I am rather disappointed you couldn't forgo your discomfort for the additional minutes they occupied, it's more important for you to know you missed some rather interesting information regarding Wrightmoor and the Edmonds. Nathan Edmonds' uncle, the Earl of Wittdam, has been the tenant at Wrightmoor for a number of years."

Mycroft's eyebrows, at first drawn together in disgust, arched as Mother shared this information. "And what does that tell us?"

"I'm not certain at present, but the number of connections between the families may indicate something." She picked up the slate and wrote the names as she described them. "There's Nathan Edmonds, the proctor representing Lady Surminster in her suit against her father over Wrightmoor; Lord Wittdam, tenant at Wrightmoor; Mrs. Simms, a lifelong friend of Lady Surminster; and her husband, the trustee for Lady Surminster's interest in Wrightmoor."

"Don't you think it odd?" I asked. "An earl renting another manor house? Doesn't he have at least one of his own?"

Both of them faced me. Mycroft shot me an expression suggesting I must be dense, but Mother seemed to be pondering my observation. In the end, she said, "A very good question. Wrightmoor might be more conveniently located, or Lord Wittdam holds some interest in the area—"

"Like the nun's chest?" I asked.

"I'd been thinking some business interest, but perhaps…" Her voice trailed off as if she was weighing such a possibility.

"Are we back to that legend again?" Mycroft followed the question with a scoffing sound.

"It may very well be a legend, but a grain of truth often lies at the bottom of such tales." Mother wagged a finger at Mycroft. "I do believe Lord Frampton, Lady Surminster's grandfather, was sufficiently convinced of its existence to ensure his daughter would inherit it if it was found."

"Doesn't it suggest we need to consider who stands to gain if the legend is real? Or from Wrightmoor in general?" I asked.

"Are you suggesting we ask, *Cui bono*? It's a basic part of our law readings. 'Who benefits?'"

"A good question." Mother stared at the list of names on the slate. "We can say Lady Surminster would be the one to most benefit from finding the chest—if the legend is true."

"What about Mr. Simms? As trustee? Would he benefit from finding the chest?"

Mother shook her head. "From what your father has told me, trusteeship is more of a burden than a benefit; but her father, Lord Thanbury, would—if he is successful in breaking the trust."

She now circled Lord Thanbury and Lady Surminster.

"If the chest was somehow related to Lord Surminster's death, I can't see how either of them would have arranged it. Lord Thanbury is too old, and Lady Surminster was his mother," said Mycroft.

I studied the list of names. "What if it wasn't about benefitting from *finding* something, but keeping it from being

THE ADVENTURE OF THE DECEASED SCHOLAR

found out?" My cheeks burned as the question brought their attention back to me again. Ignoring my discomfort, I continued. "What if Lord Surminster found something on the map that might *change* things in some way? Something possibly affecting Lord Thanbury's efforts to break the trust? Some benefit from ending or continuing the fight over Wrightmoor?"

"My guess is Edmonds has been collecting fees from the trust to cover expenses," Mycroft said. His words came out slowly, and I could tell he was thinking out loud, having taken my question in a different direction. "I've read cases where, in the end, the fees and other costs depleted whatever sum was in dispute."

Mother shook her head. "The lawyers get rich while the family is left penniless. Just like in *Bleak House*."

Her reference to Dickens' novel brought to mind my own assessment of the man's contempt for lawyers and the courts. At the time, I'd felt he'd been harsh, knowing as I did my father's own efforts to be fair as a justice of the peace. As I gained insight into this suit and Lord Thanbury's efforts to undermine his own granddaughter's inheritance, I could see how the author had developed such a perspective.

After a final moment of contemplation, Mother straightened. "Which brings us to the map. *If* Lord Surminster did find something in the library's document, the place to start is with what Edmonds showed us today. What were your impressions, Mycroft?"

I leaned forward, eager to hear what he said.

"I believe the map was a duplicate of the one taken from the library," he said. "Of course, that's based on my memory of what remained in the folder and what I saw today. The far-left sides on both were identical—or at least very close to it."

Unable to contain my curiosity, I asked, "What did this map show as the missing pieces?"

Mycroft reached for one of the school slates, and Mother provided him with a piece of chalk. On the left side of the slate, he put an "X." "The manor house. They must have used almost all the stone from the convent, including the outside wall. It's a sort of square U-shape." He boxed in the X on three sides, with the open end pointing to the slate's right side. After studying what he had drawn, he put another X almost on the right side of the slate. "The convent. Of course, this is not drawn to scale. Bit difficult to do so without proper instruments."

I put a finger in between the two points. "This is where the hill is?"

The moment I said it, without raising my gaze, I felt the glares from the other two. Mycroft, because I'd just informed him I had listened in on the conversation, and Mother because I let it slip I had.

In the question that followed, Mycroft enunciated each word as if it were its own sentence. "How do you know?"

My face burned under his scrutiny. In a small voice, I answered him. "I was listening from the dining room."

Mycroft studied our mother. "You knew about this. You had Father and I sit with our backs to the door."

"We need his insights as much as yours or mine," Mother said with a studied gaze at my brother. She turned to me. "Do you have any other questions, Sherry dear?"

I stared at the crude drawing Mycroft had made. "What about the mark on the map? What was it you saw?"

"Another possible similarity with what we found in

THE ADVENTURE OF THE DECEASED SCHOLAR

Surminster's pockets. It was drawn on Edmonds' map here." Mother pointed to a spot near the mark for the abbey.

"Odd, though," said Mycroft. "If it were on the original map, why did you find it separately in his pocket? Wouldn't he want to know where the symbol was marked on it? And what does it mean?"

Mother tapped her finger to her lips. "Let's assume the symbol dates back to when Lady Surminster's ancestor received Wrightmoor from Henry VIII. What does this suggest from that time?"

"You said it resembled a thistle," I said. "It could be for Scotland. Such as for Mary, Queen of Scots."

"All the thistle drawings I've seen have crisscrosses in the round part. This one lacks any such markings," Mycroft said.

His chastising tone forced me to drop my gaze. Mother's next remark, however, had me raise it toward her. "Sherry may be on to something. If I recall correctly, Catherine of Aragon had a symbol."

"A pomegranate," Mycroft said with the same haughty tone Charles Fitzsimmons used when he knew the answer to some question put out by a master. "I don't see—"

"I do," I said, speaking at a rapid pace and drawing in the empty middle of Mycroft's map. "The pomegranate, I mean. Only upside down, if you will. With the calyx on top."

Mother considered my sketch of the fruit's elongated circle and crown. "Yes. Conceivably…."

My elation over having possibly solved this little mystery plummeted with my brother's next observation. "What does this have to do with Surminster and Wrightmoor? And why would he tear it from the map?"

Once again, I was put in my place. He was right. Unless we could determine the meaning of the symbol, it was mere scratches on the page and got us no closer to any reason for Lord Surminster's death or his theft of the map. Mother, however, continued to consider my explanation of the symbol.

"We do know Catherine of Aragon remained Catholic even after Henry VIII separated from the Vatican and divorced her. And one of her ladies in waiting had entered the convent…"

"The nun's chest. The map may be indicating where the nun's chest is buried," I said, certain of my conclusion.

Mycroft paused to consider my statement and then deflated my enthusiasm with his observations. "The map Surminster took was from 1534. Before Catherine of Aragon's death or the dissolution of the monasteries. Most likely, before the arrival of the lady in waiting. Whatever the symbol means, it's not the nun's chest."

I dropped my gaze because I couldn't dispute his logic. Surminster hadn't pilfered the map because it marked where a nun had hidden her most precious objects. If that were the case…

"What had Edmonds hoped we might see in his map?" I asked, more to myself than to my mother and brother, as I stared at the crude map with my even cruder rendition of the symbol found in Surminster's pocket. I raised my gaze from the slate and saw the two staring at me. "I mean, why all of a sudden did he share the map with us?"

"He indicated his intention to call on us right after you saw him with Rose last night," Mother said. "Perhaps he wanted to shift our focus onto the map and away from his acquaintance with her?"

Mycroft faced me. "Mother said she mentioned '*La Lampe et le Chien*'?" I nodded. He turned to Mother. "You do know the lamp and dog were symbols for Diogenes?"

"And Miss Phillips had mentioned a Diogenes group when she shared Rose's note. Perhaps we should pay a visit to this place," Mother said.

"Let me ask about this before we go barging about like Aesop's ass in the pottery shop," Mycroft said. Both my mother and I stared at him. Rarely had my brother offered to do any activities outside his normal routine. This type of investigation was a far stretch for him. He shifted on his feet before he continued. "If this *is* some sort of low-life establishment, I need to know we'll not be exposing ourselves to any unnecessary scandal."

"Very well," Mother said. "The inquest is only four days away. It must be done quickly."

"I'm going to have to pay a call on some of those who are familiar with Edmonds and his crowd. Regardless, I doubt it will be a place where you or"—his squint at me made my spine bristle—"*you* would be welcomed. At least as you are."

She gave a thoughtful *hmm*. "Yes, I can see what you mean. I believe I have an answer. I'll work on a solution while you're gone. We should be prepared to go tonight if possible. As I said, we have no time to lose."

"What about Father?" I asked. "You can't very well tell him we're going out to hunt for Rose. He'll forbid it immediately."

"Fortunately, I have a ticket for a lecture on South American insects tonight. I'd requested it prior to leaving for

London. Some have certain medicinal properties, I believe. But I'm afraid I'll not be up to it—one of my headaches. I'll be sorry to miss it, but I know your father will enjoy it. That should give us a few hours when we can be gone without suspicion. All the more reason for us to find this place today."

I smiled at both my mother's ingenuity as well as foresight. She'd hit on the very thing that held my father's interest above all else: entomology. At home, he had an extensive collection from all over the world, but here was a chance to share knowledge with like-minded individuals. A perfect evening for him.

With our duties assigned, Mother stood, and we followed her cue to begin our latest subterfuge. Glancing at the slates, she wiped them clean. "No need to leave these about. We'll gather here after Mycroft returns."

CHAPTER EIGHT

To ensure we were hidden from view when we left on this adventure, Mycroft hired a Clarence carriage. Sitting across from her, I had a good view of Mother and had to say she made rather an acceptable man—albeit a rather puny one. Mycroft was a veritable hulk next to her. I wasn't sure how she did it, but she'd managed to lift her hair and put it under a high hat. I hoped no one pulled it off because her true gender would be revealed immediately.

For myself, I was dressed for an evening out. According to Mycroft's brief research into *La Lampe et le Chien* and similar establishments, it was not uncommon for a father or older brother to initiate a young man into this world.

The whole undertaking intrigued me. Just as Constance had introduced me to some parts of the underworld and the death of a man in our barn at Christmas had pointed to the Romani community, I was going to come face-to-face with an enterprise which some of the other students at Eton only whispered about. A few older students bragged about their visitations to certain "night houses" and the women they had seen there. As the son of a justice of the peace, I'd also overheard discussions of cases involving prostitutes. Never had I imagined, however, such a visit at the advanced age of fourteen.

Mycroft's enquiries had produced the address and some basic information about the "house." This particular enterprise specialized in French women. Unlike in England, the women signed an actual contract and were tied to a brothel, not even allowed to venture onto a street. Their main hope for freedom was convincing a client to buy their contract, tying them to a new "owner." Some enterprising young Oxford man on a trip abroad determined a means of importing foreign women to England and creating a "house" with a different offering than most. The novelty attracted a number of clients, including—it appeared— Mycroft's Oxford classmates as well as those from Cambridge. Rumors suggested more than one of his colleagues were investors in this enterprise. Mycroft concluded that Rose was one of these "imports."

When the carriage pulled to a halt, my curiosity morphed into dread. What sort of men frequented such a place? Would they be so rough we might be placing our lives in danger if we were recognized or found out? Had something similar led to Surminster's fate? And what would Father's reaction be if we were arrested or otherwise identified? I'd never see London again as long as he lived if we were.

Mycroft must have been thinking something similar

because his mouth pulled down, and he glanced at Mother. "It's not too late to go home. We could search for Rose some other way."

She glanced out the window. "Are we near Covent Garden? The area seems respectable enough. And I believe it is imperative we find Rose or someone else with knowledge of Surminster. She also has some useful information about the Edmonds. We know some connection exists between these two families, and we must uncover it."

He sighed heavily and gave a determined stare at each of us. "The first sign of trouble, we leave. If we determine Rose is not there, we leave. I'll not have my name associated with this other Diogenes group. I find their appropriation of the name offensive. The Diogenes Society is of pure intellect. This...this *group* is for drinking, cards, and women—not a whit of any type of the pursuit of knowledge."

The building was on a quiet street. At least three stories tall with brightly lit windows. The sign hanging from the building featured a lit lamp with a sheepdog sitting next to it. No hint of the old man of the legend who was said to have carried the lamp, accompanied by a dog, in search of an honest man. All the same, Diogenes was supposed to have been a rather crotchety fellow. While a perfect emblem for Mycroft and his silence-loving comrades, it seemed inappropriate for this second group.

Taking a deep breath, Mycroft reached past me and opened the carriage door. He jumped down and headed toward the structure, ignoring us completely. We were supposed to all be men, no hand to help out a lady.

Once Mother and I were on the street, she slung an arm over my shoulder as I'd seen other school comrades do. For the first time, I realized she was not as confident as she appeared. I could feel a tremble in her fingers on my shoulder. At the entrance, Mycroft faced us, as if checking to see if we'd changed our minds. Mother bobbed her head to indicate he should rap on the door, which he did, and it opened to reveal a burly policeman blocking the entrance.

Mycroft met the officer's scowl. "Diogenes."

The other man glanced past my brother at my mother and me. He pointed his chin at me. "A little young, ain't he?"

"He's older than he looks." Mycroft pulled on his waistcoat. "Besides, never too young to learn, right?"

"I suppose. Enjoy yourselves…gentlemen." He gave all three of us winks and stepped out of our way to permit us passage.

My heart drummed so fast I was certain I could hear the buttons on my own waistcoat rattle, but I followed Mother's advice from when we visited the Reading Room. I feigned an air of familiarity with such places, almost to a level of boredom.

My current fear and previous curiosity turned to disappointment as I took in the night house's front room. While more grandly decorated, it resembled more a social at our village assembly hall than any of the bacchanalia the braggarts described at Eton. Gilded white columns supported a high, domed ceiling. Gas sconces decorated many of the columns, making it very bright. Prisms hung from the lights as well, sending rainbows across the room and its inhabitants. The men, for the most part, were dressed as my brother and mother were—in evening wear complete with top hats. The women, whom some of my classmates had

THE ADVENTURE OF THE DECEASED SCHOLAR

suggested lacked some or all of their clothing, wore dresses—some more elegant than others and showing no, some, or completely bare shoulders. Velvet couches and chairs, with tables between them, lined the sides. Some, but not all were occupied.

Mycroft had warned us that we might not find those we sought. Most men visiting such places did so after the theater or opera. Mother noted because I'd met Edmonds and his companions during the first intermission, a chance existed they would present around the same time again. The smaller crowd made it easier for us to observe the patrons, but also for them to see and possibly recognize us, especially my brother. I was certain this crossed his mind. While he maintained a nonchalant stance, I noticed Mycroft's nostrils flared—a sure sign of his discomfort.

Mother's composure, on the other hand, seemed the most relaxed—even though she was posing as a man and her exposure as otherwise would be disastrous. Her gaze moved about the room as if taking it all in, and a small smile crept across her face. I wasn't sure if she was enjoying the ruse or playing the part of a youth who had found a place to his liking.

Before she could share any information from her cursory examination, a young man who had been leaning against one column pushed himself off and came toward us. He approached with a lifted chin, as if he considered all others as beneath him. His fingers held a champagne flute by its rim, letting the stem hang down. Mycroft stiffened, and I understood he recognized the man.

Planting himself in front of the three of us, the young man stared at each of us in turn. Mother met his gaze directly, and I followed her example. In a sudden burst of insight, it occurred to me this fellow—or others in the room—might have younger brothers at Eton. Should my identity become known, I wasn't sure how the school administrators would respond if the information were shared with them—although some of my classmates might actually view me with a different sort of respect.

When the man's scrutiny shifted to Mycroft, he lifted one side of his mouth in a smirk. "Holmes, old boy, I wondered when you would seek out our little group. I'm sure you'll find something to your liking. The finest from the Continent. Helped pick out some of them." He turned his gaze to my mother and me. "Tell me about your companions so I can find the…sort desired."

His voice carried an almost predatory tone, which raised the hairs on the back of my neck and sent my heart beating even faster.

"I'm not here for me, Tennyson," my brother replied with enough frost to make the other lose some of his haughty stance. "I came to help out my cousin, Jameson. He's…well, he feels compelled to find some companionship here in London. He grew up in France and hasn't had any *entré* into many circles here."

"And the boy?"

Mycroft shrugged. "I thought he needed some introduction into such…houses. Being in the country and at school, he's not had the education he should."

I involuntarily turned to Mycroft but managed to squelch the protest that rose to my lips when I realized the sort of "instruction" to which he referred. My fear returned in a different form. What if we were each expected to select one of the women here and head up the stairs at the far end or to one of the curtained alcoves lining the walls?

Tennyson turned to my mother. "Would you like me to introduce you around, then? I'm sure there are several of the...*ladies* here who would like to get to know you better."

Mother and Mycroft exchanged glances, and he said, "I think we'll just take a spot at the table over there. If there's a...*lady* who'd like to strike up a conversation, let her come to us."

"Suit yourself." He gave Mycroft another inspection. "You shouldn't be alone for long, I'm sure. I'm impressed to know you aren't as toffee-nosed as you've always appeared."

Mycroft's expression didn't change, but I observed his nostrils flaring once again. His classmate's reference to my brother's superior attitude had hit its mark. For the first time, I witnessed him as the recipient of the same type of intimidation I'd received from some of the boys at Eton—and understood both his pain and his effort to hide it. I pushed down my desire to bring Tennyson down a notch with a jab to his nose. Not the time or place.

"Again, here for my cousin," my brother said without a hint of the animosity he had to be holding inside. "Those in the Diogenes *Society* are more my crowd."

"Perhaps I was wrong about those here befriending you." He turned to Mother and bowed. "I trust you are *plus convivial*. We have little need for those like your cousin."

The man sauntered away, and the three of us took seats at the table Mycroft had indicated earlier.

My brother leaned forward and spoke in a low voice to us. "Going to get us a bottle. It will be champagne. It's all they serve in such establishments."

A thought flitted through my mind about how my

brother knew such things, but I decided it wasn't the time to ask. I had to agree. Almost all had a flute either in their hand or on a table at their side.

Once we were alone, Mother spoke to me in French. "Do you see the couple in the back corner? Is that Rose?"

The haze from the smoke and the low lights in the recesses made it difficult to determine whether the person was the one I'd seen at the opera. Her face was also partially obscured by a man's face. He was kissing her on the neck.

"Possibly. The hair is the right color, but the dress is different. It's very hard to tell," I said in French as well. "Should we ask one of the others? To invite them over?"

And what would we say if we were able to speak to the person? We'd had a plan. See if we could find someone who knew something about the Edmonds, Rose, or Surminster, but now in the midst of it all, it seemed a rather naïve idea. Despite some in the room attending Oxford and known to Mycroft, this was hardly the place to ask personal questions.

Mother glanced at Mycroft at the bar and stood. "I have an idea."

I got up as well, but she stayed me with a hand on my shoulder. "Probably best to let me do this alone. I'll send Mycroft back here with the drinks."

Mother moved across the room with a sort of swagger that almost made me laugh. Her efforts to mimic a man's stride seemed exaggerated to me, but I noticed several of the women she passed studied her without any contempt. Once she reached my brother, she spoke into his ear.

With the briefest of nods, he returned to me with three glasses and a bottle in his grasp. He handed me a flute and poured some of the wine into it. "She wants to talk to the barkeep."

I accepted the drink from him with a nod. Her logic seemed sound. The man behind the counter would know about the regulars and might be less hesitant to share information than the patrons.

"I think she wants to know about the woman in the corner," I said, keeping up the conversation in French. Taking a sip of the wine, I let the bubbles play on my tongue and appreciated the appeal of this particular drink. "It might be Rose."

Mycroft glanced in her direction and leaned over his glass.

"The one in the green dress?" he asked in French. When I nodded, he mumbled into his flute. "I can't be certain. I need to see better, but…"

"What are you two staring at?"

Mycroft lifted his head, and we both turned toward the voice. A man standing next to Tennyson glared at the two of us. Two women in evening gowns cut low to show the tops of their breasts frowned at us as well.

The man shoved off the wall, brushed off the women's attempts to steady him, and lurched toward our table. While we might not have garnered much interest when we entered, we now had the full attention of the room. I hunched my shoulders, hoping to keep my face down.

The man swayed over us. "I know you. You're one of those Diogenes *Society* swanks."

"And I know you." Mycroft stood and leveled his gaze at the drunken fellow. "Harcourt."

"There are plenty of women in this room." He swept his arm wide to encompass the space. A bit of the wine sloshed from the glass and splashed his coat sleeve. He ignored it. "No need to stare at ours."

"I wasn't. There's a young woman in the corner I thought I recognized."

Harcourt's mouth turned down. "Can't you tell she's with someone? I told you, there are plenty of others. Let me introduce you to some of France's finest imported whores."

"I believe we can take care of ourselves," my brother said.

"No, no, it's my pleasure. Or should I say *plaisir*. I bet I can guess your cousin's tastes."

His words slurred slightly, but he managed to remain steady on his feet while he scanned the room. Halfway through his survey, he stopped and smiled. "That's the one."

"He won't be interested," Mycroft said. "I'm afraid I was the one who insisted he come. I thought being around those who spoke French might make him feel more at home. You see, my grandmother was—"

"I don't give a fuck about your grandmother."

The venom with which he said this put a stone in the pit of my stomach. He seemed ready to fight, and I couldn't see the reasoning behind it. Just as at Eton, some of the boys seemed to simply want to fight and would go out of their way to insult another just to provoke a swing. While I had taken it upon myself to physically respond to the abuse my classmate Charles Fitzsimmons had directed at me, I couldn't see my brother doing the same. A display of base emotions or actions was simply not in his nature. How had he managed to survive all these years?

I watched, fascinated, as the answer to my question unfolded.

My brother stood and pointed to a seat next to our couch. "Let's set you down. I'll get you another drink—"

His conciliatory tone and offer, which might have

appealed to a sober man, however, didn't have the same effect on one at the precipice of being in his cups.

The man leaned forward to get close to my brother's face. "I don't want another drink. I want to introduce your cousin to Lizette."

He spun and crossed the room, heading in a straight line toward a young woman dressed demurely, a shawl wrapped about her shoulders. She was seated on a couch with other women similarly dressed. Of the three, she was the youngest and prettiest with a heart-shaped face and a clear complexion. Harcourt leaned over and whispered something into her ear and slipped an arm around her waist to escort her to the counter where Mother was still deep in conversation with the man who passed out the wine bottles and glasses.

I rose and rushed with my brother toward the bar and the couple heading toward our mother.

Before we reached them, the man had leaned an elbow on the bar, his arm still around the girl he'd identified as Lizette and addressed our mother. "Hey there, Frenchie," he said. Mother turned to him but said nothing. "I understand you're lookin' for some companionship. I've got just what you need right here."

Mother's eyes widened slightly, but her voice was even in her false French-accented baritone. "*Merci*, but I prefer to make my own acquaintances."

"I can testify, she's a good one. Fresh off the boat from France. Ask her yourself."

Mother turned her gaze to the girl, who gave her a small smile, then dropped her head as if unable to endure Mother's attention. "You came from Paris?" Mother asked in French. The girl's hat bobbed up and down. "How long ago?"

"A week. I think."

"Do you like it here? In London?"

A shrug. "At least they don't lock me in." She now met Mother's gaze. "There was a woman who helped bring me over. She arranged for them to buy out my contract. If you buy my contract from them, R—"

"Now, now," Harcourt broke in. "No pilfering the merchandise. Do you know how much it costs to bring a single one of these whores over? First, there's the contract, then the trip, and the medical examination—"

Mycroft raised his hand to stop the man. "We certainly can't afford that." He took Mother's arm. "I think we'll be going. This isn't exactly to our tastes."

Mother nodded and let him pull her from the bar.

Before my mother took a second step, Harcourt grabbed her arm. "Hold on. Are you saying this place isn't to your standards? I want to hear your cousin say so. Tell me to my face you don't want to go with Lizette."

Mother turned and said, "I don't."

He tightened his grip on her arm. Before he could pull her back toward the bar, she took hold of his arm, spun out of his grasp, and flipped him onto his back. The *baritsu* training Mother and I had completed during the winter paid off. In spades.

Unfortunately, the move dislodged her hat, and some of her hair hung down. Not enough for it to be noticeable to all, but enough that close inspection would reveal her true sex.

Mycroft noticed it too.

He turned to the room. "Gentlemen, it's been"—he glanced at Harcourt, wheezing from landing on his back

THE ADVENTURE OF THE DECEASED SCHOLAR

and having the breath knocked out of him—"enlightening. Please, have a drink on us."

He dropped some notes onto the bar and hustled my mother out by the elbow.

We were in the carriage and away before any of us said a word.

Mycroft straightened his cravat and gave Mother a small smile. "It appears Mr. Moto taught you well before—"

He caught my gaze and stopped himself before completing the thought. Our *baritsu* master had turned out not to be all he pretended. During my hiatus before returning to Eton, Mother contracted with Mr. Moto to teach us self-defense. Unfortunately, his time didn't end well. Regardless, he had proved a good teacher, and Mother and I both still revered his instruction and quiet ways.

My mother returned a weak smile to him. "Yes, he did. I have to say, it was the first time I'd a chance to practice that move on a person since…since our lessons. You should really consider taking up the sport."

Before I could stop myself, a chortle escaped my lips, and my brother glowered at me. The idea of my comfort-loving brother putting on a *gi's* short pants and robe formed such a spectacle in my mind, I couldn't help but laugh.

Mycroft's response, however, was gentle. "You know I don't fancy such…exertions."

"True. Not the time to discuss it anyway," Mother said, smoothing the fake moustache that had curled on one end following her encounter with Mycroft's classmate. "I do have a great deal to share with you from my conversation with the barman. Let me note that in addition to servants and household help being privy to family secrets, publicans and others in highly frequented establishments are also sources of information concerning regular patrons. In the case of this barman, for instance, I learned he wasn't familiar with Lord Surminster. Any of the Edmonds were more difficult to ascertain because they don't use their true or full names. But I was able to confirm Rose was in the corner with 'Albert.'"

"Was he aware of the rest of his name?" I asked.

Mycroft cleared his throat. "I can answer that. The man was Fenton Crandall. I don't know him well, but I do know I've seen him with Maurice Edmonds."

"Whoever was with him tonight, we must speak to her," she said. Her strong declaration made us both face her. "Didn't you see what was in her hair? She had a jeweled pin holding the hair twisted along the back of her head. A long, straight pin."

"Just how are we going to speak with her?" I asked. "I suppose we could see about 'renting' her for the evening, but she might just tell someone if all we do is interview her."

"A good point," Mother said, staring out the window. "Those poor women. Imagine being locked away in a brothel? I've read how the police will return those who escape. At least here they're allowed out…"

Before she could complete her thought, church bells chimed nearby, and Mother gasped.

"Oh, dear. It's later than I thought. We must get home immediately. Your father's lecture will be over soon, and we must be out of our dress before he returns."

Mycroft pounded on the roof, and the carriage took off at a much greater speed. The vehicle's swaying and clattering of both hoofs and wheels on the paving stones made additional talk difficult. Londoners didn't refer to a Clarence as "the growler" for nothing. The one thing to which we all

THE ADVENTURE OF THE DECEASED SCHOLAR

agreed was Mycroft would seek out Crandall to possibly arrange a meeting with Rose.

MOTHER HAD the carriage leave us behind the townhouse, and we quickly entered through the bachelor quarters' entrance and stairs. We were still in the hallway when we heard the front door open. Moving as silently as possible, Mother tossed a dressing gown to my brother and told him to keep Father occupied to give us time to change.

By the time Father's footsteps sounded on the main staircase, I was already in my nightclothes with my suit hung in my closet.

A door opened down the hall, and I heard Mother ask, "How was the lecture, Mr. Holmes?"

"Tolerable, but—" The rest of his reply was lost to me when he closed the door behind him.

When someone knocked shortly after that, I assumed it was Mycroft and called for him to enter. To my surprise, Constance stepped in and closed the door behind her. She carried a pitcher of water.

"Thought you might need some help straightening your clothes," she said and opened the wardrobe to study my suits hanging there. "I'll take your pants and shirt to press out the wrinkles. You don't want Adeline or Mrs. Simpson to see them all mussed up. There'll be questions."

"What was it like?" she asked after gathering the items. "The night house?"

She tilted her head, waiting for my answer.

I paused, not certain how to respond. True, the place had a sort of elegance, and the women were well dressed.

All the same, I'd seen some of the women brought before my father's court and knew they didn't all appear so well cared for. They were often drunk and shrunken to mere husks. Then there was the information shared by Lizette of being locked in with the only means of escape being purchased by a man.

In the end, I decided to lie for her own sake. No need to make it sound even a bit appealing. "It was dark. And smelly. The men were rough and…handy."

To my relief, she wrinkled her nose and changed the subject. "Did you find Rose?"

"We think so but didn't talk to her. She was…occupied." When she didn't move or ask more, I continued. "Mycroft thinks he knows someone who might help us arrange for an interview."

She snorted. "If Mycroft has to do the convincin', I'm not sure she'll agree."

"I know you and my brother don't get along. But tonight, he did something courageous. It was dangerous for him to go there. May still be—if word of his visit is shared with the wrong people. Some there actually knew him. Not to mention, he protected both my mother and me from some of the others. His skills at persuasion are better than you might think. They impressed me."

She gripped the clothes in her arms, and I feared they were now more wrinkled than when she picked them up. "I'll bring these back in the morning before anyone has a chance to notice them missin'. Good luck talkin' to Rose."

She left me where I stood next to the washstand. I stared at the closed door. The animosity between her and my brother was obvious, and I found myself often caught in the middle with conflicting loyalties. Why one couldn't see the qualities of the other was most disconcerting to me. While Mycroft could be arrogant, he could also be protective—he certainly had been tonight. Constance lacked refinement, but she was more quick-witted than anyone I knew outside my immediate family.

With a sigh, I crawled into bed, wishing I could provide some way of showing these qualities to each.

CHAPTER NINE

My brother disappeared early the next day. Father noted his absence as soon as he entered the breakfast room.

"Where's Mycroft gone off to?" he asked my mother and me.

I studied my plate as if the eggs and toast were some new and exciting offering. Uncertain of the pretext my brother and mother might have developed for such an early departure, I didn't want my father to expect me to answer. To my great relief, Mother had a vague, if ready, reply.

"I wouldn't know, Mr. Holmes. When you came to London during your time at university, what might you have done during the early morning?"

He stared at her, then cleared his throat, and opened his paper, almost as if hiding behind it. The lack of a response to her question suggested he didn't want to share such adventures, which made me curious as to my father's bachelor times but, more importantly, once again, raised my admiration for my mother and her ability to manipulate touchy situations.

"Plans for today, my dear?" Mother asked lightly.

From behind his paper, Father grumbled something about a meeting at a bank.

"I believe the boys and I will be going to a museum later. I'll leave word about which one, in case you wish to join us."

Once again, she had already planned an explanation for our absence, if needed, should we be able to locate and meet with Crandall.

Mycroft returned home just before noon. I wouldn't have known if Mother hadn't sent Constance to let me know I was to go to her sitting room. When I entered, she and Mycroft were already seated, each holding a teacup.

"Sherry dear, please join us." Mother pointed to a chair across from her. "Tea?"

I accepted the cup after settling myself into my seat. Taking a sip, I studied my brother over its rim. He met my gaze over his own cup. Despite my sense of loyalty and respect for him, I found myself resenting his position at this little meeting. He had gone on a brief investigation and now brought back information neither my mother nor I possessed. Taking a secondary role as Mother's assistant irritated me to the point I had trouble focusing on the current discussion.

"Crandall's club isn't in the most fashionable district," Mycroft said with a bit of a frown.

His assessment of the club demonstrated to me once again his patronizing attitude toward others, raising my resentment even more. Was there anyone to whom he bowed? Who made him feel inferior? I would like to meet them and learn their secret.

"But of course," Mycroft had continued during my own review of a mounting list of grievances against my brother. I had to focus. "Given where we have most recently visited, it is certainly a step up."

"Were you able to contact him? Get him to agree to a meeting?" Mother asked.

"He had given strict instructions not to be disturbed until three o'clock. I didn't leave a message. I considered it more suspicious if I did so than if we simply showed up."

Mother glanced at the clock on her mantel. "Then we must be leaving soon. A quick luncheon and then off to this club."

FROM THE CARRIAGE WINDOW, I studied the façade of the club where Crandall resided. "Do you think they'll let us in?"

The carriage ride wasn't far, but Mycroft had pegged it correctly as not being of the highest level—similar to comparing our townhouse with Surminster's town manor. All the same, it was well maintained with a brass plate by the door, identifying it as "The Dionysius."

"I'll make enquiries and see if he'll receive us. Of course, he might be in the middle of a card game or in his cups. If that's the case, I'm not sure it'll be worth it." He studied the club's brass plate and snorted. "Clever name. Crandall certainly does worship his wine."

"As you say, we must improvise, depending on the man's

THE ADVENTURE OF THE DECEASED SCHOLAR

condition," Mother said from her side of the carriage. The cabin swayed as my brother descended, and he thumped up the steps to the front door. More to herself than to me, she added, "If he has been drinking, he might actually be more forthcoming."

My brother spoke to someone at the door and waved for us to follow him. As we entered, he whispered, "We're to wait in the visitors' room. If Crandall finds it convenient, he will join us there. Otherwise, we'll leave a message for him."

While we waited, I explored the small antechamber. In some ways, it was a cross between a parlor and a library. A parlor because of the groupings of tables and chairs positioned about the room to accommodate members receiving various visitors to the establishment. A library, such as Father's at Underbyrne, because the chairs were leather and the walls lined with books. The only homage to the Greek god were vines and grape bunches adorning the wallpaper and carved into the fireplace.

Footsteps announced the return of the person Mycroft had spoken to at the door, but they were accompanied by a second pair of steps. Crandall must have decided to meet with us.

When the door opened, a young man about Mycroft's age stepped in. He was thin and blond, with classic features. I had no idea about his personality, but I assumed his looks alone attracted more than his share of young women. What need did he have of dollymops or other prostitutes?

"Mycroft, old chap, come to check out the facilities? I would recommend them, but I'm not sure you'd fit in. We actually *talk* here." He stopped halfway in the room when his gaze moved past my brother to my mother and me. If our presence took him by surprise, he recovered quickly enough and said, "I'm afraid we don't take women...or boys."

"They are family members. Pay them no mind. Not knowing how long this interview would take, I didn't want them to have to wait in the carriage."

Crandall glided past us, his mouth almost a sneer, and settled into the nearest leather chair. Leaning against the back, he bent his leg and set his ankle onto his knee. "*Interview* is it? No interest in our little enclave here?" He chuckled at his own joke. When none of us responded, he sobered a bit and said, "What do you want to 'interview' me about?"

"Lord Surminster."

"Couldn't stand the man. So high and mighty. I may be a second son, but my family has a good name and not a small fortune. Unlike—" He stopped himself and glared at the three of us. "You think I was somehow involved in—?" Before any of us could answer, he popped up from his chair and stomped toward the door. "This *interview* is over."

My pulse raced. Here was a possible murderer—or at least an accessory—about to slip through our grasp. We had shown part of our hand by mentioning Lord Surminster, and if Crandall left the room without sharing any information, he would certainly warn others as well as possibly destroy information vital to solving Surminster's murder. I sought for something to stop him from leaving before he shared what he knew with us.

Just as he reached out for the doorknob, I said in a loud voice, "Then tell us about Wrightmoor."

He spun about, arms crossed, his upper lip raised in a sneer. After studying me from head to foot, he said, "I have no idea what you are talking about."

THE ADVENTURE OF THE DECEASED SCHOLAR

Shock and anger radiated from the others' faces and quickened my pulse even more. I feared we would lose the current momentum my command had created.

In for a penny, in for a pound.

I took a deep breath. "We saw you. Last night at *La Lampe et Le Chien*. With Rose. And I saw Rose with Nathan and Maurice Edmonds. We know Nathan Edmonds represents Lady Surminster regarding the Wrightmoor trust, and his uncle is renting the estate. Surely you have some information you can share with us? Or arrange a meeting with Rose?"

Rather than paling as I might have expected, the man's face grew red, and his eyebrows drew together. He glared at me and then closed his eyes to open them wide at my mother. "All three of you. Have you been spying on me? If you think you can blackmail me—"

My pulse was now racing so fast I could barely make out the man's words over the *whoosh* of blood in my ears. I forced myself to remain where I stood, my gaze steady on Crandall. As much as I wanted to confirm my mother's location in case he chose to advance in her direction, any sign of hesitation or trepidation on my part might trigger his advance. Instead, I tried to recall the placement of all the items in the room—in case Crandall did move, and I had to defend myself or Mother with some object.

Before I had to do either, my brother spoke up—much to my surprise and gratitude.

"*I'm* not the one doing the blackmail," Mycroft said, stepping between Crandall and me. "Unless I can prove Lord Surminster didn't commit suicide, his sister, Sophronia Phillips, plans to share a letter written by Rose to someone named Albert, which I understand is the moniker you use at

La Lampe et Le Chien, and say it was written to me. All we want from you is to know what you know about the night Lord Surminster died."

Mycroft took two steps toward Crandall, who, in turn, straightened his spine and jutted his chin toward my brother. For a fleeting second, I feared the two would engage in fisticuffs; and while my brother was not one for much physical exertion, our uncle had trained him in boxing—the same as I. Beads of perspiration formed on my upper lip at the prospect of some brutish altercation. Beyond the obvious outcome of being thrown out of the establishment and possible bodily harm, I didn't see how this would provide us with any assistance in determining Surminster's death.

Crandall must have determined a similar result because, in the end, he ground out a single command between clenched teeth.

"Get out."

"Perhaps that's the best solution at this point," Mother said. I detected a minor tremor in her voice. From nerves or anger, I wasn't certain.

Crandall and Mycroft didn't move as she and I stepped past them and out the door. Only after we were in the hallway did Mycroft follow, shutting the door behind him to close off any additional interaction with his classmate.

Once in the carriage, my brother's face burned red, and he said to me with a tone very similar to Crandall's, "What, pray tell, did you expect from such a confrontation, you twit? If the weapon used to murder Lord Surminster was Rose's hairpin, did you expect him to confess then and there of sharing what he knew about it or Surminster's death?"

"Of course not." The urgency I'd experienced during

my brief altercation with Crandall had dissipated, and I'd fairly collapsed into the carriage seat when I ascended. Mycroft's remark, however, revived my determination to resolve the intrigue we'd encountered around Lord Surminster's death. I returned my brother's glare and provided the logic behind my verbal confrontation with Crandall. "Do you know how they catch rats? I've seen workers do this in the barn when Uncle Ernest needs them for an experiment. These animals build burrows with more than one entrance. If you put a trap at one end and send something through the others—water or smoke, for example—they will run straight into the trap."

"And where," Mycroft said with a sneer rivaling the one Crandall had given me, "do you think he will be flushed out to?"

"I'm hoping to his accomplices. If Crandall was involved in Lord Surminster's death, he'll most likely seek them out. Tell them that we are aware he has knowledge of the man's murder."

"Then we should stay and follow him," Mycroft said.

Mother spoke for the first time since we'd left the club. "I think I have a better idea. We'll discuss how that little interchange was not the most prudent later, but I do believe I can make some other arrangements."

She stepped from the carriage, returning several minutes later.

Once we were moving, she said, "I've paid a cab driver to wait for Crandall, take him where he requests, and then report back to me on his destination."

I pondered this for a moment before identifying a problem with her plan.

"How will he know it's Crandall?"

"This particular driver regularly carries those from this club and is familiar with the man. And given his reaction, I doubt Crandall will wait long before running to report to others. So, we shall go home and have tea as we await the news from the driver." She leveled her gaze on me and added, "While your logic appears sound, I would suggest you refrain from such independent decisions in the future. Had we been aware of your plan to ask such a question, we would have been prepared for his response. It could have gone much worse. How would we have been able to explain to your father any physical assault if such an attack had occurred?"

"Hear, hear," Mycroft said and might have added more had Mother not stared him down.

The rest of the trip I passed in silence, watching the street scenes pass without seeing them. While Mother's tone wasn't harsh, I had still felt the sting of her disapproval and the reprimand her words contained. All the same, I'd not been wrong to call the man out—and Mother hadn't disagreed with the result, only my approach. We had only a little bit of time to unravel all the connections between these families, and somehow Crandall might just uncover a portion of it.

The driver's information would be key—but waiting for him to bring it would test all of our patience.

FATHER surprised us by joining us for tea.

"How was the museum?" he asked.

"Crowded," Mother said without missing a beat. "We

didn't stay long because of it. Always a problem during the holidays. And your day?"

"I met with an old school chum Jonathan Sires. Wanted to talk to me about investing in silver mines in South America."

Mother's cup paused halfway up to her lips. "Silver mines? I had no idea you were interested in such prospects."

"Hadn't thought much about it until he approached me. Always seemed to have a good head for business. Been very prosperous at it. Should have seen his offices."

Mother simply smiled and gave a quiet *hmm*.

For me, the small, noncommittal sound was as obvious as if she'd waved a red flag and shouted, "Beware!" A small knot formed in the pit of my stomach. I'd read more than one newspaper report of a group of investors losing their funds to fraud or simply bad luck, like a ship and cargo lost at sea. Dickens had described debtors' prison in great detail. I had no desire to observe such accommodations first-hand.

Father must have caught the implication in Mother's response as well.

"I didn't commit to anything. But it did sound interesting. I asked him to share a bit more with me. In fact, he's invited us to dinner."

"Tonight?" she asked.

"Of course tonight." He paused and studied her. "Did you have other plans?"

"No, no," she said. "How lovely. We'll leave about seven?"

When my father turned to study the small pile of sandwiches on a plate in the center of the table, the three of us held a silent discussion. Should there be additional investigation this evening related to trips Crandall made from his club, it would be up to my brother and me. While she might regret not accompanying us, I suspected she would be more concerned if my father went to dinner alone with Sires.

We had only a few hours for word to come about Crandall's movements, if any, before she would have to leave for the evening. As if in answer to our concerns, Constance entered with a note on a silver tray.

"This just came for you, ma'am."

Mother took the note, read it, and said, "From Mrs. Simms, thanking us for tea the other day."

This time, Father made the noncommittal *hmm*, and Mother slipped the note up her sleeve. I was certain she didn't want him to accidentally read whatever was written there. My desire to learn what she now knew dried my mouth, making it difficult to swallow the bite of sandwich there. I forced myself to choke it down and concentrate on the conversation my mother and father held regarding whether to accept an offer from the owner of land adjacent to ours. He had some acreage he was seeking to sell.

"Apparently, he's in dire straits," Father said and gave a little *tut-tut*. "An addition to his house cost him more than he had anticipated. The soil, you know. Not stable enough to hold the weight. They had to dig the foundation deeper than planned."

Mother echoed Father's sentiment with a *tsk-tsk* of her own. "So much money and work buried underground. Nothing on top to show for it. I do hope Underbyrne will not suffer the same fate."

"No worries there. It was built on stone."

"Good to know," she said and took a sip from her tea.

She then glanced toward the mantel and drew in a breath. "Oh my, will you look at the time? I should go

THE ADVENTURE OF THE DECEASED SCHOLAR

upstairs. I'll need to get ready."

With that announcement, she rang a bell and requested Constance to have the tea service removed and to join her in her dressing room to assist in her preparations for a bath and dinner. Soon, Mycroft and I were alone in the drawing room.

"*La Lampe et Le Chien*," Mycroft said.

I glanced at the door to ensure we were alone before I responded. "How do you know? Were you able to read the note?"

"Where else would he go?"

While Mycroft's deduction was the most probable, I couldn't eliminate several other options, which I enumerated.

"Edmonds' office? Edmonds' home? Maurice Edmonds' home?"

"Possible, but not probable."

Constance stepped into the drawing room and whispered, "Mrs. Holmes would like you to go to her sitting room for a moment."

We were up and moving toward the door so quickly, Constance jumped back to avoid us running her over. Mycroft, having taken the steps two at a time, was breathing heavily by the time we reached her room.

At Mother's invitation, we pushed through the door at almost the same time.

"Please shut the door, but do *not* slam it," she said from her chair next to the fire. "No need to call attention to this conversation any more than you have."

Once secured within the room, I said, "He sought out Edmonds, didn't he?"

"*La Lampe et Le Chien*?" Mycroft asked at the same time

as my question.

A smile played on her lips. She was obviously enjoying our display of anticipation and competition. After a moment when the only sound was Mycroft's still-labored breathing, she said, "Lady Surminster. Or Miss Phillips. Anyway, their house."

My brother and I could only stare at her. Neither of us had considered this possibility. I found my voice before he did.

"Why would he go there?"

"I suppose we could speculate," she said. "Without more information, it would be mere guessing."

"And where would we get additional knowledge?" Mycroft asked. "I'm beginning to feel a breath on the back of my neck. The inquest is in three days, and we have yet to ensure the decision."

He sank into a chair on the other side of the fireplace. For the first time, he mentioned the panic he had to be feeling related to this whole mess. I glanced at Mother. She ran her hand over her hair. She had to be suffering the same concerns and frustrations her son felt.

"Do you think I'm not aware? And don't you think if there were any way I could determine who Crandall was visiting within the family, I would do so? They are in mourning. In seclusion. And I must attend a dinner with your father. Just how do you suggest I break it to him I can't go because I need to visit Lady Surminster when he has expressly indicated we must leave it to Scotland Yard?"

After considering both my brother's and mother's thoughtful postures, I spoke up. Given their reactions to my outburst at Crandall's club, I hesitated, but neither had offered a solution, and one seemed obvious to me.

"Mycroft could go." The glower my brother gave me resembled the one he'd shot at me in the carriage after we left Crandall. I pushed on despite the trepidation I experienced from his reaction to the first part of my suggestion. "Not to Surminster's, of course. But to the Simms'. He could visit their home on some pretext while you prepare for dinner. Mrs. Simms would know if Crandall had visited the family, and whom."

"Possibly," Mother said, tapping her finger to her lips.

"No," said Mycroft. "If I appear, they'll seek to link me in some way with Cora. You and Father may feel the need for me to marry one day, Mother, but even you said not with her."

"I'm afraid they're already seeking a way to have you and Cora meet again," she said. "I received a note from Mrs. Simms earlier today thanking us for the tea and asking us to check for a handkerchief Cora has misplaced." She picked up an item from the table next to her. "And she had. It's an old ploy. A way to either ensure a call to their home or arrange a second visit."

I stared at the white cloth in her hand, amazed at the devious workings of the female mind. Had it been Mrs. Simms or Miss Simms who had left the handkerchief?

"Where did you find it?" I asked.

"Between the cushions next to the armrest. Miss Simms sat there if I recall correctly."

I didn't imagine Cora to have thought of leaving the article by herself. Surely her mother had instructed her in the ruse? All the same, I was grateful to the ladies for providing a means of learning more about Crandall's connection to Lord Surminster's family.

During this brief discussion, Mycroft had been silent,

but he spoke now with great conviction. "No. I'm not going over there. No matter what's at stake. I go to the house with that-that linen trap, and I'll have to endure more of those two women. I could survive whatever scandal Miss Phillips produces better than any more communications with the Simms family."

Mother massaged her temple. My brother's intractability was common family knowledge. During the past few days, he'd been pushed to his limit with respect to moving beyond his routines and the solitude he craved. Even if he did agree to visit the family, he might be so bent on exiting as soon as possible, he'd fail to collect any of the information we sought. On the other hand...

"I'll go." I tapped my hand against the chair's arm, ready for the inevitable rebuke. Before they could respond, I decided to strengthen my case with an outcome both would find acceptable. "My return of the item should discourage Mrs. Simms from pursuing Mycroft. At the same time, they could hardly turn me out without showing some courtesies. I can ask about Crandall's connection as well as Mycroft."

My brother had been preparing for a second volley of protests. As the leeway of my offer became clear to him, his brow smoothed.

Mother tilted her head and nodded. "It could work. You should go shortly to ensure your return before I leave. Please have Constance come to help me prepare."

MOTHER HAD BEEN correct about the Simms' economic situation. The townhouse was on Baker Street. While still a respectable area, the buildings were narrower than my uncle's on Grosvenor Square. I also noted brass plates, indicating professional (doctor, lawyer, and the like) offices occupied many of the residences' first floor. I couldn't recall a single such office in our area.

The maid who answered the bell pulled back her chin at the sight of an unaccompanied young man at the front door. Given my fashionable dress, I wasn't a servant or tradesman who could be told to seek out the back entrance. And while I had arrived in the carriage waiting on the street, the interior was too dark to determine if I was alone or if someone waited for some type of response before descending. I decided to use her confusion to my advantage.

"If you please, ma'am, I'd like to speak to Mrs. Simms," I said, handing her one of my mother's calling cards.

Another squint toward my transportation and then at the card, and she stepped aside to let me enter. While I waited, I found myself comparing the residence's interior with the feel of the overall neighborhood. Both coincided with my mother's original assessment. "Fashionable, but not the best quality." The same could be said of the foyer's wallpaper, the rug running the length of the room, and even the clock on the wall. All meeting certain standards but showing more than a few years' use.

A flurry of footsteps from upstairs announced the response of more than one person to my arrival. I assumed both the Simms women were making their way to greet my mother—or possibly Mycroft if the maid had said a young man was at the door. I couldn't repress a grin, knowing they would be most disappointed to find me instead of either of the other two.

"Welcome, my dear—" Mrs. Simms said when she stepped into the front hall.

She had extended both hands—I'm sure with the plan to grasp both of her guest's. She pulled to a stop so quickly, Cora almost ran into her. I held my hand over my mouth and coughed to keep from laughing out loud. The young woman's own jaw dropped open, and I had to cough a second time when the first thought flitting through my mind was how much she resembled a dead fish.

My father's training in social convention, however, provided me with the remedy for the obvious consternation the two were experiencing. "How do you do again, Mrs. Simms?" I bowed to the lady. "We met at Lord Surminster's home the other day. When my mother received your note about the lost handkerchief, she decided to send me to return it as soon as possible. Unfortunately, she couldn't do so herself because of a prior engagement tonight. She didn't want Miss Cora"—I glanced over the woman's shoulder to her daughter, who still seemed not to be able to grasp the change in events—"to be without such a lovely item."

Finishing my little speech, I retrieved the linen cloth and held it out to her.

"Yes…well…thank you," the older woman said. She snatched it from my hand. "Please let your mother know I appreciate her efforts to return it promptly."

The woman's rather curt response telegraphed her plan to dismiss me as quickly as possible. Mother had planned for such an event and instructed me in what to say should I be presented with such a scenario. "She wanted me to pass on another message as well."

"A message?" She glanced about her as if uncertain whether the news might require more privacy. In the end, she seemed to decide it did because she waved her hand

THE ADVENTURE OF THE DECEASED SCHOLAR

toward a door. "Why don't we sit down? I'll have some tea brought in."

As a gentleman, I allowed the two to lead the way. Another grin threatened to surface, and I was grateful to have their backs to me. Mother had been right about the mention of a message. With the offer of tea, I would have more time to gather any intelligence about Crandall.

Once seated, Mrs. Simms summoned the tea. After the maid had left the room, the older woman faced me. "You said you had a message from your mother?"

"She would appreciate more information about Lord Surminster's internment. She assumed it would be Sunday."

"I don't understand." The woman's brows drew together.

With a brief nod, I said, "I did think it a rather odd question myself." I'd been instructed to develop a more confidential attitude by agreeing with whatever she reported. "Then she explained with the next Sunday being Easter, she wondered whether the funeral would be a private affair, or if others could attend."

"Definitely private," Mrs. Simms said.

A pause occurred as tea was served to the three of us.

"In particular," I said, taking up the original conversation again, "she wondered about any of Lord Surminster's friends. As you know, my brother, Mycroft, was close to Lord Surminster at Oxford. Surely he had other friends who would like to join in the procession?"

"I-I don't think Lady Surminster has mentioned any such plans."

"Of course, she hasn't been thinking clearly," Cora Simms said, breaking into the discussion for the first time. She must have recovered enough from her disappointment to feel the need to contribute as well. "She's still in shock about the-the tragedy."

"My brother offered to contact some of his classmates, if needed. Of course, some are very much aware of the events—like Maurice Edmonds, Nathan Edmonds' cousin. The one at Oxford, you know."

"Both gentlemen have been by. Particularly to meet with Miss Sophronia and Zachariah—the future Lord Surminster."

At the mention of the deceased man's brother, a shiver once again ran down my spine. I felt for the young man, only a few years older than I, who now carried responsibilities beyond his years. This concern suddenly focused my thoughts on the people surrounding, and possibly advising him.

"Without a father, I suspect Master Phillips seeks out their counsel—as he might an older brother. Or does he have any uncles or cousins who might serve in such a capacity?"

Mrs. Simms twisted the handkerchief I'd passed to her earlier and glanced at her daughter. I'd obviously touched on a sensitive subject. I forced myself to appear nonchalant about the topic, although whatever she had to share would be most interesting.

"While I have the utmost respect for the Lord Wittdam and his son, Jared, his brother's sons—the cousins—are not..." She peeked at Cora before continuing. Cora nodded at her as if to show support for what she was about to say. "They aren't cut from the same cloth as the earl or his son."

"The same with some of their acquaintances," Cora said and sniffed.

Before either could say more, the front door opened,

and a gentleman entered the room. He was about my father's age but showed a much more fit frame. His coloring suggested much time out of doors in some physical activity—most likely hunting given his social position.

"Good afternoon, Mrs. Simms, Cora," he said, nodding to the two women. He then faced me. "And you are...?"

"This is Master Sherlock Holmes," Mrs. Simms said. "Master Holmes, my husband, Mr. Simms."

I stood and bowed to the man.

"He did us the favor of returning Cora's handkerchief"—the woman held out the now limp, wrinkled piece of fabric in her hand, glanced at it, and closed her fist around it—"she'd lost at their home when we visited."

"My family met Mrs. Simms when we paid our respects to Lord Surminster the other day," I said, retaking my seat. I added a second part as a way of prodding the ladies to share about the Edmonds' or Crandall's visit. "Mrs. Simms was just saying some of his other friends from Oxford had also visited."

"Yes, several had," Mrs. Simms said. "But there was one rude young man who made such a scene today. Showed up demanding to see Miss Phillips. It took Hamilton and two of the footmen to escort him from the house. All the while he shouted she must tell Edmonds he had better watch himself."

"How terrible," I said with a shake of my head. "I hope he didn't disturb the family greatly."

"When did this happen?" Mr. Simms asked.

Another silent exchange between the two women.

"About four, wouldn't you say, Cora?"

I forced myself to breathe normally. The time was about

right for Crandall's visit. As we already knew, he was friends with Nathan Edmonds, but...

"Why would he be asking for Miss Phillips if he had a message for...I'm sorry, which Edmonds was he seeking?" I asked.

"I assume it was Lord Jared," Mrs. Simms said. "He's been with Miss Phillips and the young Lord Surminster as much as convention allows."

Cora spoke again before her mother could say more as if to either correct or warn her. "Of course, it's hard to tell when there are so many with the same name." She glanced out the window. "It's getting rather late, and we have an engagement this evening. We shouldn't keep you any longer. I'm sure Mrs. Holmes will worry if you are not back before long."

"Yes," said Mr. Simms. "I must be going too. I just came home to let you know I have an appointment at my club. Don't expect me for dinner."

"I do need to speak with you later, Mr. Simms," his wife said. "The milliner's bill has arrived, and—"

Simms glared at her, cutting her off. I was surprised she'd bring up such a private matter as an expense in front of a guest. Perhaps she considered me less of a guest, given my age, or that he would be more receptive in front of others? Her husband, however, didn't agree with such an indiscretion in either case.

"We'll discuss it later," he said. "I'll escort Master Holmes out."

Once outside, I forced my steps to remain calm since Mr. Simms was with me. I also repressed the urge to tell the cab driver to hurry to avoid alerting the man to my eagerness to share what I had learned with Mother. When the cab turned a corner, however, another hansom passed mine at a faster clip—with Mr. Simms inside. I followed his example to hurry on, eager to share my news.

CHAPTER TEN

"Pity Crandall didn't use the full name," Mother said.

She studied her image in the dressing table mirror situated on one side of her sitting room. Her transformation had taken me aback when I'd entered. While she'd dressed for special events back in our county and to go to the opera here in London, her current attire surpassed the elegance of any of those occasions. Her hair was swept up and had some pearls strategically placed within it. The arrangement displayed a bare neck and shoulders. The necklace and earrings, a matching set of sapphires, reflected the blue in her eyes and the shimmering silk in her gown.

I stared at her one breath more.

"Is there something wrong?" she asked and glanced at her reflection again.

Breaking through my amazement, I shook my head. "No. It's just...you're stunning."

"Thank you, my dear." She glanced in the mirror again. "You know how I prefer the practical to the elaborate, but

THE ADVENTURE OF THE DECEASED SCHOLAR

your father made a special request for tonight. He desires to present a very prosperous image. I'm not sure I agree, but he has been more than patient with us as we've dealt with this Surminster matter, and I decided to humor him tonight."

"Did Constance do your hair? I mean the pearls and…" I didn't even know what to call the rest of the arrangement.

"I had to instruct her in the beginning, but she's a quick learner." She frowned at her reflection. "We'll have to give this Gordian knot linking Surminster, Edmonds, and Crandall some additional thought. Unfortunately, it will have to wait."

She rose and kissed me on the cheek. "Thank you for braving the Simms ladies. I think what you learned is very important."

I followed her out of the room but remained upstairs, watching her descent from the second-floor landing. While she had noted her preference for the practical, she still carried herself with the grace and ease of a lady—head high, back straight, and an upward tilt to her chin.

Constance took a spot next to me by the stairs. I turned and gave her a smile.

"Mother said you did her hair. Well done."

Her cheeks flushed. "Thank you. It ain't—er, isn't—easy to get the hair through the pearls. She taught me a trick, though. Usin' a needle. Course them's not real pearls. Just paste, she told me. Has a whole box of 'em. Said they belonged to her mother."

I nodded, recalling a portrait I'd seen of my grandmother Charlotte. Her hair had been done in an elaborate style with many more pearls than my mother had used for this dinner.

She glanced away from me, studying my parents' backs as they stepped through the door to a waiting carriage.

"They look so elegant-like," she said. "Like them we saw at the opera."

Her gaze remained on the empty foyer, but I could tell her focus was inward—not on the floor below. Hoping to draw her out of whatever thoughts she now considered, I decided to offer her some entertainment during the hours until my parents' return when Mother would require her assistance in retiring for the evening.

"I was wondering…" I said. She startled and faced me. Her cheeks flushed again, as if I'd caught her in some wrong deed. "I thought this might be a good time to teach you how to play chess."

"Chess?"

Her question suggested she had never heard of the game, but she'd seen my family bent over the board numbers of times. Deciding I had simply broken into her thoughts, I continued. "You're so terribly clever, I know you would pick it up right away. Then we can play other times, and—"

"A lovely idea," she said, and I bounced on my toes for a second. I stopped, however, immediately with her next statement. "But I thinks I'm going to lie down for a little bit. When your mother comes back, I'll have to help her undress, and then I'll have to get up in the morning. Even if she sleeps late, I still have duties."

My gaze dropped to the bit of carpet between us. Once again, I'd forgotten the differences in our situations. Of course, she had work to do. At Underbyrne, we had a whole household staff (albeit small) to attend to the many housekeeping duties. In town, the staff was much smaller, and given her position as the youngest and least experienced, they were certain to assign her the hardest tasks. For her, the absence of my parents—particularly my mother—offered an opportunity for at least part of an evening off.

"Yes. I understand," I said when I raised my gaze. "Do you need me to warn you when they arrive?"

"No," she said quickly. "Mrs. Simpson is sure to let me know. She keeps me on a short tether most times."

Her voice took on a harsh tone in reference to our housekeeper. Of course, the woman had always been deferential to my family and me. After all, she was our employee. But Constance…

"Has she been mistreating you? I can tell Mother. She'll have a word—"

"No. Don't," she said, not letting me finish. "Sometimes, I feels like the old biddy is watchin' me. Waitin' for me to blunder—what so's she can tell me how I did it wrong."

I nodded, understanding her concerns completely. Having been under Mycroft's—and Father's—scrutiny all my life, I found it sometimes difficult to remember, much less observe, all the rigid codes they held regarding proper comportment. Mother, too, wasn't above correcting my behavior, but somehow her remarks didn't affect me the same way.

"Get some rest," I said, hoping I sounded amiable and not put out at her rejection. "See you in the morning."

With a wave, she left in the direction of the servants' rooms.

Once alone, I considered my options and decided some time on the violin would be the best. Mycroft had squirreled himself away somewhere and probably wouldn't complain about the noise as long as I kept the door to my room closed.

Besides, I found my efforts on the instrument freed my thoughts to wander. The process was fascinating to me. While part of my brain focused on the notes, my fingering, and the sounds produced, another part could review information, rearranging ideas to knit them into a pattern—just as the jumble of musical tones, when aligned correctly, would make a beautiful etude, aria, or whole concerto.

This observation was still on my mind as I practiced a new piece Mother had proposed for a duet—with her on the pianoforte. My thoughts shifted first to the opera. First, because Constance had mentioned it, and second, because we'd seen Rose with Nathan and Maurice Edmonds there. And then how Mrs. Simms had noted Crandall had shouted to Miss Phillips to pass a message to Edmonds. I doubted the young woman had many dealings with Maurice, Nathan's cousin. But Lord Jared Edmonds, the son of the Earl of Wittdam, would have been around a lot more if an engagement was in the future. Of course, Nathan Edmonds had been the one who had arranged for the preparation of Lord Surminster's remains as well as the postponement of the coroner's inquest.

The consideration of Nathan Edmonds returned me to his sudden interest in sharing the map with the pomegranate symbol. We'd assumed the small piece of paper with the same symbol found in Surminster's pocket had been torn from the map he stole from the library, but what if he had drawn or copied the symbol himself to keep as a reference?

It might be possible to examine the drawing and determine if it came from the stolen map.

THE ADVENTURE OF THE DECEASED SCHOLAR

Without another thought, I put away my violin and bow and rushed to Mother's sitting room. The last time I'd seen the scrap of paper was when Mycroft had drawn his recollection of the map on the slate. As soon as I got there I searched the tabletop, under the slates, and checked the other surfaces in the room. Several items had been moved and rearranged as Mother had prepared for the dinner tonight. Perhaps Constance would recall where it had been placed?

I rapped on her door but received no answer.

After what she had shared about Mrs. Simpson watching over her, I feared calling out her name. I rapped louder and whispered to her.

Unfortunately, I must have made more noise than I had desired. To my great dread, Mrs. Simpson poked her head out of her own room.

"Is the girl not there?"

Her judgmental tone made me cringe, and I feared I'd made Constance's relationship with our housekeeper more difficult than ever. At the same time, I didn't appreciate the attitude she showed toward my friend.

"Her name is Constance," I said. "She was going to lie down, but maybe she's elsewhere."

"Lying down, is it?"

Mrs. Simpson banged on the door and called her name loud enough for all the other servants to open their doors in response to the fuss in the hallway.

When she still received no answer, she opened the door. Facing me, she said, "She's not here. Bed's still made. I would guess she's not been 'lying down' since last night."

"I just remembered. After saying she'd lie down, she then said something about working on her reading. I thought she meant here, but she must have meant the library. I'm sure that's where she is."

I rushed away before Mrs. Simpson could suggest she join me or remark on my friend's cheekiness in accessing the family library.

Once on the ground floor, I paused to consider where she might truly be. I returned to Mother's room, even though I'd just come from there. When looking for the image of the pomegranate, I'd noticed some of her things were out on her dressing table. In particular, a hairbrush and an open box of pearls. Closing my eyes, I recalled the scene when I reported on my conversation with the Simms ladies. Mother had done a final inspection in the mirror, but neither of those items had been present on the table when she rose to join Father.

Perhaps Constance had simply returned them after she had helped Mother dress her hair? But returned them from where? Surely Mother had completed her toilette here?

I picked up the box of pearls. They still filled its bottom. Without recalling how many Mother had used, I had no way of knowing whether more were missing. My hand shook as I placed the box back onto the tabletop as I ran through a number of reasons Constance would have taken some—if that was what happened. They had no real value. She told me herself they were paste. More importantly, I couldn't believe she would steal from us, from Mother, from *me*.

If she took some, she was using them for some purpose. The hair was one possibility, but they could be used to adorn dresses. Or other feminine items like reticules, hats, or fans. My pulse quickened, remembering the fan and hat we'd discovered in the classroom the other day. I spun on my heels and raced up to the top floor, unsure of why I would think she was there. She wasn't, but on checking the top of the old table where the fan and hat had been, I found her maid's uniform.

Staring at the discarded dress, I had a hard time fathoming her actions. Like the paste pearls, the items had little to no value. She'd noted some items in the room could be sold for a fair sum, but I saw nothing missing. At this point, I determined she wasn't in the house and had appropriated some of the pearls and the hat and fan in order to enhance herself in some way. My next step was to return to her room and determine how she had been dressed when she left.

A creak from the hallway interrupted my plans. Someone was using the bachelor stairs. I'd heard of servants having secret rendezvouses with those from other households—or even less savory characters, and decided to investigate the noise, but not empty handed.

Searching the dark room, I spied a broken table leg lying on top of a desk. As good a club as any. With as much stealth as I could muster in my hard-soled shoes, I crept to the staircase leading directly to the alleyway. The table leg raised over my head, I waited for the person to emerge. My plan wasn't to strike them immediately but to shout a warning and only club them if I thought it was necessary.

I could make out a shadowy figure now on the stairs, and my palms dampened. I gripped the wood tighter to avoid its slipping.

One, two...three.

"You. Stop there," I said in what I hoped was both a gruff and menacing tone.

Constance squealed and covered her head with her arms.

Dropping my weapon to my side, I stared at her. "Wha-what happened to you?"

Her ginger hair still held the pearls in an upsweep similar to the one Mother had worn, but some of the tendrils had worked themselves loose and hung below the hat from the classroom. She was wearing the same dress she'd worn to the opera, and the fan hung from her wrist. But I stared at her face. Even in the dim light, I could see how she'd powdered it, adding bright pink spots on the cheeks, red lips, and black around the eyes. Only she'd been crying, and tears had washed the powder and rouge off the center of each cheek and outlined it in black streaks. My first concern was she'd been attacked. I saw no marks, however, on her clothes.

She sniffled and swiped the back of her hand under her nose. "Nothin'…"

After turning her back to me, she continued to weep silently, her quivering shoulders the only clue to her distress.

"You didn't dress up like that, disappear from the house, and come back crying because of nothing. If someone hurt you—"

My hand gripped the table leg tighter. If whoever made her cry had been in front of me, the person would have been clubbed before drawing another breath.

My short speech must have hit some nerve because she straightened her spine and spun about to face me. "No one hurt me. I was just—just—humiliated."

I studied her overall appearance, imagining it as she would have first prepared herself, and saw she'd made a serious attempt to present herself as older, more sophisticated—and possibly above her station. With this review, I developed a theory of where she'd been and why.

THE ADVENTURE OF THE DECEASED SCHOLAR

"You went back to the opera house, didn't you?"

She dropped her gaze and nodded. Drawing in a shaky breath, she said, "I thought I might be able to find that George fellow. Convince him to hear me sing."

"Did he…" I swallowed, finding it hard to pose the question, but pushed myself to ask it. "Did he turn you down?"

She shook her head.

"He offered you a position in the company?"

Biting her lip, she shook her head again. Her lower lip, still in the grip of her upper teeth, trembled. With another shuddering breath, she said, "I didn't get past the door. The man there thought I was…" Her voice took on a stronger whimpering tone, but she forced out the rest before bursting into a howl. "He thought I was a street trollop."

I shifted my weight from one foot to the other, unsure how to respond to the sobbing girl before me. A part of me wanted to embrace her, let her know it would be all right. I raised my free hand halfway but stopped myself. Pulling her toward me would surely mean the powder and other cosmetics would stain my jacket and possibly lead to more questions from my parents. I dropped it to my side.

The other part of me considered her predicament not as dire as her current emotional state suggested, and should she view it from this perspective, she could calm herself a bit. According to what she'd shared, her humiliation was limited to a doorman.

"I'm sorry, Constance, he treated you so horribly. I'm sure there are a lot of made-up women who show up at the stage door who are what he thought you were. We both know you're not."

She raised her head and gave one final sniff. Her eyes

were still red-rimmed, but they were no longer teary, and her next words carried none of her earlier mewlings. "What do you mean, 'made-up women'?"

My mouth went dry, as I understood how her view of the situation wasn't the same as my own. I paused and sought the most delicate means of pointing out the difference. "Perhaps you noticed, my mother—"

"She put her hair up, and I just borrowed some of her pearls—"

"But, you see, she doesn't rouge her cheeks—or at least as much as you've done."

"Miss Augustin did." Her hands jammed onto her hips. "I saw her. You did, too."

"But that was for the stage. The actors wear heavy makeup so their expressions can be seen from the back of the theater."

"Oh." Her hands sank to her side. She stared at me, and her lip trembled again as her comprehension of my explanation grew. "Oh—oh, no."

She buried her head in her hands and sobbed once again. "I'm such a buffoon."

"You're not," I said. This time I did reach out to pat her shoulder. "But you need to change and clean up before Mother gets home. I'll tell Mrs. Simpson I found you. You've been in the library. Practicing your reading. Understand?"

She drew in her breath. "Lors, you mean the old crone knows I stepped out?" The fire I'd always attributed to her character returned.

My own trepidation returned as well. I had no desire to harm our friendship by disclosing my earlier interaction with our housekeeper.

"She only knows I was searching for you. I'll make certain she knows I've been with you. Just clean yourself up and be ready for my mother's return."

When she stepped to the classroom door, I asked, "How did you know about these stairs?"

She faced me, rather slowly.

"Adeline," she said, referring to one of the London maids hired for our time here. I knew the girl. She seemed demure enough around us, but maybe she wasn't all she appeared. "She likes to step out of a night. Has always offered to take me too, but I've always turned her down. I haven't gone out until tonight. I was too scared Mrs. Simpson would catch me and tell your mother."

I nodded, glad I was the one who caught her—at least for now. Another thought occurred to me. "How did you get to the theater?"

"One of them cabs. Adeline told me how to hail one and how much it'd cost." A smile played on her lips, and a small rock formed in the pit of my stomach. Had she stolen from my family? "I borrowed it from a wallet I found." The rock grew. "From the Edmonds fellow what come the other day. I fetched him his coat, you know. When he left. After the way he gave you the evil eye, I figured he owed it to us."

I pinned my own evil eye on her. "Is that all you 'borrowed'?"

"Well, I might've found some other interestin' papers. I couldn't very well give them to you without tellin' you how I comes by them. Now that you know, I'll show them to you later."

She turned and slipped into the room. I stared at the closed door, rooted in place—curiosity about what she had found comingled with a fear of how we might be implicated in some crime against this man should he find himself light a few items. Would he be able to trace their loss back to us?

With great effort, I shook myself and went in search of Mrs. Simpson. We had enough troubles without turmoil among the servants.

Mrs. Simpson gave me a rather skeptical squint when I explained how I'd found Constance asleep by the fire in the library, which was why she hadn't heard me when I first searched for her. But as I was her employer's son, she had to outwardly accept my explanation and my assurance the girl was now in her room, awaiting my mother's return.

While I wanted to go to Constance's room to let her know what I'd told Mrs. Simpson, as well as to press her on what she'd found in Nathan Edmonds' pocket, two occurrences held me back. After she thanked me for the information, Mrs. Simpson made directly for the servants' stairs, certainly to check on Constance's whereabouts. I hoped I'd stalled long enough for my friend to have washed her face and changed. The second was the arrival of my parents.

I could still see the hem of Mrs. Simpson's dress on the stairwell when the front door opened. The woman turned and bounded down the stairs to greet her employers with more agility than I thought she possessed. I followed at a more sedate pace to give Constance a little more time to prepare herself before attending to my mother. I had no worries she would be able to return the pearls without my mother suspecting they had been "borrowed." After all, the girl was an expert pickpocket. Replacing the pearls in the box required much less stealth.

THE ADVENTURE OF THE DECEASED SCHOLAR

The lines about my father's mouth and mother's tightly pressed lips signaled the evening had not gone well. My welcome stuck in my throat when they turned in my direction. Adeline had opened the door and helped my mother with her cape, and Mrs. Simpson held out her arms for Father's coat.

"Did you have a nice dinner?" our housekeeper asked.

"Yes." Mother clipped the word. "Very pleasant."

Regardless of what had upset them, they wouldn't discuss it until alone. Father's rules of etiquette required any such disagreements not be aired in front of the servants, although I'd learned from Constance, the staff were fully knowledgeable of all that transpired in the household.

Mycroft stepped into the hallway from the library, and we all faced him. He read the situation as well as I did and stopped just outside the doorway.

"I-I heard voices," he said. "Just checking to see if you had returned."

"Were you expecting someone else?" Father asked.

"No, no."

I truly felt for Mycroft. He seemed to have something on his mind to share with our parents, but he quickly ascertained it was not the time to do so. Having stepped into the hornet's nest, he now sought to extract himself as quickly and safely as possible.

"Actually, I was going to bed," he said. "I've been reading about—er, history. Yes, found an interesting book on the Tudors. Well, good night."

"Mr. Mycroft," Mrs. Simpson said, halting my brother in his tracks once again, "have you been in the library long?"

The question constricted my throat even tighter. My

breath fairly wheezed through the opening. I'd failed to confirm the library was empty, and now would be caught in a lie. Not that I was worried for myself, but I had no idea what the consequences might be for my friend.

The woman stepped between my brother and me, prohibiting me from signaling him to reply in the negative.

"Long enough," he said.

My throat eased a little.

"You didn't see Constance in there?"

"Why would I see her in the library?"

Hoping to stop this line of questioning before my lie was exposed, I said, "You didn't see her because I already found her there, and she went to her room."

They all turned to me now, and for the first time, I was able to see around Mrs. Simpson, but it made no difference. Everyone would see if I signaled my brother. I feared heat was rising in my cheeks—a sure giveaway of being caught in a lie. Mother, however, seemed to have sensed this problem and spoke up, taking the focus away from me.

"I'm very tired. Adeline, please bring up some hot water."

"Should I send Constance to assist you?" Mrs. Simpson asked after one last glance in my direction.

"I'll fetch her," I said, perhaps a little too quickly. In an effort to justify the offer, I said, "That way, Mrs. Simpson can arrange for the water…for both of you."

My parents gave me a curt nod and moved toward the stairs. I'd only taken a few steps toward the servants' stairs when someone knocked. The six of us froze, exchanging glances, and Father waved a hand at Mrs. Simpson, indicating she was to answer the door.

THE ADVENTURE OF THE DECEASED SCHOLAR

Before she could announce him, Inspector Roggens stepped inside.

"Good. You're all here," Roggens said, letting his gaze rest on each of us in turn. "Saves me the trouble of asking to send for any of you."

"Excuse me, Inspector," Father said. "It's late, and it's been a trying day. Whatever questions you have about Lord Surminster, can it not wait until tomorrow?"

The man shook his head. "I'm not here about Lord Surminster. I need to ask about what you might know about a Mr. Fenton Crandall."

My throat squeezed shut again. This time, I feared I might pass out, which would only bring our family under greater scrutiny from Scotland Yard. After all, someone dropping unconscious at the mention of a name would surely suggest some connection, if not guilt.

Was that what lay behind Roggens' question? To observe our reactions?

Mother seemed to suspect some ulterior motive behind the inspector's call because she spoke up almost immediately. "How does any acquaintance with Crandall involve us?"

"Because he was murdered today, and you, madam, along with your sons were among the last to see him alive."

CHAPTER ELEVEN

Somehow, I managed to make my legs work well enough to follow the inspector and my family into the drawing room. My anxiety stemmed from both the news about poor Crandall as well as what would surely be my Father's eruption after the visit. He'd been in a foul mood when he arrived home, and Inspector Roggens' pronouncement simply added kerosene to the fire. As I joined my brother on a settee next to the fireplace, and my parents sank onto a couch on the other side, I hazarded a glance at my father. His jaw was working as if he was trying to keep from cursing at all of us, including the man from Scotland Yard. I could only hope whatever he had come to share didn't push my father too far.

Roggens stepped to the fireplace, clasped his hands behind his back, and rocked back and forth on the hearth rug. As he had in the entryway, he let his gaze rest for a moment on each of us.

Finally, his mouth turned downward, and he said, "I

THE ADVENTURE OF THE DECEASED SCHOLAR

understand Mrs. Holmes and your sons paid a visit to Fenton Crandall."

Before any of us could answer, Father broke in. "Who the devil is Fenton Crandall?"

He then took his own turn eyeing each of us, and the only thing keeping me from squirming or averting my gaze was sheer terror. I once had come across a rabbit in the woods. While they usually darted away, this particular one fixed his stare at me, as if frozen in place. Now I understood why the rabbit hadn't run. His fear had paralyzed him.

Mycroft cleared his throat and spoke up.

"He—" He coughed again, as if the answer were lodged in his throat. When he spoke again, his voice was stronger. "He's a classmate of mine. From Oxford. But not in the same college. I only knew of him from his association with another classmate. Maurice Edmonds."

"And you visited him at his club today?" Roggens asked.

Mycroft nodded, but Mother responded to the question. "We all did, Inspector. Mycroft, Sherlock, and I."

"And where was I when this occurred?" Father asked.

His face was now a deep vermillion, and both his body and voice trembled.

Despite Father's apparent rage, Mother maintained a straight back and kept her voice steady when she faced him. "With Mr. Sires. I'm afraid I misled you, Mr. Holmes. We didn't go to the museum."

"And just how many other things have you misled me about lately?"

He obviously had forgotten his edict about discussing private matters in front of the servants—or perhaps he didn't place Inspector Roggens in the same category as Mrs. Simpson.

Mother opened her mouth as if to answer, but Roggens interrupted. "Before we move on to that topic, perhaps you can tell me more about your meeting with Mr. Crandall. According to the club's butler, you had a rather heated discussion with him."

My heart drummed in my chest. Just how much had the butler overheard? Had he accused me of provoking Crandall?

"I'm afraid he did become rather angry, but only because he was confronted with the truth," Mother said.

Father twisted himself to face her directly. "What sort of truth would you know about this man?"

"Squire Holmes," Roggens said in a strong voice. "If you will allow me to ask the questions here."

Mother placed a hand on her husband's arm. "Perhaps it would be better if we three answered the Inspector's questions alone. You weren't aware of our visit with Crandall, and it's clearly upsetting you."

"I. Am. Not. Going. Anywhere."

Roggens cleared his throat—loudly—and the two of them shifted their focus to him. The contrast between them —one steaming and the other cooler than ice—telegraphed a mounting tension within the room. Roggens shifted from one foot to another. Mycroft studied his shoes, and my stomach roiled to the point I feared I might have to excuse myself.

"You admit going to Crandall's club?" Roggens asked, focusing on my mother.

"Yes. We went there because we hoped he had information regarding Lord Surminster's death."

"And why would you think that?"

"Because he'd been seen with a woman named Rose the

THE ADVENTURE OF THE DECEASED SCHOLAR

previous night, and she had been in the company of Nathan and Maurice Edmonds the night before that."

My insides felt as if they were dissolving. A few more questions and Father would learn of our visit to *La Lampe et Le Chien*. If he was angry at the news we'd been to see Crandall, he would be apoplectic at this new bit. Even though he was in good health, I feared he might have a stroke right in this room. Barring that event, I worried for our health once he learned of that adventure.

"You see," Mother said, leaning forward a bit. I could see she was caught up in reviewing what we had learned, unconcerned about her husband's reaction at the moment. "As I mentioned to you, Lord Surminster was murdered by a sharp instrument penetrating his brain through his ear. And Rose was wearing a very long, ornate pin in her hair when we saw her with Mr. Crandall."

"This Rose woman wore a hairpin," Roggens said.

It was a statement rather than a question, which suggested Roggens was not surprised by either the name or the pin. I was certain this observation wasn't lost on either my mother or brother, but Mother continued explaining our visit.

"That's why we went to see Crandall. To arrange a visit with Rose. Unfortunately, he was not willing to share much with us and basically threw us out. We understand he did visit Surminster's home later—in case you wish to learn more about his whereabouts today."

"Speaking of whereabouts, can you all share with me where you've been this evening?"

"I can answer that question," my father said. He seemed eager to enter into this discussion and display some control over the interview. "My wife and I had dinner at a friend's home. We just arrived. My sons were at home all evening."

Roggens faced my brother and me. "Were you?"

The inspector's intense gaze sent another wave through my lower abdomen, but a second later, a small flame of anger ignited. Whatever had happened to Crandall hadn't been our doing. We might have questioned him (even threatened him), but if he was murdered, we hadn't been there or done it.

When he continued to stare at me, I spoke in a rather abrupt and harsh tone, "Yes. All evening. And so was my brother."

"How do you know? Did you see him?"

I paused only a breath because I hadn't actually. I'd been too involved with Constance's disappearance and return. But I also knew my brother. He didn't leave the house unless absolutely necessary. Especially at night. He preferred his quiet solitude, which was why Mother's efforts to drag him to the various entertainments she'd accepted on his behalf had been such a burden on him.

In the end, I stretched the truth just a little with an emphatic, "Yes."

"Most certainly," Mycroft said at the same time.

"And there are others in the household—the servants perhaps—who can back up that statement."

"Of course," Father said and rang the bell for our housekeeper.

Without a doubt, Mrs. Simpson had been nearby, probably eavesdropping from the dining room, because she appeared in the doorway almost as soon as Father touched the bell.

"Mrs. Simpson," Father said. "Did you see my sons this evening?"

"Of course, sir," she said with a nod. "Master Sherlock was looking for Constance, and I helped him into her room. Mr. Mycroft came out of the library the same time as you arrived home."

Father waved his hand in front of him, as if erasing an invisible slate. "No, woman. Mycroft. Did he go out?"

"I can't say I saw him until you came home, but he was in the library then." She faced me. "But Master Sherlock said Mr. Mycroft wasn't in the library earlier when he found Constance there."

I held her stare, regretting ever having created this alibi for Constance without first checking on whether the library was actually vacant or not, but knowing both my friend and my brother required my corroboration of having occupied the same space simultaneously—each unaware of the other. I weighed the consequences of being caught in my lie. While I couldn't be certain, most likely Constance would face anything from a demotion from her post as lady's maid to a position where Mrs. Simpson would have her more under her thumb and scrutiny to an immediate return to Underbyrne and removal from the household entirely. On the other hand, Mycroft's situation appeared much less dire. Surely if not Mrs. Simpson, at least one of the servants had seen him during the evening?

I faced the inspector.

"He may not have been in the library when I found Constance there, but I know my brother. He's not been out all evening."

Father raised his hand to stop any further conversation

and turned to Mrs. Simpson. "Thank you for your observations. That will be all."

When the door closed again, the lines around Roggens' downturned mouth deepened. "There are at least two men at *La Lampe et Le Chien* who would disagree. They claim to have seen him there tonight."

My thoughts reeled. While the man was focusing on the current night's events, I had no doubt he would next reference our visit to the night house the previous evening. More to explain to our father. I glanced at my parents. Mother remained still, but her face seemed paler to me. She had to be seeing where the man's questions would lead. Father, on the other hand, appeared to be seeking to understand what sort of establishment the name implied.

Mycroft jumped to his feet, obviously aware of all the implications. While he made no move toward the man from Scotland Yard, Roggens stepped a little to the side. My brother towered over the smaller man, and his voice held a menacing tone.

"I have not set foot outside this home this evening. Who would dare to suggest I was anywhere else?"

"But you are familiar with the place?" Roggens asked, his gaze now fastened on my brother.

Mycroft lifted his chin. "I've been there once. Last night. For about thirty minutes. I have not returned."

"During the visit, you almost got into a brawl with..." Roggens flipped through his notes. "A man with the last name of Harcourt."

I could see the man lying on his back on the tavern floor, wheezing from having his breath knocked out of him from Mother's *baritsu* move. He certainly had an axe to grind with my brother. Had someone convinced him to lie just to get Mycroft in trouble?

"I'd hardly call it a brawl. We had a few words, but he was in his cups. I decided not to stay, but he tried to stop me, tripped, and fell backward. When he did so, I left."

With great effort, I restrained myself from slapping him on the back for his ability to blithely fabricate the events of the previous evening. Would his ability to present such information with such flare never cease to amaze me?

Roggens' frown deepened, and my admiration for my brother turned to dread when he continued to press him. "You left alone?"

Again, my brother had a ready answer. "No. I escorted two other patrons out. As I said, not everyone there was sober, and I was concerned for the safety of the other two."

"Your 'cousin' and a 'boy'?"

His voice carried a snide tone when he referred to the description of the two "patrons," and while he kept his gaze on my brother, I had to wonder if the inspector already suspected my mother and me as being the other two in his company. His thorough research garnered my admiration.

As much as I desired to transmit at least some of these thoughts in a glance to my mother, I feared Roggens might pick up on any such communication and possibly consider it an admission of guilt. I focused instead on the inspector, seeking to keep as blank a face as possible.

"Correct," Mycroft said. "I'd brought two others I'd met outside along. They'd asked for my help to gain entry. I felt responsible for their safety. When things became heated during the discussion with Harcourt, I insisted they leave with me. But it has been the one and only time I have visited the establishment."

"We can return there later. More importantly, you disagree with those at the pub who say you returned this evening to look for Rose?"

"Most definitively."

Mycroft dropped into his seat as if to emphasize his innocence.

"Excuse me." Mother broke into the conversation before Roggens could ask his next question. "Perhaps you can share when and where Crandall was found? We might be able to better indicate where we were in relation to the gentleman."

The man paused to browse through his notebook. He had to know where Crandall's body was found. I surmised he was using the action to make a decision.

Before Roggens could respond, Father spoke up. I risked a glance in his direction. His face was no longer flushed, and his voice was steady when he said, "As a professional courtesy. I am, after all, an officer of the court as well."

"But not in London," the man said. He shook his head, and the hand holding the notebook dropped to his side. "He was found in the alley behind a row of houses near the docks. About two hours ago." He focused on my brother. "Plenty of time to make it here."

"And what time do the men at *La Lampe et Le Chien* say Mycroft was there?" Mother asked. "Because I can assure you, he was here until eight. Mr. Holmes and I didn't leave the house until then, and I saw him just prior to our departure."

"You're saying the men at *La Lampe et Le Chien* are lying?"

"Blatantly," Mycroft said. "As I already shared, there was a bit of a row last night. Bad blood has existed between

THE ADVENTURE OF THE DECEASED SCHOLAR

Tennyson, Harcourt, and me for a while. I'm a bit of a loner, and they have taken offense to my reserved nature. My guess is that they see this opportunity as some sort of retaliation."

"Inspector," Mother said, interrupting the exchange, "can you share how the man was found?"

"Neighbor went to toss some garbage and found the man."

"Interesting," Mother said, tapping a finger to her lips. "And just how did he die?"

All of us focused on the inspector. He gripped the notebook so tightly I could see his knuckles growing white. "Madam, I came here to ask questions, not answer them."

"I simply wished to learn the cause of death because it might very well help us share where we were at the time it occurred. You see, if rigor has not yet set in—"

"I *know* about rigor, madam. But again, I'm asking the questions."

Father stood. "Now see here. I'll not have you speak to my wife in that tone of voice. She has been helpful in a number of recent murders in my parish, and I'll not have her treated as either a criminal—which she is definitely not —or as some dimwitted female."

My gratitude for Roggens' annoyed response overflowed. At least for the moment, he had become the object of my father's wrath and perhaps had now spared my mother, brother, and me from any repercussions for the near future. To my surprise, the Scotland Yarder paused and surveyed the four of us. Father remained standing, fists clenched at his sides. Perhaps the inspector realized he had lost control of the interview, or perhaps he felt he might gain more from sharing a bit of information with us.

Either way, he grimaced and said, "If you must know, he was stabbed. In the neck."

Mother drew in a breath as if it were not the answer she had expected, and I had a similar response. Given the circumstances of the other two deaths, I hadn't anticipated such a violent end. A stab wound to the neck would create a foul mess with blood spattering both the agent as well as the whole scene. Not to mention requiring the murderer to be next to the victim.

"With a knife?" she asked.

Roggens' gaze shifted to my father, who still stood, with his arms now crossed in studied silence, before answering. "No, with a long, straight pin. We know because it was still in his neck."

"Did it have a jeweled head? A large enamel butterfly?"

The man paused and stared at her. "How did you know?"

I kept my gaze down to avoid the inspector seeing my distress. She had been the one to notice the pin in Rose's hair, and in her haste to determine Crandall's death, might have implicated herself as being at *La Lampe et Le Chien* with Mycroft. Her reply, however, soothed my concern.

"Because it's the pin Sherlock reported seeing in her hair outside the opera—which I already reported to you. Although I don't see how useful it would be as a weapon unless—" She stared at the Scotland Yarder. "Are you referring to the base of the neck? Here?"

She dipped her chin to her chest and placed a finger in the hollow at the top of her spine, just below her hairline. When she raised her gaze, the man's face showed she'd made the correct assumption.

"Of course," she said, more to herself than to the rest of

us. "A direct thrust upward into the medulla oblongata would effectively immobilize as well as kill. Although no one would allow such an attack unless they were incapacitated."

She focused again on the inspector. "You need to check Crandall's stomach contents. I believe you will find he was drugged—either by a sedative, or drink, or both. Unless you find some indications of a struggle on Crandall—I saw none on Lord Surminster—they were not conscious when they were murdered. Whoever did this had both knowledge and skill regarding human anatomy." She shifted her gaze to my brother. "Are you familiar with any of your colleagues who might have such training, Mycroft?"

My brother started as if poked by a hairpin himself. "You mean medical training? Well, a medical sciences program exists—which has been improving, I'm told—but I don't know of anyone reading for such a degree."

Mother faced Roggens again. "I would suggest you seek this Rose woman. Ask her about the hairpin."

"Would love to, but it appears she's...disappeared."

Mother's paled at that news. As I was certain, my own face did as well. What had happened to the woman?

She stood and brushed her skirt. "I'm afraid we can't be of more help for you tonight, Inspector. Yes, we did have words with Fenton Crandall. None of us was at *La Lampe et Le Chien* tonight, and those whose statement says otherwise are acting from an ulterior motive. I would suggest determining whether any of those at the establishment or his club have any medical training. They would be the ones most likely involved in poor Crandall's murder. Also, make an effort to find this Rose woman. She appears to know all the parties involved. Now, if you'll excuse me, it's getting late, and the news is most upsetting. Allow us to escort you to the door."

Mycroft and I stood in response to Mother's own rising.

Roggens opened his mouth and shut it after he glanced at each of us. His shoulders slumped, an indication he recognized he'd somehow been bested by my mother.

After the door closed behind him, Mother clucked her tongue. "I feel for Crandall's family. Murdered. By the docks. Hardly an appropriate place for a young man of his standing to be found. What could he have been doing there? Most likely, it will be hushed up in some way."

She took a few steps toward the stairs, but Father remained rooted where he'd taken leave of the inspector. When he failed to follow, she turned back around to him. A shiver swept down my spine as I read the thin-lipped expression on his face. She may have been able to best the man from Scotland Yard, but her husband was a different matter.

"I suggest we return to the drawing room," he said.

We trailed after him back into the room, and I feared Mother's skills at appeasing him would be sorely put to the test. In the past half hour, he learned of our acquaintance with another dead student, our having tracked the mysterious Rose to a night house, and my brother actually visiting such a place. I prayed Mother and Mycroft had solid explanations to offer because if they admitted the truth—which my father wouldn't find acceptable—there would be no way to avoid his wrath.

He now took the spot the inspector had commanded only a few minutes before. Once we were all seated, he clasped his hands behind his back and said, "Apparently you have been inserting yourselves into matters I have strictly indicated are not our affair, and as a result, you have put Mycroft under even graver suspicion."

Mother straightened her back and met his gaze. "I'm afraid, Mr. Holmes, we didn't insert ourselves as much as we were forced into the situation by Lord Surminster's family. As for any suspicion cast on Mycroft, I think we can agree it has been reasonably addressed. The original threat of scandal, however, still lies ahead, should Miss Phillips decide to follow through. The only way, as I see it, to avoid such concerns is to find the true culprit—which I believe we can narrow down given what I just shared with Inspector Roggens."

She faced my brother. "Are you certain you know no one who would have such knowledge? Perhaps someone who has already left Oxford?"

"Can't think of a one," he said without even pausing. "As I noted, few seek such training at Oxford. There's been a push to revise the program, but few students are interested in treating—let alone touching—ill people. Better left to surgeons, you understand." He paused, glanced in our mother's direction, caught her squint at his remark, and added quickly, "Their prejudice. Not mine."

"Can we return to the point at hand," Father said, perhaps a little bit louder than required.

He had to be as frustrated as Roggens with my mother's insistence on reviewing our current knowledge of the situation rather than showing the contrition he might expect from a guilty person brought before his bench.

"I think we've covered it," Mother said, rising from her seat. She placed a hand on Father's arm. "It's been a long day for all of us. Why don't we all sleep on it? I'm sure things will be more settled in the morning."

He opened his mouth, probably to protest that nothing had been covered or settled but closed it when Mother stepped toward the door. I filed out after my parents and brother. Constance waited at the top of the stairs to help my mother change. Before she stepped into the sitting room, my friend beckoned to me. I thought she was going to ask me about what I had shared with Mrs. Simpson, but instead, after a glance around, she handed me a book.

"Thanks for borrowin' it to me," she said with a smile.

I didn't recall loaning her a copy of the history of Tudor England but accepted it with my own smile in return. Once alone in my room, I opened the inside cover and found a torn piece of paper. The thickness and yellowing of the parchment indicated its age. Unfolding it, I held it next to a light and recognized it as part of a map. Drawing in my breath, I forced myself to maintain my composure and not go running into my mother's room. I held in my hand a portion of the map Lord Surminster had stolen from the library at the British Museum.

As much as I wanted to share this with my mother, it wouldn't be possible tonight. There was one other person, however, who would be as interested and at least as helpful in determining what to do with Constance's little theft.

CHAPTER TWELVE

Mycroft peered at me through the crack of his opened bedroom door. After he turned his gaze toward the ceiling, he stepped back and allowed me to enter.

"I'm tired," he said with a deep sigh. "Whatever you want, can't it wait until morning?"

"Constance just gave me something she took from Edmonds' pocket the other day. I think you'll be interested."

Another deep sigh, followed by an outstretched hand. I placed the folded map onto it. He carried it to a table by the fireplace, raised the light on the gas lamp, and opened the paper. Once he'd run his hands across the parchment to smooth out the image, he faced me.

"She took this from Edmonds?"

I nodded. "It's the missing map, isn't it? The one from the British Museum?"

"Looks like it," he said in an almost absentminded mutter.

He smoothed his thumb over his jawline as he continued to stare at the paper. I thought I could hear the scratch of stubble as he did so. He took so long in raising his gaze, I had to suppress a desire to pull his hand away from his face and shout at him to tell me what he found.

By the time he finally did look up, I felt as if my lungs would explode from pent-up exasperation. "Why would Edmonds be carrying this in his pocket?"

"Maybe he wanted to compare it with the one he showed us? Or he forgot he had it. Just tell me how it compares with what he showed you and what was in the library."

He turned to the table and ran a finger along the even-cut right side. "This is a complete edge. Even you can tell that. So's this." He ran the finger over the bottom part. "But this"—he ran his finger along the left side—"you can tell it was torn, but there is a part missing between what remained at the library and what we have here."

"Which is?"

He raised and lowered his shoulders. "I would only be guessing—which I abhor doing. What I can tell you is in the piece Edmonds showed us is…nothing."

A shriek bubbled inside me, and I pushed down the desire to snatch the map from the table and rend it into pieces before tossing it into the fire. I took several deep breaths and let my gaze follow the straight edges he'd pointed out as well as the jagged one he still let his finger rest upon. He raised his hand to his chin again, lifting his finger from the parchment. When he did so, I glimpsed a small mark where it had been.

"Really, Mycroft, the least you could have done was to clean your hands before touching this."

He glowered at me and thrust his hand within inches of my nose. "They are, you twit."

Instead of arguing with him, I glanced around his palm to the paper. "Then what is this mark?"

I brought the lamp closer to the ripped portion, almost at the bottom edge of the paper, and studied what I had thought at first was a smudge. "This is…" I picked up the paper to hold it closer to the flame. "This is part of the map, I think. Maybe a straight line?"

Mycroft bent forward, his cheek close to mine. "I do believe you're right. Missed that the first time."

He straightened and closed his eyes. "That part of Edmonds' map didn't have a line. There was one"—he opened his eyes, placed the paper on the table, and drew his finger down an imaginary line on the wood further to the left of the ripped edge—"over here. It marks the boundary between two properties."

"You mean between Wrightmoor and Mrs. Simms' family property? Which one do you suppose is correct, then? This one with more land on Wrightmoor, or on the Simms' estate?"

"Only one true way to find out," he said and met my gaze. "Check out the properties."

I blinked at him. "Go there? And how do you propose we get there without Father finding out?"

"A major problem," he said and stretched. "As Mother has noted, things may appear different in the morning. Let's discuss it with her then."

BREAKFAST the next morning was a subdued affair with everyone keeping their heads down and thoughts to themselves. The rattling of Father's newspaper became the most pronounced sound in the room. When he pushed his plate back and opened the paper wide in front of him, my brother and I signaled to our mother the need for a conference after the meal by widening our eyes and glancing in the direction of her upstairs sitting room.

She shook her head in response. Whatever had transpired in their bedroom while Mycroft and I had studied the map seemed to have dissuaded her from further efforts in the area for the moment.

As if in answer to a prayer I had even yet to form, Mrs. Simpson appeared with a letter on a salver. Father lowered his paper, read the note, and asked, "Any plans for the day?"

Mother put down her teacup and smiled at him. "Did you have something in mind?"

"Sires has invited me to his club for the day. Wants me to meet some of his associates."

"I see."

Something in her tone raised my gaze to her. I couldn't put my finger on why it gave me concern. While the remark appeared noncommittal, I had a feeling it was anything but, and not a topic I could raise with her even when we were alone. Certain discussions remained between my father and her, and their reticence this morning indicated this was one.

More than an hour elapsed before we finally gathered in Mother's sitting room. Father had gone off for a day with his friend, and we spread out the parchment, pointing out the differences noted and our conclusion about the property line. She listened to our discussion and then glanced at the door over her shoulder as if expecting someone to enter.

THE ADVENTURE OF THE DECEASED SCHOLAR

When she turned her attention back to the map, she asked, "What do you propose we do with this bit of information?"

I glanced at my brother and read the same reaction on his features as those flitting through my mind. We'd assumed our mother would know what to do. She always did.

"Mycroft thought we should go there," I said after a mute prompting from my brother. "To see which map is correct."

Another glance at the door. "I can't go. Not today."

"We could," I said without waiting for my brother to suggest an alternative. "Mycroft and I."

"Do we even know how far away Wrightmoor is?" she asked.

"I looked it up in Bradshaw's while we were waiting for Father to leave," Mycroft said. "There's a train at noon. Gets us into Bristol after two. Then we must catch the train to Plymouth. Wrightminster's stop is about an hour from Bristol. That's the town. Wrightmoor is outside."

While the information was presented in a rather matter-of-fact manner, I could read some hesitation in his voice. Some quick addition indicated we would be gone at least all day—if we were able to catch a late-night train back to London. Mycroft would have to leave home. For at least a day. While I doubted he had any major plans, this meant he would once again have to break his routine—a big inconvenience to him.

Mother shook her head. "Your father would most certainly note your absence, and what sort of excuse could I give to cover it? We've been caught in too many lies this week for him to trust me now."

"He's going to be out all day with Mr. Sires and his

friends?" I asked. Mother nodded. "What if you met him and suggested a night out? Just the two of you? By the time you came home, we would normally be in bed anyway."

"Dinner out?" Mother said in a rather thoughtful way. "A nice thought. We haven't been out just the two of us in I don't know how long. Thank you, Sherry dear. It might be good in a number of ways."

Had she plastered a gold star on my forehead, I couldn't have been more pleased with myself or her praise. Until I glanced in my brother's direction. A deep ridge bracketed each side of his down-turned mouth. He most likely had hoped Mother's reluctance to allow us to travel outside of London would have prevented the trip. The prospect of its fruition produced a less than favorable response.

"If you are going to make this trip, we'll have to be sharp about getting you ready and to the station on time," she said. "I'll have Cook prepare you a knapsack for the trip. I'll say you are going on a picnic with some acquaintances. Just in case your father asks any of the staff."

As we were leaving her room, Mother called to Mycroft, asking him to stay for a moment.

I left them to quickly change for traveling.

Once on the train, Mycroft leaned back in the seat, obviously preparing to get in a nap before we arrived in Bristol. A sense of foreboding swept over me as I settled onto the seat for the trip. We had been in a similar train car with "something to eat on the road" only six months ago when our father had called us back to Underbyrne following our mother's arrest for murder. Although we were headed in a different direction for a different purpose, the familiarity of the whole situation brought a cold sweat to my upper lip.

THE ADVENTURE OF THE DECEASED SCHOLAR

Hoping to break the mood, I asked, "What did Mother want from you after I left?"

He paused in his efforts to adjust his coat over him as a makeshift blanket to reply with a dismissive wave of his hand. "She asked if I'd been in contact with Colonel Williams."

"Uncle Ernest's friend?" I asked. Colonel Williams had appeared at Underbyrne at Christmas, presumably to visit our uncle. The true intention of his arrival and his identity led to the unraveling of our whole holiday. "Did she say why?"

Another pause, this time with a studied glance at me before resting his head back upon the head-high cushion. "Presumably to get in touch with him herself. She asked for his address."

"I wonder what for?" I said aloud, but more to myself than to my brother. I then directed the next question to him. "Do you think that means Uncle Ernest will be joining us for Easter? Maybe she wants to invite the Colonel and Chanda for dinner?"

He cracked one eye to glower at me. "It should be apparent to you by now she doesn't clear her social calendar with me. Now, because of your clever suggestion, the two of us are heading out into the hinterlands in search of heaven-only-knows what. My whole day has been disrupted, including our evening. You will, as a result, allow me a few hours' rest before we go gallivanting about the countryside."

Following his announcement, he pulled his hat over his face and was soon snoring away.

The anxiety I'd experienced when we'd boarded our car continued to disrupt my thoughts. They kept returning to Mother's apparent distraction during our discussion in her sitting room and how she'd noted she couldn't possibly accompany us today. At first, I'd considered the remark related to Father's warning about becoming involved in Lord Surminster's (and now Crandall's) death. Now, however, I speculated on other reasons—with the added information regarding her enquiry about Colonel Williams. Given his contact with the government, there was the possibility of gaining some service or information from that source. Or, as I had already mentioned, inviting him for Easter dinner.

The continuous turning of these points, with no clear resolution, gave me a headache. After deciding only time and more information would produce the answers, and in an effort to break my circling thoughts, I opened the knapsack to see what Cook had packed for us. To my delight, I found, in addition to sandwiches, apples, and several wedges of cheese, some hot-cross buns fresh-made that morning. When I pulled two from their paper wrapping, the scent of cinnamon and sugar filled our compartment.

I'd just finished the first and was licking the icing from my fingers when Mycroft removed the hat from his face and asked, "What's that smacking noise?"

"Cook made hot-cross buns. You want one?" I asked, tipping the sack to show him. "Or something else?"

He studied the contents and held out a hand. "I'll take the last two buns. Put them in a serviette. I refuse to slurp my fingers like a common laborer."

By the time we arrived at the seaport, only the apples remained. The Bristol train station, while not nearly the size of the one we'd left in London, was still impressive with high ceilings and a tall clock tower in the middle. With the near-empty knapsack thumping on my back, I hurried to keep

THE ADVENTURE OF THE DECEASED SCHOLAR

pace with my brother's long strides as we found the next train to Wrightminster.

Never having been to this particular seaport, I would have enjoyed spending a bit of time in the city. Many of the ships from the West Indies arrived at the port, and the idea of seeing the tall sailing ships intrigued me. I had to content myself with catching whatever views I could from the train window as we chugged close to the coast at points.

From the far side of our compartment, I caught images of land stretched out in undulating greens, browns, and touches of color—marked at times with rises cutting off the view to the land beyond. The scenery prompted me to rejoice in having the forethought to wear boots instead of my dress shoes, and I couldn't help but hold this over my brother.

"Do you see what awaits us?" I pointed out to the moors passing by. "I'm glad I wore my boots."

He glanced down at his own shined shoes and frowned. "I hadn't thought about that. I suppose if we're going to be seeking some sort of boundary marker, it might just require such equipment. I might be able to purchase a pair, but we may need the funds for a place to stay if we aren't able to catch the last train tonight." He stared out the window at the rather wild terrain passing by. "Not to mention explaining them to Father."

I wasn't sure if he was referring to newly purchased ones or the ones he was wearing, should he ruin them, and a thought occurred to me of more pressing matters than possible damage to his footwear.

"What do you propose we do when we get to Wrightminster?" I asked.

He pulled back his chin and glared at me. "What do I suggest? This little expedition was your idea."

"You mentioned it first. Your exact words were we should go there to 'check out the properties.'"

"I wasn't exactly including me in this. I thought you and Mother—"

"This time, it isn't she and I. And she was far too distracted to help us much with a plan. We need to come up with it ourselves."

He watched the scenery out of the window. "I suppose," he said after what seemed like ages, "the best approach would be to at least see if the boundary is marked. A fence or something to indicate where one property ends and another begins."

"To determine if it follows the newer line? The one in the map Edmonds showed us?"

Another study of the countryside. "The most we'll be able to do is find the property line, if there is one, and report back when we get to London."

"Seems like a long trip for that. Surely there's a way for us to find out a bit more about the two properties?" I took his cue and studied the verdant landscape through the window. With a gasp, I faced my brother. "Remember what Mother said the other day about barkeeps and publicans? If we want to know about what goes on in an area, we should speak to the publican."

"She also said we should ask the servants, but I can't believe either group will just open up to two strangers."

Sitting back against the cushion, I exhaled the excitement I'd let build with the last thought. He was right. Villagers tended to be rather closed to outsiders—at least those in our village—and would certainly suspect anyone

THE ADVENTURE OF THE DECEASED SCHOLAR

suddenly asking questions about those in the manor houses. Unless, of course…

"What if we were to share we were friends of Surminster—and the Simms? By now, they know about Lord Surminster's death. We could say we were traveling back to London at the end of holiday and hoped to extend our condolences to the Simms."

"They're in London. Who are we supposed to talk to?"

"We'll act surprised we missed them and say we'll see them there. But having come all this way, perhaps we can see the properties, as Lord Surminster and Mrs. Simms always spoke of them."

"And get someone to take us out there." He rubbed his chin with his thumb and gazed out the window. "I am beginning to feel a little peaked. A bit of something might prove useful before we head off to the estates."

As much as I wanted to hire a wagon and take off to Wrightmoor, I had to agree an hour in the local pub might just be what was needed to pave the way there. As long as it was still light enough to see what we had made the trip to confirm.

The Duck and Hound, located near the train station, reminded me of the pubs I'd seen in our own village. Both catered to the county's farmers and laborers. We clearly didn't resemble such patrons. My boots, traveling clothes, and knapsack lacked the dirt and wear of a hard day's effort, and Mycroft was even more out of place with his shined shoes and suit. I'd encouraged him to put his Oxford pin prominently on his lapel to give a little more credence to our story of seeking out school chums.

We'd agreed to try to engage the publican first. While I felt the entire room staring at us when we entered, I focused on my brother's back in an effort to ignore them as he made his way to the bar. After some discussion on the train, we decided it best to appear as out of place as we now knew we looked—two swells out of their depths here among the moors. While we might be viewed with contempt, the locals might consider us harmless enough to share more than they might otherwise.

Approaching the bar, my brother ordered two beers and asked about the possibility of something to eat. The man slapped two mugs in front of us and suggested the meat pies —made fresh.

When he brought those back, Mycroft asked, "Are you familiar with Wrightmoor? We stopped here on our way back to London to speak to the family. We heard about their loss and hoped to express our sympathies in person."

His Oxford accent was so strong, I feared the keeper might not understand him.

"The family at Wrightmoor?" he asked as if he needed to confirm my brother's question. "You mean Lord Wittdam?"

"Lord Wittdam?" He pulled back his chin in surprise. "I was referring to Lord Surminster. I just got a letter from a classmate. He said Lord Surminster met with an untimely end, and I—"

"Lord Surminster hasn't resided at Wrightmoor for ages. It's Lord Wittdam what's there."

"Oh, dear me. I did so hope—Wittdam? I know a Jared Edmonds from Oxford. His father is Lord Wittdam. Is the earl there now? It wouldn't do at all not to stop by and pay my respects."

"Certainly, the earl's there. He's getting on in years and doesn't leave the house much."

THE ADVENTURE OF THE DECEASED SCHOLAR

"Capital. Capital. Is there someone we can hire to take us out that way?"

The publican searched the room behind us and shouted over my brother's shoulder. "Hey, Arnold, these gents need a carriage out to Wrightmoor. You interested?"

Once again, I felt those in the room fix their gaze on the two of us, and a twitter of laughter passed through the patrons. I directed my focus to the meat pie now in front of me. Breaking the upper crust with my fork, I examined the filling. An aroma of onion and beef rose with the steam rising from the hole. With that encouraging scent, I took a forkful and found, to my surprise, the crust had a flakey, buttery consistency and the gravy just the right amount of seasoning.

Before I could take another bite, a man spoke behind us. "Sure, I can take you. Ain't no 'carriage,' but there's room for the two of you."

"Excellent, my good man," Mycroft said. "Allow me a few minutes to finish this delightful repast, and we'll be on our way."

Arnold's "carriage" turned out to be a dog cart, but as promised, it offered the space needed for the two of us, with my brother joining the driver in the front and me riding with my back to them on a seat facing the opposite direction. The horse pulling the cart was a sturdy work animal, and we set off to the estate at a steady pace.

Arnold turned out to be a talkative fellow. While Mycroft preferred peace and quiet, he continued to play his part of the Oxford gent and kept the man engaged, steering the conversation toward both Wittdam as well as the Simms.

I was grateful for Mycroft's efforts because the nearer we drew to the two properties, the more uneasy my stomach became. As much as I wanted to blame it on the pub's cook, the more likely suspect was my own concern about what we would find. Should it turn out to be a wild goose chase, we would have wasted a day needed to gather the information for the inquest—now less than two days away.

At one point, our driver pointed to a stone wall reaching as far as could be seen to our right. "This marks the beginning of Wrightmoor."

The wall was low, and spaces in it could be seen where the stones had fallen away.

"Looks like it could use some repairs," my brother said.

"It's been there for hunners of years. Used to be around a nunnery. Their convent was up ahead there." He pointed to a heap of stones casting shadows in the afternoon light. "Had been given to a Lord Frampton, then it passed to his daughter Lady Surminster. The original Lord Frampton, he took most of the stones to build the manor house. It's over the hill. Can't see it yet."

"Why'd they take the stones? Not just rebuild on this spot?"

"Way they tells it, even though it wasn't a convent no more, it was still sacred ground. There be bones there. The nuns what died were buried under the chapel. Didn't want to disturb the dead. Also, they say Frampton kept the Catholic. The minute Mary became queen, he'd whipped out his crucifix and declared he'd been keepin' the grounds safe. Course by then, there weren't naught left of the nuns or the nunnery, and not long after, he said he'd been Protestant all along. Managed to keep both his head and his property. Not so easy to do then."

"Fascinating," Mycroft said. "I had no idea about the nuns."

THE ADVENTURE OF THE DECEASED SCHOLAR

"Yep. Folks say their spirits still come back sometimes to hold chapel. And then there's the nun's chest. Afore they were all chased away, they buried a bunch of jewels somewhere on the grounds. Never been found."

With my back to my brother, I couldn't very well see his reaction to the mention of this particular story, but I felt his spine stiffen. The reference intrigued him as much as it did me. Was this what Lord Surminster had discovered on the map?

We climbed the rise and now had a good view of Wrightmoor as well as a glimpse of the roof of a smaller manor house just visible to the left and farther along the road. Lady Surminster's inherited property both intrigued and disappointed me. Given the age of the structure, I had imagined a castle-like architecture, which it definitely had. Much larger than the Devonys' Hanover Manor near Underbyrne, it sported the turrets, arched doorways, and gables I'd expected, as well as the heavy stone walls from the abbey's original buildings. What I had not anticipated was how poorly maintained the residence appeared. Moss and plants had taken root among the roof's tiles, and the gardens were overgrown. The moors had begun to reclaim their own.

"I do say," Mycroft said after he completed a survey of the property similar to my own, "I'm rather surprised at the state of the manor house. Is Lady Surminster not aware of its condition?"

"Hasn't been out here since the tenants moved in," our driver said. "Lady Edwina, of course, lived here. Back when Miss Lillian—er, Lady Surminster—was a girl. Lord Surminster, her husband, came out here some. Enjoyed the hunting in the woods there."

"I understand there's a trustee, Simms is the name I believe, who oversees the place."

The man pointed to the roof I'd spotted earlier. "That's Simms' house. Him and his family live there."

My brother craned his neck to study the area between the two properties.

"I can see where it would be convenient to have the trustee on the adjoining estate. How far does this one extend?"

"See the line of hedge?" The man pointed again. This time, to a row of overgrown bushes and brambles running the length of a trough before the rise cut off all but the Simms' roof. "Used to be the line. But I hear Simms sold a piece of his land a while back because, like I said, Lord Surminster enjoyed hunting in the woods. Used to have a lot of parties here. Guests would go huntin.' I was one what helped carry the game back. Course I had a bigger wagon than this."

The man continued on with a series of tales of hunting parties past, including one where one guest's horse fell and landed on its rider's leg. Another where the largest stag the man had ever seen had met its demise. And one about how a feral hog had ended the life of three hunting dogs in a poorly managed event.

After he finished the story, he turned onto the drive leading to Wrightmoor's manor house. As we passed the rather unkempt greens and gardens, I was struck again by how it had been allowed to overgrow. Then again, I wondered at the costs for maintaining the property. Beyond the game and hunting Arnold mentioned, just what did Wrightmoor offer in terms of income? What would happen to Lady Surminster should she need to rely on this estate?

THE ADVENTURE OF THE DECEASED SCHOLAR

The cart pulled to a stop just behind a bend in the drive leading directly to the front of the manor.

"I's can go to the front if you wish," Arnold said to Mycroft. "Or drive on over to the side. Seein' how's this isn't a fancy carriage. I don't know which you'd druther."

Mycroft seemed to consider his options, then said, "From what you say, the earl doesn't seem to stand on a lot of ceremony. Perhaps we'll just drive on up to the front."

While the earl might not stand on ceremony, his butler, dressed in full livery, did. When he opened the door under the manor's arched entrance in response to Mycroft's knock, he glanced at the two of us and then at the dogcart behind. Arnold touched the brim of his hat to the old man, who simply scowled at him and then at us.

"Deliveries in the back," he said and pushed the door to close it.

Mycroft halted the door's movement, held out a card, and said, still in his very-Oxford accent, "We're here to pay a visit to the earl. Friends of Lord Jared, you know."

The butler read the card and opened the door wide enough for us to enter. The foyer was as impressive in its dimensions as the exterior with a wide, sweeping stairway to the right, a chandelier hanging high overhead, and the most extensive collection of hunting trophies I'd ever seen outside of the British Museum. Beyond the expected deer and stag heads, a number of standing displays lined each side of the hallway. These presented naturalistic scenes with various creatures. Squirrels, raccoons, and a fox were fixed about a tree trunk. A deer and fawn stared at me in front of a bush. I caught sight of what looked like a bear farther down.

While we waited for his instructions, the butler stepped

around us and waved at our driver. "Pull around to the side. Can't have a dog cart sitting in front of the house."

I had the urge to ask the man just who would see the cart, given we hadn't passed more than a half a dozen wagons on the road, and not a single carriage, but as we wished to interview the earl, I sealed my lips instead.

The butler directed us to what I assumed was the receiving area. The room presented a vault-like quality with a high ceiling, tall windows opening to the front, and a bench opposite them. After taking a seat, I watched Arnold direct the horse around the circled drive to a smaller lane leading off to the side.

Mycroft sank onto the bench next to me and groaned.

"My backside is never going to be the same. First that underpadded seat on the train, then the ride in the cart, now this bench. Next time we take a trip like this, I'm bringing a cushion with me." He moaned. "And we still have the trip back. I'll be attending lectures standing up for the next month."

Before I could respond to his remark, the butler entered. "Please follow me. Lord Wittdam will see you in his workroom."

The room turned out to be in one of the manor's towers. A journey up a winding staircase led to a stone chamber filled with more stuffed animals—although not in the completed stages I'd observed below. Despite the open windows in the room, the air still held a strong chemical smell, including—among other scents—a garlicky odor with undertones of naphthalene.

When the butler announced us, a short, thin man wearing a pair of heavy glasses stared at us from behind a wire model of a deer. He pushed the glasses to the top of his

THE ADVENTURE OF THE DECEASED SCHOLAR

head and stepped up to us. Taking a heavy glove off his right hand, he extended it to my brother. "Mr. Holmes. What a surprise. I'm afraid my son is not here at the moment. In London, you know."

"How unfortunate," he said, shaking the man's hand. "We were on holiday in Glastonbury and heard the news of Lord Surminster. I thought to pay respects, knowing your acquaintance with the family."

"Yes," the man said with a shake of his head. "I just sent a note to Walter about what a sad state of affairs this has been for the family. First Lord Surminster's father, then this tragedy. At least Lady Surminster has an income from this property. Walter has taken good care of her and it."

"Walter? Walter Simms, the estate's trustee, you mean?" Mycroft asked. Lord Wittdam nodded. "Yes, heard he's been an excellent administrator. We understand he even expanded the property a few years ago."

"Quite right. That's what interested me in renting here. As you can tell, I have a passion for taxidermy. And the game here is so plentiful. Of course, Walter has kept me well supplied. I've given him permission to continue to hunt as desired because he always brings me the best specimens. Clean kills with only the smallest holes to be repaired."

"Our father has an interest in entomology and has a very extensive collection." I spoke for the first time since our introductions. "But he doesn't truly mount them himself. You have exceptional skills."

"Thank you. Been interested in taxidermy all my life. Mammals, for the most part. As you can tell"—he swept his arm wide to encompass the room—"exhibiting them in more natural settings has become my passion lately. This is my latest creation. This deer will be the centerpiece on the stand over there."

Following his indication, I approached a platform already adorned with a sapling trunk and tall grasses. On one side was a large stone.

After studying the empty scene, I asked, "Where will the deer go?"

"I plan to position it between the stone and the tree. Its head will be turned to be looking out. Of course, there will be other creatures as well. A fox will be at the bottom of the tree. Some birds in the branches. Perhaps some other creature, if Walter brings me another."

Touring completely around the platform, I paused when I reached the backside. "What a well-shaped stone. Almost square. Wherever did you find it?"

The man shrugged. "I told one of the stable hands to procure a square one. Easier to attach a specimen on a flat surface. You'd have to ask him where he got it."

Raising my gaze from the exhibit, I said, "I do hope we're not disturbing you greatly."

The man glanced down at the deer form and then back at us. "I am at a rather delicate juncture at this point."

"Perhaps we should leave you then," I said.

His back to the earl, Mycroft gave me a puzzled, wide-eyed stare warning of my breach of social conventions. I was more concerned, however, about locating the stable hand. I wouldn't be able to tell Mycroft until we were free of the house why we needed to learn where the stone had been found.

CHAPTER THIRTEEN

As we stood on the drive, waiting for the butler to inform Arnold to return with the donkey cart, Mycroft straightened his spine, pulled on his waistcoat, and glowered at me. "Can you please now share with me what was so important you bordered on insolence in the manner in which you took your leave?"

"The stone," I said with great effort to keep my tone even and slow when the words wanted to spill themselves out of my mouth in a rush. "Remember the pomegranate symbol from Lord Surminster's pocket—?"

"It wasn't in Lord Surminster's pocket. It was in the suit on the other man."

"I don't care if Lord Surminster had it stuffed inside his mouth. The importance was the symbol. It was carved on the stone for the new display. The one the stable hand brought him. The carving had been on the bottom, buried in the dirt. I can tell by the discoloration on that part. No one could have seen it. When he put it on the stand, the bottom was on the backside of the display. We need to learn where he found it."

Mycroft opened his mouth as if to add to his earlier rebuke but instead simply stared at me as if digesting what I'd said to him. "We must speak to Arnold at once."

Given my brother's abhorrence of physical activity, he surprised me by sprinting down the drive toward the path running along the side of the house. I raced to catch up with him to learn what he told the driver.

The donkey cart was rounding the corner when we reached him. Arnold reined the horse to a stop and stared at the two of us as we came panting up to him.

"I say, my good fellow," Mycroft said in a more coherent accent than he'd used previously. I hoped the man would put it down to his being partially out of breath. "Do you know any of those who work in the stables here?"

Arnold stared at him as if considering the earl's complete staff. Finally, he said, "There's Roland. He comes into the pub on Sundays. Has a fancy for Gloria, one of the serving girls."

"Any chance you can locate him now? We need to speak with him."

The man sighed, glanced at the stables, and then at the roadway. The shadows were stretching long. He had to be thinking of getting back to town. I saw our chances of learning about the stone slipping from us.

"There's half a shilling in it for you if you can locate the stable hand who brought a stone to Lord Wittdam," I said.

I didn't know which stare made my stomach tighten more. My brother gave me a glare warning me I had overstepped myself again, while our driver's mouth lifted in a smile, suggesting avarice more than any other interest. I feared I'd overplayed our hand by putting such a high price on the information—and Mycroft telegraphed the same fear back to me.

The man's smile widened, and he said, "I'll be right back."

He slapped the reins against the horse's back, and the donkey cart jerked and rattled toward the stables at a speed that made me glad I wasn't seated on the back. I most certainly would have landed face-first on the ground with the first turn of the cart's wheels.

Mycroft spun about to face me. "Will you ever overcome your impulse to step in when tact is needed?"

"He wasn't going to go. I could read it in his face. Did you see how fast he agreed when I offered him the money?"

"And what do you propose we use to pay him?"

"We have the funds. If needed, we'll take a second-class car instead of a first."

I got another scowl at that suggestion and most likely would have received a long lecture on the condition of his backside if a commotion from the direction of the stables hadn't drawn our attention to the donkey cart racing back toward us. It almost ran us over, but we stepped back just in time.

The poor workhorse huffed from his exertion, and I feared our return trip would be longer given how much energy the poor animal had spent in those two short sprints.

"The one what found the stone is Percy," said Arnold, puffing almost as much as the horse. "He's out in the fields right now. They said he'll come to the pub tonight. I told 'em you'd give him half a shilling, like me."

Once plodding our way back to Wrightminster and the

pub, Mycroft asked, "Do you know when's the last train to Bristol?"

The man glanced up at the sky and asked, "What does your pocket watch say?"

"A little past five."

He shook his head. "Will be at least an hour for us to get back to the pub. The last train will have left by then. You can stay at the Queens Hotel for the night."

At this pronouncement, Mycroft turned in his seat and gave me a stare to inform me the shilling I'd squandered on the information would probably result in some suffering on my part.

With our gazes still locked, I asked, "When's the first train in the morning to Bristol?"

"One of the earliest trains from Bristol to London leaves at eight o'clock in the morning," Mycroft said, also without glancing away from me. "You know we won't be back in London until almost noon."

"You should be able to catch that one, then. There's a train to Bristol at six," Arnold said.

My brother's eyebrows drew together, and I foresaw a full litany of laments from him about having to rise so early to catch a second-class compartment. Regardless, I shrugged back at him, considering both inconveniences worth the price.

At the pub, we took a seat at a rather secluded table in a corner. Mycroft ordered a single meat pie for himself—in all likelihood, to punish me for spending our funds on a whim. I pulled the two apples, now bruised but still edible, out of the knapsack and munched on them.

"Should we go ahead and ask for a room?" I asked when

I had only the two cores in front of me. "We have no idea how soon this Percy will appear."

"I'm surprised he's not setting the road on fire for half a shilling."

"Just how long are you going to hold this over my head?"

"When I feel you have suffered a shilling's worth."

The retort I formed in response died in my throat when a man entered and glanced around the establishment. He wore a laborer's heavy pants, boots, and jacket—all with bits of straw attached to them. After scanning the room, his gaze settled on us, and he moved toward our table. Mycroft noticed my attention was elsewhere and checked over his shoulder.

The man snatched off his hat and whispered, "I'm Percy." I slid over on the bench, and the man took the space I'd been occupying. "Arnold said you had half a shilling for me."

"Once you give us the information we want," Mycroft said. "We have an interest in a stone you gave to the earl. He's putting it in a display he's working on at the moment."

"You want one like it? I can get you—"

"We want to know where you got it."

The man screwed up his face and stared at my brother as if he'd sprouted a second head. "Where I gots it? Out in the fields. The earl showed me the size he wanted, and I picked it out from the ruins."

"The ruins? You mean the old convent?" I asked.

The moment I spoke, I watched Mycroft's eyebrows draw together. I'd shown too much enthusiasm. The man might very well demand more than the agreed price, and my brother would be certain to seek additional means of punishing me. I could very well wind up sleeping on the floor of the Queens Hotel tonight.

"Aye. The old convent."

The next question slipped from my mouth before I could stop it. "Would you be able to show us the place?"

"Aye. Tomorrow—"

I saw our chance of investigating whether the stone marked what I hoped slipping away. If we were to leave on the morning train, there would be no chance to visit the area.

"What about tonight?"

"Tonight? Some say there are spirits out there. It's a graveyard, you know."

"You can show us and then wait in the wagon until we return," I said. "You did come in a wagon?"

"Aye. A tuppence more. I has-ta brings you back to town."

Eight pence seemed a small price to pay for what I thought might still lie where the rock had been.

"Come on," I said, standing up from my seat.

Mycroft stared at me but rose and followed us to the street. I was certain he surmised what I thought we would find. My greatest concern focused on how, in the morning, the town would be buzzing about the two swells who'd paid an enormous sum to look at a hole where a stone had been. Hardly a way to keep a secret if we did find the chest.

Percy's horse had a little more vigor than Arnold's, despite, I was certain, having been pushed to make the village in record speed. We were all able to sit on the front

THE ADVENTURE OF THE DECEASED SCHOLAR

bench, allowing me a different perspective of Wrightmoor's grounds. Unlike Arnold, Percy wasn't a talker, and so the ride back to the estate was a very silent affair. A bright moon shone overhead, making the moors' contours visible, and with the exception of the wheels turning and the horse's plodding hooves, only cries of night birds carried by the wind emanated from the shadows.

At last, the horse stopped along the side of the road and, in the distance, I could make out the convent ruins, their stones shining white in the moonlight. Percy jumped off the bench and took off toward what was left of the abbey, lantern in hand.

I leaped off as well and called after him. "Do you have any tools in the wagon?"

"Only what we carry in case a wheel breaks or the wagon gets stuck in the mud," he said, facing us.

"That includes a shovel, then. Can you fetch it for me?"

With a groan, he returned, opened a box attached to the side, and handed me a shovel. He didn't offer to carry it, which he might have done for another penny, but I had no doubt Mycroft had firmly locked his purse.

Resting the handle on my shoulder, I followed our guide once again, taking care to follow his lead to avoid the ankle-turning stones and low plants lurking on the ground. After only a few yards, I realized Mycroft wasn't behind me. I turned to find him leaning against the wagon's side.

"Aren't you going to help search?" I asked.

"This is your wild goose chase." He shook his head. "I'll give you all the glory."

I shrugged and hurried to catch up with Percy. He held the lantern out to help avoid the worst of the possible vegetative snares, and given his familiarity with the area, we made the slog in what I considered good time.

When we came to what had most likely been an outer wall, given its length and still-apparent straight line, he stopped and pointed to a spot on the ground just inside what would have been the convent's interior.

"Here."

The six-inch depression created by the stone appeared to be more recently disturbed, but not so recent as to leave any foot or other prints in the grass or dirt. Plants had also begun to fill in around the hole's edges.

"Did it take much to pull it out?" I asked. "It looks like it was buried rather deeply."

"I thought so at first," he said, scratching the back of his neck. "But when I pushed on it, it moved easier than the others I tried."

I studied the wall's remains. A gap occurred in its stones, almost directly in front of the hole Percy had shown me.

"Most likely it fell off the wall there," I said, indicating the space.

Hesitating a few moments, I considered the two spots—the one where the stone had lain for some time and where it had originally rested. I wanted to plow straight into the task but feared Percy or Mycroft would soon announce it time to return. To make prudent use of their patience, I needed to determine what the stone most likely marked.

The pomegranate symbol would have been on the inside of the convent wall. While it might have marked something buried beneath it, it would have required the nuns to have taken apart a bit of the wall to do so. A more likely scenario would be if something was buried just in front of it. I stepped to the empty space where the stone had toppled

THE ADVENTURE OF THE DECEASED SCHOLAR

from the wall and stuck the shovel into the ground. The earth was hard but penetrable. Pulling out the spade, I gave it a stronger thrust and was able to dig up what I considered a sizeable chunk, but Percy apparently didn't appreciate my effort as much as I.

"Gimme that." He held out a hand. "You hold the lantern so's I can see. If we have to wait for you to make the hole, we'll be here all night."

I didn't object. While I was no weakling, he certainly was more skilled at this. I also wasn't sure how I would explain to my father the blisters I would most likely develop from the task.

True to his word, Percy made progress to a considerable depth in less than half an hour. The hole wasn't wide, but it was deep. After one particularly strong push, the shovel hit something hard.

When it did so, he faced me and gave me a studied look. "What's down there?"

"I-I don't know. Truly I don't. It could be a stone, you know."

He dropped the shovel by the side of the hole and said, "It ain't no stone, and whatever it is, it don't belong to you."

My heart and thoughts raced, and with great concentration, I reviewed my options. I could run back to Mycroft and the wagon with the goal of making it there before Percy, but his familiarity with the terrain put me at a disadvantage. On the other hand, if I could convince him I was not a thief, I might actually complete my task.

"You're right. This is Lady Surminster's land. If we find anything, we should give it to her. Help me dig it out, and you can come with us to London if you like. Present it to her." He stared at me as if contemplating whether a trip to

London would be worth his while. I decided to entice him further—through his pocket. "She'll probably give a reward if you do."

That possibility put new fervor into the man, and soon, the hole was wide enough to completely uncover the item. As I had hoped, it was an old metal box. The rust on the handle and rivets visible on its top indicated it had lain in the ground for an awfully long time. Percy grabbed the handle and tugged. It disintegrated in his grasp. He wouldn't be deterred, however, and using the shovel, leveraged the chest from the hole.

I feared the whole thing might crumble from the extraction, but it remained in one piece and soon lay on the ground between us. I was more than a little disappointed in the size. The word "chest" suggested something much bigger than the item about a foot square and only half as tall. But even in the lantern light, I could make out the pomegranate symbol etched into the top and knew what we had found.

"It's the nun's chest, ain't it? The one what everyone says don't exist," the man asked. "Should we takes a peek?"

I held the lantern close to the box and studied it. "There's a keyhole." I pulled on the top. "And it appears locked fast. We might have to break into it, and all we have here is the shovel. I think it would be best to at least take it back to the wagon. I think between the two of us—"

Percy hefted the box onto his shoulder. "No more than three stone," he said and took off toward the road.

I stared at his back, the box riding on his shoulder, and marveled at his ability to carry a weight of forty pounds, before rushing after him with the lantern and shovel.

Mycroft must have taken advantage of his time alone to

stretch out on the wagon bed because I saw his head pop up when we rustled through the undergrowth back to the road. He took one look at what Percy carried and shouted, "Good lord, you actually found something."

"Aye," said Percy. "And I'll be gettin' the reward from Lady Surminster for it. For now, I'll take me fee."

When my brother glanced from the stable hand to me, my only reply was a shrug. Any explanation would again have to wait. He descended the wagon and counted out the coins into Percy's outstretched hand. After Percy slid the box onto the bed next to the empty knapsack I'd left behind, Mycroft took the lantern from me to hold it close and examine the chest for himself. He ran his finger over the two pomegranate symbols and ended his observation with, "I suppose we should take it straight away to Lady Surminster as Percy suggests." He straightened and passed the lantern back to me. "They might break their seclusion for this."

"Off to London, then," Percy said, already on the wagon bench.

Before either of us could step into the wagon, the man slapped the reins on the horse and took off at a speed that, while it might not win the Derby, left us behind coughing in the dust stirred up from the road.

My brother spun on his heel to face me. The ochre glow from the lantern I still held gave his flushed face an orange tinge. His cheeks puffed in and out in a manner similar to a dragon's. I was grateful he couldn't breathe fire because I would have been ash with the first blow. His hands formed into fists. While I didn't think he would actually strike me, I gripped the shovel in my other hand tighter—just in case.

After several more exhalations, he was finally able to

sputter out a question. "You twit. Just what did you promise the man out there?"

"He wasn't going to help me dig—"

"And so you told him there would be a reward?"

"I suggested it was possible. After all—"

"What makes you think he won't open it and take whatever's inside for himself?"

"I suppose it's possible, but regardless—"

"Or report us to the earl?"

"We didn't steal anything. We don't even have—"

He threw his arms up into the air and took off down the road, throwing a comment over his shoulder. "I suppose we will make it back to town in time for the train."

"We should be able to hire a first-class cabin," I said to his back. "There's no point seeing to a room at the hotel by the time we get there."

He paused for a second as this bit of information registered, shook his fists at the heavens, and continued on without checking to see whether I followed.

Although the donkey cart ride from Wrightminster to Wrightmoor took a little more than an hour, it didn't take much longer to return on foot. All the same, when we reached the train station on the edge of town long past midnight, Percy's wagon wasn't in sight.

Mycroft paused to allow me to join him as he surveyed the area.

"Do you suppose he took the horse and wagon to the stable?" I asked.

"Most likely just headed on to the next village," he said. "It's not like this is the only train station in the area."

"Should we do the same?"

"I'm not walking another step." He pulled out his watch

THE ADVENTURE OF THE DECEASED SCHOLAR

and checked the time. "Hardly worth it to see about a room at the hotel, and the public house will be closed."

He trod up to the train station, stepped onto the platform, found a bench, and stretched out on it. I followed his example, extinguishing the lantern and placing it and the shovel beside my own bench.

MYCROFT CONTINUED to snooze on the ride to Bristol, while I silently wished trains offered some sort of refreshment for passengers. I regretted having eaten both apples the previous night, but even more, the sad sandwiches we'd purchased when the train station opened. The bread was old, and I wasn't sure what had been inside. They now sat like stones in the pit of my stomach. Of course, the thought of the reception we'd receive when we finally made it home didn't help my digestion either.

What exactly would we find there? Particularly, the state of Father's mood? He would certainly be aware of our absence, and I had no idea what tale Mother invented to explain it. I could only hope she would be able to convey it to us in some manner before he had a chance to question us. We didn't even have the chest to demonstrate our trip hadn't been in vain.

Given my growing apprehension about my parents' reaction to our disappearance, I fairly jumped when we stepped off the train in London, and someone called our names. With Easter only two days away and many enterprises closed for Good Friday, a large number of travelers filled the platform. Mycroft and I stopped amid the push of passengers and porters under the tall rounded arches and sought out the caller. Nathan Edmonds, Lady Surminster's proctor, waved at us from the platform entrance.

"How do you suppose Edmonds knew to look for us here? Did Percy actually make it to London so much earlier than we?" I asked.

"Or he telegraphed someone here with the news he'd found the chest. I suppose we'll know soon enough."

Nathan jogged toward us, a wide smile on his face, and we met at the front of the platform.

"I'm so glad I was able to catch you," he said, panting a little from the exercise. "I have a carriage waiting."

"Very kind of you," Mycroft said, "but I think we should hire one to take us home. They are bound to be waiting for our return."

My brother took a step to pass him. As he did so, Nathan grabbed his arm and pulled a revolver from inside his coat and poked it into Mycroft's side. "If you both will please follow me to the carriage."

I glanced around, seeking someone who'd caught the man's act or seen the weapon. My survey, however, was fruitless. The crowd simply parted and flowed around us, paying no attention to two men and a youth standing still on the platform.

Edmonds must have caught my furtive attempt to attract someone's attention because he spoke directly to me. "Try to run away or call out, and I'll shoot your brother. At this distance, I can assure you, it will be fatal."

"Do as he says," Mycroft said with a slight growl in the low tone.

I nodded and stepped around in front of the two as Nathan directed.

My vision of the scene before me, of passengers rushing

THE ADVENTURE OF THE DECEASED SCHOLAR

to and from the platform and out into the main station became distorted. The throng's sounds grew garbled as if underwater. I was buffeted more than once by someone rushing past, but I had no reaction other than to push on ahead, according to Nathan's harsh, whispered instructions.

Once inside the closed carriage, Nathan positioned himself on the seat facing backward to now point the revolver directly at us. As far as I was concerned, the instrument was as large as a canon with the capability of eliminating both of us with a single shot. My mouth had dried, but I was able to pry my tongue from the roof enough for a few words.

"Where are you taking us?" I asked, glancing toward the window. The shades had been pulled down, making it impossible to identify any landmarks.

He lifted one side of his mouth in a crooked smile. "You'll see. There's someone terribly interested in seeing you."

"Obviously not to thank us," Mycroft said. "Would it be the earl's son Jared or Mr. Simms?"

"Or both?" I asked.

"I'll let that be a surprise," he said. "I do have one question, however. Which one of you stole the map from me?"

Mycroft gave me a sideways glance. I saw no reason to bring Constance into this. Edmonds hadn't enquired about missing any money after visiting us and might not even be aware she'd taken both.

"I did," I said before Mycroft could provide another answer. "While you were in the drawing room with everyone, I went through your pockets. I do it all the time. You learn a lot by reviewing people's pockets."

"Like what you found on poor Clement?"

"Clement? Is that the name of the man who drowned the same night as Lord Surminster? How did you know him?" Mycroft asked.

"I'll let your host answer any questions."

Nathan settled back in his seat but never lowered the revolver. A cold sweat formed on my upper lip. With great effort, I forced myself to run through different scenarios for overcoming and escaping from our captor. My *baritsu* training had included disarming an attacker, but while I might avoid being harmed, I wasn't so certain of Mycroft. Regardless of any move or attack strategy I considered, it ended with Nathan firing at my brother. With no viable alternatives, I resigned myself to continue letting him think he had the upper hand until some opportunity presented itself.

When the carriage stopped, Nathan motioned with his weapon for me to open the door. I blinked in the bright sunlight flooding the darkened cabin, and considered whether Nathan might be as blinded as I. Would the momentary disorientation be enough for me to overpower him? A second later, a voice to my left quelled that thought.

"Messrs. Holmes. How good of you to come."

The pronouncement caused me to turn to the left and get a good view of yet another revolver, this time held by a much older man.

"Good afternoon, Mr. Simms," I said.

I stepped onto the ground and waited for Mycroft to descend the carriage. We now each had our own escort from an alleyway to the back of a house in a drab row of lower-class buildings. The scent of fish and garbage wafted over me, suggesting we were near the Thames. I glanced at

Mycroft but couldn't read whether he had the same thought as me. Was this where Crandall had been found?

We entered through the kitchen, the remains of several previous meals scattered about on the table and drainboard. Whoever lived here could certainly use a housekeeper. Given the odor of spoiled food floating about us, I hazarded a guess it had been some time since anyone had tried to clean the room. Through the doorway, I could see what would have been a dining room for the narrow house. A table occupied the center with the remains of a card game scattered across its surface. In addition to the cards, dirty glasses and cigar ashes littered the stained green baize covering.

Instead of entering the main part of the house, we filed down a narrow flight of stairs. Without any light, I had to feel my way with a hand on the rough stone wall, testing each step with my toe before putting my weight upon the uneven wood slats.

As soon as I reached the bottom, Mr. Simms grabbed my arm and led me forward until my hips hit what appeared to be a table. "Light the candle you'll find there. Remember, we both have weapons, and I am an excellent shot even in the dark."

The moment the candle shed its yellow glow into the gloom, I spied three details that made my knees go weak. The chest Percy had so unceremoniously commandeered last night rested on the table. Percy was also there. Tied to a chair, a handkerchief tight across his mouth. I didn't think it was needed. His head drooped onto his chest, which rose rhythmically with his breathing. He had to be drugged or drunk. Next to him, a woman was bound in a similar manner. I understood why Roggens hadn't interviewed Rose.

"I believe you all know each other," Mr. Simms said. "Percy arrived a few hours ago, having taken a direct train to London from the next village. He even telegraphed ahead to Lord Surminster's house, stating he had a treasure to share with them. Luckily, Jared has been vetting their mail during the family's seclusion, and Nathan intercepted both at the railway station."

"So, Jared is part of your little group too," Mycroft said.

"Actually, my cousin hasn't a clue," Nathan said. "He told me about the telegram, and I volunteered to meet the fellow. No reason to upset the family if the whole thing was a hoax."

Simms waved his gun between me and the chest on the table. "Go ahead. Check out the treasure. We have."

I stepped to the table and lifted up the heavy metal lid. Inside I found a set of ebony beads, a small book, and a metal crucifix. "I suppose a rosary would be considered a 'treasure' by a nun. Were you disappointed?"

Simms laughed. "You don't get it, do you? Did you truly think I cared about some legendary fortune?"

"It's about the shift in the property lines," Mycroft said behind me. "That's what Lord Surminster saw on the map. You sold land to the trust. And not because the previous Lord Surminster liked to hunt as everyone believes. He probably wasn't even aware he was hunting on the estate's own land. Pretty easy to agree to the purchase at any price when the buyer and seller are the same. Did you need the money so much?"

"Do you know what it's like to have four daughters?" Simms asked. His voice shifted into a strange falsetto.

"'Papa, I need a new gown.' 'Walter, we must arrange for a ball. How will they ever marry well if we don't invite the right sort to meet them?'"

"Surely, you can't blame it all on your daughters. I think you've been using funds from the trust for a while," my brother said.

Simms, his face flushed, spun about to face my brother. "I have expenses. Do you have any idea how much work it is to run another property? And see those rents coming in when you have so little? I tried to explain it to him, but the old man wouldn't listen."

"The old man?" I asked. "You mean old Lord Surminster? You killed him too?"

The man shrugged. "I had no choice. Of course, I've progressed since then. The first one was rather…inelegant. But the poison was effective all the same."

I tried to swallow, but the lump in the back of my throat prohibited the action. Lord Wittdam had noted Simms' skill in making almost invisible holes in the specimens he provided for his taxidermy. Did he consider a hatpin through the ear or the back of the neck "elegant?"

"Now, if you would be so kind as to take your seats"—he used the revolver again as a means of pointing to two chairs next to the unconscious Percy—"I'll leave you for a time. We have to prepare for the coroner's inquest tomorrow. And you, Mr. Holmes, will be the star witness."

"You want me to tell them how he was murdered?" Mycroft asked.

"Oh, dear, no." Simms pulled a sheaf of paper from his breast pocket. "You're going to report how Lord Surminster was distraught. Had been for some time. How he'd confided in you about a love affair gone wrong and, in the end, committed suicide, leaving behind a note now in your possession."

My brother's mouth fell open, and he stared at the older man. "You would have his family lose all?"

"Oh, hardly all. Wrightmoor is a lovely estate. You've seen it. And once Jared weds Sophronia, things will return to the way they were before. I'll run the trust, and Nathan and I will continue to enjoy the profits as the lawsuit drags on. Of course, the future Lord Surminster will be only Zachariah Phillips, but he will be well cared for by the trust."

"And if I refuse?"

"That's why young Sherlock will remain here. Any problems with your testimony tomorrow, and he'll meet a fate similar to Crandall's—or Lord Surminster's—I haven't decided which."

Edmonds directed Mycroft to one chair and, after a poke in the back from Simms' revolver, I stepped to the other between my brother and the unconscious Percy.

Simms had a number of talents, I observed. Including the ability to truss a person tightly to a chair—perhaps from having practiced on dead game. Of course, a shot animal's blood didn't circulate, and I could feel my feet and hands growing numb. This thought inspired a means to create an opportunity for Mycroft and me to escape.

"You might not want to tie us too tight," I said, as Simms turned his attention to Mycroft. "You'll want us to be able to walk tomorrow. Cut off our circulation, and you'll have to carry us. Difficult to explain when you take my brother to the inquest."

The man paused and glanced at the two of us as if trying to decide whether what I said was true.

Nathan spoke up. "He's right. You can give them what you gave the others. That'll keep them quiet until needed."

What you gave the others.

I suddenly knew why Lord Surminster and Crandall had been so docile when pierced with the hairpin. They'd been drugged—but not poisoned. My uncle's experiments with poisons hadn't found one that didn't lead to convulsions, vomiting or other violent reactions. Hardly "elegant." And while several different drugs would achieve the effect, the one that would hardly raise an eyebrow if purchased was…laudanum.

Perhaps he'd added a bit of gin to it? Or poured the gin down their throats after?

Simms approached me first with a little vial. With my hands and feet now immobilized, he had no problem seizing my head by the hair. I twisted about in his grasp, trying to prevent the bottle from entering my mouth. He didn't succeed until Nathan drew my attention to the weapon he pointed at my brother's head. "There are always others who can bear witness at the inquest, Master Sherlock."

With that, I let him tip the bottle into my mouth. Wrapping a hand tightly about my nose and lips, he held it there until I swallowed.

As the fog announcing the opium's coming oblivion washed over me, the voices of the two men drifted through the mist.

"I don't understand why we don't just get rid of them now," Nathan said.

"We need the older to convince the coroner's jury of the suicide. And someone to stay here with the other three when we go to the inquest."

"I know just the men. The ones that brought Rose here

when we disposed of Crandall. Couldn't very well let her go to the police. Not good for their business. But what about afterward?"

"I'm afraid the three men will have a terrible argument over the chest and the woman here in the basement. Will do themselves in—all four."

CHAPTER FOURTEEN

Someone was shaking my bed. I moaned and tried to turn over to ignore whoever was trying to wake me, but I found it impossible to move. I opened my eyes, and my surroundings floated dimly in front of me. A single candle stub sputtered in its holder on a wooden table in what appeared to be a...

Basement.

Despite a still-muzzy brain, I took an inventory of my situation. I was sitting up. Tied to a chair. But someone kept moving it. I turned my head, and a wave of nausea swept over me. I sputtered into the gag in my mouth, forcing back the bile threatening to rise. Without an exit for the vomit, I could easily choke, solving Mr. Simms' problem for him.

Once I regained my composure, I focused on who had awakened me in the first place. Percy was seated in his chair, the leg of which now touched the side of mine. I could easily read the terror in his wide, red-rimmed eyes. Beyond him, Rose's terrified eyes shone. With a very deliberate and slow movement, I checked my left side and saw Mycroft's chair was now vacant. They had planned to force Mycroft to attend the inquest in the morning. Had a whole night passed? Just how much laudanum had been forced on me?

Another boot of my chair called me back to Percy's panicked demands. Again, I swiveled my head to him. He mumbled something through his gag. While I couldn't make out anything intelligible, I understood him all the same. They had come for Mycroft, and when they returned, we would all be eliminated.

And Percy expected us to avoid such an end at all costs.

I had to think. But pulling together ideas made me recall the mudlarks who extracted debris from the silt uncovered when the Thames was at low tide. The muck sucked their feet and legs up to mid-calf, making each step a tedious process....

I pushed the unbidden image aside. Escape meant concentration, not recollection.

Mother always based her plans on mathematics, and I now used this approach to my current situation. First, the variables. I was tied to one chair. Percy to another. They were both wooden, but while Percy's had a thick, sturdy frame, mine was much less solid. How the man had managed to work himself close enough to kick mine once again pointed to his strength as well as the desperation fueling it.

If he was to give mine a push hard enough...

I jerked my head to one side in a "come here" motion. The movement almost made me pass out, and I desperately hoped Percy understood my directions. I wasn't sure I could do it again.

He seemed to have gotten my message because he

jerked his chair into mine. It scooted a bit across the floor, but I feared he might not have the leverage needed to get mine to tip. With the next thrust, I pushed my toe down to add to the momentum. The chair rose onto three legs but landed upright with a *thump*. My breaths came in snorts through my nose to keep my stomach calm. I nodded to Percy to try again. Somehow, he managed to put a little more effort into the next one, and with a heavier shove from my foot, the chair teetered on the three legs, and I fell onto my right side. My head fairly exploded with the impact.

As soon as I gathered my wits, I completed a brief inventory of the new situation. I now lay with my cheek against the basement's stone floor. In addition to my head, my shoulder ached from the fall. Most regrettably, I found my legs and arms still held fast. I was even more helpless than before.

Or was I?

I twisted my left wrist—the one that had landed on the side up in the air.

It moved.

The fall might not have broken the chair, but it had loosened my bonds a bit. I twisted again. The rope burned my skin, but thanks to the laudanum's lasting effects, the pain was tolerable. I continued to twist and pull on the cord. Wetness slicked the ropes. Sweat? Blood? Or both? I couldn't see and decided it was for the best.

When the lashing slackened more, I added pulling on my hand to the twisting. When my hand slipped free, I pushed the gag to my neck and panted in lungfuls of air. Percy made a high-pitched sound, bringing me back to the task. While I now had one free hand, I still had the task of undoing the knots and bindings, which remained a slow process as I lay on my side.

Releasing Percy was much easier. Some old tools littered the table next to the candle. As I cut his bonds, he told me how he'd been awakened when they came for Mycroft but pretended to be asleep. My brother had been very groggy, but they managed to get him up the stairs, warning any efforts to escape would end in my death, and someone would be watching us.

"Do you think it's true?" Percy whispered.

"They're 'ere," Rose said in a heavy French accent. Percy and I turned our attention to her. "I 'eard zem laughing. I know this 'ouse. They are in the front, playing *cartes*."

"Could we sneak out?" I asked. "Would they see us?"

She shook her head. "The door. It is locked. When they first brought me 'ere. I tried."

I studied the odd bits of furniture scattered around the room before ending at the table where the chest still rested. "Then, we'll have to make them open it for us."

"Each of you, take a chair and wait to one side of the steps. Use the wall to hide in the shadows. I'll use this one and hide underneath the stairs." Pointing to the chest, I asked Percy, "Do you think you can throw that against the door?"

"Not from here, but if I get up the stairs…"

"Throw it hard enough to make some noise and run down as fast as you can. I'm going to put out the light as soon as you do. Let's hope they both come down to check out the crash."

I picked up my own chair and the candle and took the place I designated.

When Rose was hidden, Percy carried the chest almost

two-thirds the way up before he heaved it over his head to the door. The *thud* was loud, but its landing on the stone floor (missing my head by inches in its descent) was deafening. Footsteps pounded on the floor overhead. My stomach jerked, and I held up two fingers to indicate at least two were checking on the commotion. Percy had barely scurried next to Rose before the key turned in the lock, and I blew out the candle.

Despite the gloom, enough light shone through the door to distinguish two hulks rushing down the stairs. With a rather primal yell, Percy swung his chair at the first figure. The second turned as if to run upstairs. I reached through the open steps and grabbed his ankle, pulling it toward me. With a scream not unlike Percy's, our second captor fell backward and landed on top of his companion. Before either could rise, Percy, Rose, and I beat at the two until neither moved.

Only then did we turn them over, and I confirmed their identities as Harcourt and Tennyson. Belatedly I recalled Edmonds mentioning the two had brought Rose here. Her boot landed in the side of Harcourt, and she'd drawn back her leg to land a blow in Tennyson's when I pushed her backward. She staggered on her feet and cursed at me in French. The two prone figures moaned, and I feared they wouldn't be out for long.

Percy picked up the ropes that had bound us, but I held up my hand to stop him. "There's no time. I have to get to the coroner's inquest right away. Before Mycroft destroys his life as well as Surminster's."

"And how do we do that?" Percy asked.

"I suppose we take a cab."

"You gots money?"

I shook my head and what I could see of the room swam about me. Placing a hand on the side of the staircase, I lowered my head and took deep breaths. As my vision cleared, the two unconscious men almost at my feet came into focus.

"I know someone who does."

Kneeling next to Harcourt, I searched his pockets and pulled out a few coins and banknotes. "Should be more than enough."

Rose did the same to Tennyson and smiled at whatever she'd recovered from his pockets.

At the top of the stairs, I took the time to put a chair under the knob to at least delay the two men for a while, if they should wake up. "I need to catch a cab," I told Rose in French. "Which way is best?"

She pointed to the front of the house. "This way."

Once on the street, I turned to ask Rose for more directions, but she was already halfway up the block, running away from us and the house as fast as she could in her boots.

"You wants me to catch her?" Percy asked.

I shook my head and regretted the move as my vision swam again. "We need to get to the inquest. But if she's trying to get to the docks and maybe find a way back to France, we should probably go in the same direction. We just need a street busy enough to find a cab."

As we rushed up one street and across to another, I heard a bell tower chime the hour. Eleven. I had no idea when the inquest would start, but I assumed we needed to hurry.

When several cabs passed us by without stopping—one driver even sped his horse faster—I glanced at Percy and then at my clothes. We were both filthy, having dug up the

THE ADVENTURE OF THE DECEASED SCHOLAR

chest back in Wrightmoor, and then suffered various scuffles in the basement. I placed my hand on my cheek and recalled the spill I'd taken earlier. We hardly appeared the sort to be able to pay for a ride to the next block—let alone to one of the better neighborhoods.

"No cab is going to stop for us," I said.

Percy nodded. "Don't look too respectable, do we?"

"I need to get home. And fast."

My heart quickened, and sweat dampened my brow. I didn't know whether these were reactions to the laudanum leaving my system or to my concern for my brother. If they were to return and find us missing...

"I gots an idea," the stable hand said. He was staring at a pub sign across the street. "Should be someone in there what gots some sort of rig who can take us. Fast. For the right price. You stay here. The ways you look, you'd scare old Scratch himself."

His description must have been accurate, for when he returned with a rather rough-looking laborer, the newcomer stared unabashedly at me. He asked no questions, however, once I showed we had the funds to pay his price for the ride to—?

I paused. I had no idea where the inquest would be. Neither could I give him Surminster's address because I wasn't certain who I might encounter there. In the end, I gave directions for our family townhouse. Either my parents would be there, or someone would know where they went to attend the inquest.

The driver Percy had recruited let his mouth drop open when I told him where I wanted to go, but with the assurance of funds, we were soon in a small cart darting through London traffic toward the townhouse.

My foot tapped a drumbeat faster than that of our hired horse. I imagined entering the inquest and demanding to share my story. Given my current state, however, I wondered if they would even let me in. Perhaps—?

"Why'd you free me?" Percy asked, breaking into my thoughts.

"Pardon me?"

"I left you and your brother on the road in Wrightmoor. You could've left me and the woman in the basement, but you didn't."

Several reasons flitted through my brain about the decision—from needing him to assist in escaping to his being the one to bring me out of my stupor. But in the end, I gave him the most honest and simplest.

"I couldn't very well leave either of you to Simms. As for leaving us behind in Wrightmoor, you thought you were doing the honorable thing by returning the chest to Lady Surminster."

He dropped his head and spoke to the cart's floor. "The reward. I wanted it for myself. That's whys I drove off."

I shrugged. "All I've cared about is making sure Lord Surminster's death is redressed. I never wanted a reward for finding a treasure."

"Which weren't no treasure anyways," he said with a shake of his head. "I guess I gots what I deserved."

"No one deserved what Simms did to us, and if I have my way, he'll get his due."

THE RECEPTION I received when I entered the townhouse wasn't as I had imagined. No one came rushing at my call, and I had to go into the kitchen before I found Cook, pounding her fists into a mound of dough on a table.

At my greeting, she raised her head and shrieked.

I backed toward the door when she rushed at me, but she caught me up in her beefy arms and pressed me to her chest. Between the flour dusting I received and her embrace, I could barely gasp out my question. "Where is everyone?"

"They gots your brother's note and rushed out to meet you," she said. "Except for your mother. There was a big row between her and the squire. In the end, she wents off alone, but I don't know where."

A moan escaped my lips before I could stop it. A note from Mycroft? Simms' and Nathan's doing for certain. For whatever reason, Mother didn't trust the missive and had probably gone to the inquest. But where? In our village, the inquest was often held in the main tavern because it had the most space. But this was London. The process could be different.

Part of me wanted to rush into the street and jump onto the wagon where Percy still waited, but I needed a plan—and a destination. I quickly ran through different possibilities and determined too many existed for me to eliminate them all in time. One place, however, existed where Mycroft would not be: wherever the note said he was.

Rushing from room to room on the main floor, I checked for the note that had sent the family flying from home. Nothing. Then on to the second floor and my parents' room. On a table by the fireplace, I found it. It stated we would be arriving into Paddington at one. The clock on the mantel struck half-past noon. If Simms wanted my family away from the inquest, it had to begin at one. Of course, Mycroft's testimony might not be the first. I had, at most, an hour to find it. Before him, the coroner would most likely call other…

Witnesses.

Like Inspector Roggens.

I took the stairs to the main floor two steps at a time and fairly flew out the front door. Cook ran after me and shouted as I jumped into the wagon, "Where are ya goin', Master Sherlock?"

"Scotland Yard," I said to her and the hired driver at the same time.

Both stared at me, but I faced the driver and nodded at him. "That's right. Number four Whitehall Place. Or rather behind it."

To my good fortune, the inspectors' headquarters was not too far from Grosvenor Square, and we reached the brick building in less than thirty minutes. Given its reputation, I was surprised by the rather low, narrow building housing it. Two uniformed officers stopped me when I jumped off the wagon and rushed toward the entrance.

"I must get in," I said. "I need to speak to Inspector Roggens."

One of the helmeted men stared at me, his gaze taking me in from my scraped cheek to muddy boots. I shifted my weight from one foot to the other, knowing my appearance marked me as the type of thug they often arrested. After a second review, he turned and shouted into the building's interior.

"Is Roggens here?"

A voice called back, "He's out. Went to some hearing."

"The coroner's inquest?" I asked, fairly bouncing on my feet. My heart beat faster as I hoped for the answer. "Where is it?"

THE ADVENTURE OF THE DECEASED SCHOLAR

The two exchanged glances, and the one who'd answered me shrugged at the other and pointed to a building behind me. "The courtroom's in there."

I sprinted away, shouting my thanks behind me. No one detained me as I pushed opened the door and ran inside. When an entire room of men in black robes and white wigs frowned at my abrupt entrance, I understood my mistake. I'd attended enough trials where my father presided to know a criminal courtroom when I saw one. This was not the coroner's inquest, and other than Inspector Roggens in the witness stand, I recognized no one there. Bright scarlet now flushed the Scotland Yarder's face. My sincerest desire in that instance was to simply disappear in a puff of smoke. Instead, I swallowed, bowed my head, and backed out of the room, bending at the waist for the mile between where I'd stopped and the door.

My fiasco in the courtroom sucked the wind out of me. With boots made of lead, I trudged back toward the wagon.

Percy jumped down and jogged up to me. "Where are we goin' now?"

I shook my head, unable to explain how I'd run out of ideas. As we continued back to the wagon, Percy followed at my side. Unable to meet his gaze, I focused on the ground, blinking to clear my vision.

Finally, I raised my head. "I suppose we can try Surminster's. Perhaps I can persuade—?"

A vise gripped my forearm, stopping me in my tracks. I turned about to face Inspector Roggens. "Just what was that performance in there, Master Sherlock?"

My mouth opened and closed several times as I reviewed how much of an explanation to share with him. I needed to get to the inquest, and he might require more of an explanation than I had time to spare.

Percy saved me the trouble. "We needs to get to the inquest for Lord Surminster. They are goin' to make Mr. Mycroft lie. He's only doin' so to keep Master Sherlock and me safe."

The inspector glanced from me to Percy and back as if assessing our credibility, and then to the wagon we'd arrived in. "And you were going in that?" He shook his head. "Will never get you there on time. Come on."

He dismissed the wagon, giving the patient driver an extra shilling for his troubles, and called to one of the two helmets at the entrance.

I'd never ridden in the back of a police wagon before and found the overall exhilaration of the adventure greater than the less-than-pleasant aspects of traveling as the criminal element does. The box's air was probably less than wholesome, and I wondered if I was breathing in some miasma that might come back to haunt me. Of course, given my shabby condition, I might also have contributed to the overall ambience. All the same, it allowed us to share our story with the inspector without an audience.

I explained in short terms how Mycroft and I had gone to Wrightmoor to check out a discrepancy in the estate's property lines—leaving out how we came to know of the shift—and in the process had discovered the chest. Percy picked up the story and explained about taking the chest to London, being met at the station, and I finished with Simms and Edmonds' plans for Mycroft's testimony at the inquest.

"They told you all this?" Roggens asked.

I nodded. "I think Simms considers himself too clever to

THE ADVENTURE OF THE DECEASED SCHOLAR

be caught. And when he returned from the inquest, we'd be eliminated."

"Hold on there," Percy said. "Edmonds said the old man what drowned the same time as Lord Surminster was named Clement?" When I responded in the affirmative, he slapped his knee. "Clement was the gamekeeper at Wrightmoor. I met him at the pub when he was waitin' for a train about a week ago. Said he had business in London. When he didn't come back, we's figured he'd met a bit o' raspberry and stayed a while because of her."

I glanced at Roggens. His brow furrowed as if he was putting all the information in order. "Simms killed both men, you say?"

"And I think Lord Surminster, Vernon's father, as well—with arsenic. The Earl of Wittdam uses an arsenic mixture in his taxidermy. I smelled it when we were in his workshop. Most likely, the previous Lord Surminster learned of Simms' deceit just as his son did. Only for whatever reason, Simms decided on a more exotic death for the next two. He used the term 'elegant' when he discussed them."

When the horses stopped, we followed Roggens out of the wagon and up the stairs into another court room. Finally, I was in the correct hearing. I recognized the coroner presiding over the proceedings and also spotted my mother among the spectators from the brightly colored silk scarf she wore about her neck. She stared at me with rounded eyes as I followed the inspector down the aisle to the front of the room. When she moved to stand, I raised my hand to stay her.

Had he not been sitting between Simms and Edmonds, I might not have identified Mycroft. My usually immaculate brother wore a day's growth of beard and the wrinkled, muddy clothes he'd worn on our adventure to Wrightmoor. While these aspects of his appearance disturbed me, the manner in which he stared straight ahead made my heart beat faster. Just how much laudanum had they forced on him?

"What is the meaning of this, Roggens?" the coroner asked when the Scotland Yarder stepped to the barrier between the court and the spectators.

"Excuse me, sir, but I'm here to arrest Mycroft Holmes for the murder of Fenton Crandall."

A gasp escaped me before my whole body stiffened. Mother leaped to her feet, and several of those in the room whispered to their neighbors, creating a general droning that drowned out the current witness. While the coroner shouted for silence, Roggens signaled to Mycroft to come with him. With the slow, precise movements of a man in his cups, he stepped from between our two captors and prepared to shuffle down the aisle toward the Scotland Yarder.

Before he had taken two steps, Simms grabbed my brother's arm. "See here. This man is a witness."

"Don't care. I've got two witnesses who say he was looking for the deceased and had quarreled with him earlier." He waved at my brother again to step into the aisle and then spoke to Simms again. "Let him go, or I'll arrest you for obstructing justice."

A uniformed officer appeared from somewhere and moved next to the bench where the men had been sitting. Simms glanced at the policeman, released his grip on my brother's forearm, and gave him a little shove.

Mycroft stumbled but moved to the aisle, repeating one word over and over, "But. But…"

I, on the other hand, couldn't even fashion that single syllable and stood rooted to the spot while Roggens gripped my brother's arm.

"Hand me your nippers," he said to the officer beside him.

The uniformed man passed him a rather evil-looking device resembling a miniature iceman's tongs attached to a bar shaped like a "T." Roggens inserted my brother's right hand between the tongs and fiddled with the T-bar for a moment until the device tightened about Mycroft's wrist. With his suspect thus detained, Roggens led him from the room with the T-bar.

The entire court had hushed as they observed my brother's arrest, but as the three men pushed past me, their buzzing comments returned, only louder—although I wasn't certain if what I heard wasn't the ringing in my own ears.

Only when my mother stood and made her way to the aisle did I regain command of my limbs and trailed out behind her. Percy fell in beside me outside the courtroom, whispering something, but I was unable to comprehend anything he said. As if in a trance, I reeled out into the bright sunlight and blinked to bring everything into focus. My brother was almost at the same police wagon in which we'd arrived in what seemed only a heartbeat ago. Mother was already on the street, seeking up and down the thoroughfare, most likely for a cab to follow the wagon.

I kept shifting my gaze between the two, uncertain which to join. Until a few minutes ago, I had considered Roggens on our side. He'd listened to my tale about what had happened and appeared to believe it. What had occurred between the wagon and the courtroom? How could he think my brother had murdered anyone? And in such a bizarre manner?

Remaining immobile, I could merely watch the scene unfold, seeking to make sense of it all. Until Percy shoved me to the ground and shouted toward the police wagon. In the next second, the tableau shifted once again. I landed on my good cheek, the one not injured in the fall in the basement. Percy lay on top of me. His weight pressed me into the street's hard-packed earth and stones, and the only thing I saw when I opened my eyes was a pile of horse manure only inches from my face. My first thought was I was glad I hadn't landed on top of it. My second was Percy had tried to cover me in horse manure on purpose, and I struggled to get away from both him and the excrement. He wrapped an arm around me and held me fast.

The next moment, several gunshots thundered from behind me, and I tried to turn my head enough to determine who was shooting at whom. Unfortunately, Percy's body kept my head pinned to the ground. My only view was of people's boots and shoes running in various directions. Amazingly, not one stepped on the pile.

One pair of shiny boots positioned themselves on each side of it, and a voice overhead said, "It's all over now. You can get up."

As soon as Percy's bulk was gone, I turned over and sat up to search for my mother and brother. I discovered a knot of police officers on the steps of the courtroom building but didn't recognize anyone. Turning to focus on the wagon, I found another group of people, with only two uniforms among them. I distinguished my mother's back in the cluster. She was kneeling on the street over—

Mycroft.

THE ADVENTURE OF THE DECEASED SCHOLAR

My scattered impressions melded into an understandable whole and made my empty stomach churn. Forcing myself to my feet, I pushed off Percy's hands and those of the officer who sought to detain me and rushed to my mother's side.

Blood ran through her fingers as she pressed the silk scarf she'd been wearing into my brother's upper arm. I knelt beside her, in part because I doubted my knees would hold me upright. He lay on his left side while Mother pulled back the scarf to examine his still-manacled right arm. He moved as if to adjust his weight, but Mother placed her hand on his shoulder.

"Lie still, dear," she said. "The more you move, the more blood you will lose. I'm going to place a tourniquet to slow the bleeding."

White-faced, he moaned, bit his lip, but quit wiggling. The pain must have been intense for him to feel it in his drugged condition.

"H-how is he?" I asked.

Mother turned to me. "It was a through shot in the muscle, from what I can tell. It didn't hit the bone or an artery. It should heal with no problem."

She glanced farther into those standing and kneeling about, and only then did I see Roggens was also on the ground, but he wasn't moving. My stomach gave another churn.

Turning back to me, she said, "I've bound Mycroft's wound. I should check on the inspector." In a lower voice, she whispered to me. "I had just hailed a cab when the shooting started. Get him in it and home before they stop you. I'll distract the officers while you do so."

She worked herself around my brother and knelt with

her back to Mycroft and me. Glancing over her shoulder, she called to the two uniforms still standing by me. "Officers, I need your help."

As soon as they stepped away, I pulled on my brother's shoulder. "Come on. We're getting out of here."

Percy must have been behind me the entire time because when Mycroft fumbled, he helped lift him and positioned himself in front of the handcuff still on my brother's wrist. Once in the cab, Mycroft rested against the hansom's back and groaned. His face was gray and slick with sweat. I opened the slit in the cab and told the driver to hurry. I would double his fee.

"Always spending money," he said, his speech slurred, and ended with a disturbing teeth chatter.

While he was still conscious, I feared he was on the precipice of shock. I pulled off my jacket, placed it over him, and ordered Percy to do the same. The cab offered no room for me to have him elevate his feet, but at least I could keep him warm, as Mother had taught us.

Arriving at the townhouse, Percy and I supported him up the steps.

When we entered, Mrs. Simpson was the first to see us and screamed at the sight. "Come quick, everyone."

Father, Constance, and several maids came running. My father's face broke into a smile when he saw us, only to pale when he focused on Mycroft's face.

"W-what happened?" he asked.

"Edmonds shot him," I said. "He needs to lie down. Mother should be coming soon, and the police may be with her."

Without any additional questions, he pointed to the library. "In there. Put him on the couch." He faced Mrs.

THE ADVENTURE OF THE DECEASED SCHOLAR

Simpson. "Bring in plenty of hot water, a basin, and Mrs. Holmes' medical bag."

"I'll get the bag," Constance said and was gone before we could even acknowledge her offer.

Percy and I moved to the library with Mycroft. When we reached the door, someone knocked at the entrance. Everyone froze. A second pounding had us hustling into the room where I shut and locked its door before anyone answered the knock.

By the time we had Mycroft on the couch with his feet elevated, Father called through the door. "Did you tell the cab driver you'd pay him double?"

I swallowed, opened the door, and nodded, unable to answer over the lump in my throat.

"Spending money like it was water," Mycroft mumbled to the ceiling.

Percy joined us at the door and dipped his head. "Please, sir. He was worried about Mr. Mycroft. His color ain't so good."

Father stared at each of us in turn, nodded, and stepped back to let Constance into the room. She tiptoed to me and whispered, "Was it the coppers?"

"I hadn't paid the hansom driver."

She set Mother's bag on a table next to the couch. Pointing to my brother's still-bound hand, she said, "I can take that off."

She fiddled with the T-bar end of the cuff, and a click followed a moment later.

When she pulled out Mycroft's hand, he moaned with relief and whispered, "Thank you."

Despite my concern and worry, relief passed through me. For the first time, my brother acknowledged his gratitude to my friend. I could only hope this might be some turning point for the future.

Before I could say more, Mother joined us, followed by a maid carrying the basin and a pitcher of steaming water. She glanced at those in the room and said, "Constance, I need you to stay and help me. Sherry dear, go to the drawing room with your father and explain to him what has happened. And you—"

Percy touched his head as if to tip his hat. "Percy, ma'am. Master Holmes and I escaped the basement together."

I could tell Mother had many questions, but she shook her head and said, "First things, first. Adeline, will you show Mr. Percy to the kitchen where he can clean up and get something to eat."

The maid curtsied, and the two of us followed her to the library door. Before exiting, I turned to share one more bit of information with her. She and Constance were already helping him out of his jacket.

"They gave us laudanum," I said. "Be careful about giving him anything else for the pain."

"Sound advice," she said as she dipped a cloth into the basin of water.

My father was pacing the room in front of the fireplace. He paused when I entered and surveyed me from head to foot. "Come here, son," he said at last.

I traversed the room with more than a little trepidation. I had no idea what my mother had shared with him or whether any answers I gave would contradict what he already thought he knew. When I reached him, he turned my head to examine the cheek I'd scraped on the basement floor.

"Are you"—his voice cracked, and he started over—"are you injured anywhere else?"

"I walloped my head when I fell. That's when I hurt my cheek. And the ropes cut my wrists when I pulled out my hand."

He inspected my arms when I held them out. They were raw, and his touch made them burn. Running his hand over my skull, he found a bump and fingered it, making me wince. "But no broken bones?"

When I shook my head, he pulled me to him and squeezed me almost as tight as Cook had done earlier.

"After not finding you at Paddington, Constance said she knew where you might be. She'd found an address in Edmonds' pocket. When I found the basement and saw—"

He stopped and took a deep breath as if to gather himself. I pushed back to be able to meet his gaze.

"You went to where they'd held us? Was Harcourt still there?"

He shook his head. "The house was empty. But it was obvious someone had been bound by ropes there. I feared we were too late. That they had—"

Another tight embrace followed, which was broken by another knock at the door. My stomach dropped. It had to be the police.

"Two men are at the door. One's a policeman," Mrs. Simpson said when she entered. "Should I let them in?"

Father straightened his back. I recognized this stance. He used it when he entered his courtroom, ready to battle for justice and the law. "Did they show a warrant?"

"No, sir."

"Then I'll see them in the doorway. Don't let them in."

I doubted many housekeepers were as prepared for

meeting an officer of the law as Mrs. Simpson. We'd had more than our share of visits and searches by our local constable in recent months, and she had experience allowing entrance only to those with Father's permission.

While he wouldn't approve of my following him, he didn't notice when I positioned myself in the drawing room doorway for a clear view of the potential confrontation.

I recognized the police officer as the one who had assisted Roggens in Mycroft's arrest. He had his helmet under his arm. Without it, he was much younger than I would have guessed—barely more than twenty. His mouth, topped by a sparse moustache, was a straight line.

The other man, dressed in a suit, carried himself as Inspector Roggens had. A wariness as if always on guard. He had to be from Scotland Yard, just like Roggens.

"Good afternoon, sir," the Scotland Yarder began.

"Squire. Squire Holmes, if you please," Father said, in an effort I assumed to set the appropriate tone for the meeting.

"Yes, si...Squire. Inspector Harrison, Scotland Yard. I am here about one Mycroft Holmes."

"I don't know where he is."

Our two unexpected visitors glanced at each other before the man continued. "It's a pity. A true pity. You see, he left the scene of a shooting, and we had hoped he would provide us with a statement."

"If he appears, I will have him contact you, Inspector. And you are...?" Father asked the uniformed policeman.

"The name's Douglas."

Father had his hand on the door as if preparing to shut it, when Mother called out from down the hallway. "Officers, do you have news of Inspector Roggens?"

For the first time since I'd seen her at the inquest, I inventoried her current state. Her skirt was covered with dust at the bottom and in patches about the knees where she must have knelt beside Mycroft and Roggens. Her hands were still stained with blood, as were the front and sleeves of her dress. Her hair had come undone, and strands hung about her face and down the back of her neck. Even her face had smears of dirt and blood.

Despite her disheveled appearance, both bowed to her. The officer said, "He's been taken to a nearby surgery. We're still waitin' for word."

"And the despicable man who shot him?"

"Both of them under arrest, ma'am. Already accusin' the other of killin' Lord Surminster."

"Did they mention Fenton Crandall?"

Another glance at each other, perhaps more than a little surprised at her knowledge of the events. The inspector spoke this time. "Yes, ma'am. Also sayin' the same about him. That's why I came, ma'am. To let you know Mr. Holmes is no longer under arrest. Really never was." At my parents' stares, he shuffled his feet and glanced about him. "If you please, Squire, ma'am, we'd prefer not to discuss this on the street."

At Mother's nod, Father opened the door to let the officers enter.

The policeman shuffled his feet before speaking. "You see, Squire, Roggens did it to protect Mr. Holmes. Your son, there,"—he pointed past Father and in my direction. My face burned having been caught eavesdropping—"he explained to the inspector how his brother was bein' forced to provide false evidence at the inquest. To stop him,

Roggens arrested him. Only way to get him out of the inquest before he committed perjury."

Father's frown turned upward, and he actually chuckled. "Your Inspector Roggens is a clever man. A clever man." He thrust out his arm and shook both men's hands vigorously. "Thank you. Thank you for the good news."

CHAPTER FIFTEEN

I was surprised at how similar my family's Easter observances in London were to those at Underbyrne. Mother, Father, and I breakfasted and dressed for church services. Mycroft was, of course, excused.

Londoners dressed in their finest crowded the streets, and I remarked on this to Mother.

"Yes," she said, nodding to one of our neighbors we passed on the street. "I understand it is becoming a tradition. There are even parks where people go to 'parade,' if you will. A chance to see and be seen. One of the biggest is Battersea."

Father touched his hat to another passing neighbor. "Battersea? That's a ways away."

"I didn't say I wanted to go. I merely noted it was a popular place today. I'd prefer to remain home today and tend to Mycroft. Although he appears to be healing well."

I raised my face to the heavens in a gesture of thanks, then let a shudder pass through me as I recalled the scene from yesterday. "Have we heard about Inspector Roggens? Perhaps we can visit him?"

"Capital idea," Father said. "Very clever fellow in the end. Arresting Mycroft. I'll make enquiries, and perhaps tomorrow we will be able to see him."

Tomorrow. Easter Monday.

Another sort of chill passed through me. I was halfway through my spring holiday. Then the return to Eton.

A group of urchins ran between the well-dressed strollers, begging for pennies. On most days, they might have been chased away, but given the benevolence of the day, many were treated with a coin or two. Mother and Father had supplied me with several in the event we came across such children. Knowing Constance's own past of having to sing on street corners or beg for funds to help feed her younger brothers and sisters, I never refused any who came my way.

When we arrived home, we found Mycroft sitting in the drawing room. Mother scolded him for being out of bed, but he defended himself saying, "I cannot take another mouthful of the gruel Mrs. Simpson insists I eat. I decided if I came downstairs and had Easter dinner with the rest of you, I'd get a decent meal."

We quickly changed, and he joined us in the dining room for the meal we were all anticipating as much as he. While we were still at the table, Mrs. Simpson arrived to announce Mother had a visitor. She read the note on the back of the calling card and passed it to Father. After perusing it, he frowned and shrugged at her, as if to say, "It's your decision."

"I think we shall have dessert and tea in the drawing room, Mrs. Simpson." Mother stood and let her gaze rest on

THE ADVENTURE OF THE DECEASED SCHOLAR

each of us—an invitation to join her. "Miss Phillips has come. I think we all deserve to hear what she has to say."

If she hadn't expected to see us all, Sophronia Phillips displayed no surprise when the whole family entered. In fact, her face displayed no emotion whatsoever. The week had taken a toll on her complexion, and her black crepe mourning dress only accentuated her lack of color. More striking were the dark circles under her eyes and the downward pull of her mouth. Nevertheless, I had only to remind myself of how her efforts to blackmail my brother nearly cost him his life to push aside any feelings of sympathy for the woman.

After taking our seats and exchanging rather stilted greetings, Miss Phillips smoothed out her skirts and said, "I appreciate your receiving me. This has been a trying week for us all, but thanks to you, the family name and fortune have been redeemed. We're all very grateful."

The maid Adeline arrived with the tea, and cups were passed around, saving anyone from having to respond immediately to this less-than-full apology. For myself, the tea wouldn't cool the scorching heat in my stomach.

Mother, however, seemed to find an appropriate response. In a calm voice, she said, "We really didn't have a choice, did we? Your threat to ruin my son was exceedingly clear."

"You had to be aware of my desperation? You—all of you—seemed to discover what the authorities couldn't—or wouldn't."

"And your first thought was to extort us? You couldn't have simply asked us to help?" Mother asked.

"I couldn't take the chance you'd refuse." A small smile

crept across her lips. "It all turned out well in the end, don't you think?"

"A man was killed because he visited you. My oldest son was shot, both he and his brother suffered through a night of horror where they were drugged and trussed up in a basement, and the rest of the family was put through more than a day of anguish where we had no idea what had happened to them. How is this all 'well'?"

The woman paused, and pink tinged her cheeks as Mother's recital of the consequences of her actions confronted her with the unpleasant truth. "I-I—"

Before she could articulate more, Mother said, "As part of our research, we learned Lord Wittdam, the father of the man everyone assumes will be proposing to you, is living at Wrightmoor."

"Yes, I believe I may have mentioned—"

"Did you not think it odd an earl would live as a tenant rather than on his own estate?"

"Jared explained he had known Mr. Simms since school, and there was also a strong friendship between the two—"

"Did he also mention Stoneger Abbey, the Wittdams' estate, is in disrepair? In such a dismal state, it is uninhabitable? I'm afraid the present earl is more than just eccentric. He's addled."

"The taxidermy," I said, feeling the others turn their gaze to me. "He had the window open in the room when we visited him, but I detected the smell of arsenic and naphthalene, among others."

"Yes, I'm afraid the chemicals have affected his judgment," Mother said. "He made some rather bad investments and basically lost the family's fortune."

While Mother shared this bit of information about the

earl, her gaze turned to my father for an instant. Was this warning about bad investments and lost fortunes not just meant for Miss Phillips? Was it a vague warning to Father regarding Sires' proposed opportunity? Father may have seen such a connection as well because he shifted in his seat.

Miss Phillips' protests, however, broke into these thoughts.

"You're wrong. Jared has assured me—"

"I have it on the best authority. A family friend who works in the Home Office—Colonel Williams—did some research for me. I'll be glad to share his report with you." Miss Phillips' face shifted from pink to vermillion, and her back stiffened as Mother continued. "Surely someone from Scotland Yard shared with you that Mr. Simms and Mr. Nathan Edmonds murdered your brother. They made it appear a suicide to break your family and force a marriage between you and Jared Edmonds. Such a union would ensure the trust remained within their control. Most likely, their plans also included the demise of both your mother and her father after the marriage. While the trust would still pass to you and your brother, Jared's uncle would remain as trustee with the assets still under his control."

"You're wrong. Jared loves me." Sophronia blinked rapidly as if to prevent tears spilling down her cheeks. "He's not. He can't be—"

"I'm afraid he has been as much a pawn under Simms' control as your father and brother. I have no reason to doubt Jared's professions of love. I would caution, however, to avoid any engagement to him until all matters have been settled and a contract arranged between you both. At some point, Lord Thanbury will pass on—naturally, I hope—and I would hate to see Wrightmoor be lost or fall into another's hands because of imprudence on your part."

"You have given me a great deal to think about," Miss Phillips said. "I had no idea—that is—my whole family appears to have been deceived, and by such—we trusted them—took what they said at their word."

Her voice cracked at the end, and tears formed again in her eyes. A little sympathy for her did break through—at least when I considered the events from a larger perspective. She, too, had been manipulated, and her father and brother, murdered. Glancing at my father, I observed the lines around his mouth and eyes had softened. My brother, on the other hand, shifted in his seat, as uncomfortable around this demonstration of female emotion as always. Only my mother seemed unaffected by Miss Phillips' display. I'd learned she could perceive another woman's true feelings and motives better than I. Was her lack of sympathy the result of skepticism on her part regarding Miss Phillips' sincerity?

Mother allowed the younger woman to whimper for another moment before saying, "I shared all this with you to assuage my own conscience. This is, after all, a day of reconciliation—when sins are forgiven, and we are made right with God. Remember, I could have allowed you to learn this on your own, most likely after your marriage to Lord Jared—a very cruel lesson indeed. I do hope you will consider our talk and actions today the next time you wish to abuse another to do your bidding."

Mother rose, and we joined her. Miss Phillips, after a moment's hesitation, did the same. She glanced about her as if uncertain what to do. Mother pointed to the entrance. "The door is there. Please see yourself out."

The younger woman provided the tiniest nod before retreating to the hallway. We remained where we were until we heard the front door open and close. I stepped to the window and watched Miss Phillips ascend her carriage.

No one commented on Mother's actions as we, too, exited the room. She did, however, turn to my brother. "You're looking a little peaked, my dear. I would suggest it best for you to return to your room and bed."

He grimaced at the suggestion, but he and I both knew it was useless to argue with her. No doubt remained on that point after her discussion with Miss Phillips. Father retreated to the library, and after considering my options, I decided to seek out Constance. There had been no chance to speak alone since she helped Mother tend to Mycroft.

Unable to find her, I enquired after her with Mrs. Simpson.

She pursed her lips as she always did when sharing unpleasant news. "If you hurry, you might catch up with her. She left only a bit ago. It's her Sunday half-day, you know."

I stared at her while I grasped what she had shared. I decided I needed more information. "Constance went out? Alone?"

"Oh, my no. Adeline invited her to Battersea Park with her brothers. To show off their bonnets."

"Bonnets?"

Again, I could only stare at our housekeeper as I remembered the hat Constance had found along with the fan in the old schoolroom. Was she dressing up to go out as she had for the opera? I'd hoped the treatment she received at the theater stage door when she had made up her face and dressed in her version of a "lady" would have put her off any efforts in that direction. I didn't know Adeline well and her brothers not at all. Mother wouldn't hire anyone with serious flaws, but I'd learned through my interactions with Constance that girls are wont to do foolish things—like stealing a few pounds from a guest to pay for a cab ride to the opera.

"Master Sherlock?" Mrs. Simpson asked. "Are you all right?"

My gaze refocused on our housekeeper, and I realized I'd been analyzing Constance's actions for longer than social convention allowed. My face burned at my lack of manners. "Yes. Sorry, Mrs. Simpson. I was…I think I'd like to see Constance's and Adeline's bonnets before they go too far."

My apprehension over Constance's imprudence sounded loudly in my ears—like the bells on the fire wagons as they rushed down the street. A number of scenarios, many ending in unfortunate outcomes, played through my mind, and I determined to seek the girls out to ensure their safety.

Unfortunately, like Constance, I wasn't familiar with the city, and while Adeline served as her guide, I had none. To avoid floundering about amid all those parading through the streets for Easter, I needed someone to provide me with directions to the park. Despite a mounting sense of urgency on my part, I forced myself to consult my brother for directions.

When he answered my knock, I stepped in and shut the door behind me. He put the book he'd been reading by the fire on the table beside him. "Why the serious face?"

"I need to know how to get to Battersea Park."

"Planning on showing off your bonnet? Why don't you

THE ADVENTURE OF THE DECEASED SCHOLAR

take a cab? You seem to enjoy spending Father's money on such indulgences."

"Please," I said. "I'm trying to catch Constance. She and Adeline left for the park with Adeline's brothers, and I don't think it's a good idea for her to be out with someone she doesn't know—even if it is Adeline's brother."

He picked up his book and said to the page. "It's the middle of the day, and they are surrounded by crowds out to show off their Easter finery. Nothing will happen."

"I know you don't care much for Constance. That you think she acts above her station. But she was the one who knew how to release the nipper from your wrist. Helped Mother tend your wound. And most of all, she's my friend. You know the whole city. The quickest route. Please, tell me how to get to the park."

He turned his gaze to the book on the table, but I could tell he was considering what I had said to him. After the mantel clock ticked for an eternity, he raised his good hand and pinched the bridge of his nose. "Go past Buckingham Palace and along the side of Belgravia. If you need to, ask for the Victoria Bridge. Cross the bridge, and you'll be in the park."

I rushed to him, but then recalled his shoulder and stopped before I hugged him or shook his hand. "Thank you. If Mother or Father looks for me, tell them I took a walk in the neighborhood and will be back shortly."

"The girls will be fine. I assure you. But go and leave me alone."

To avoid any questions from my parents, I used the bachelor's entrance as Constance had the other day. Once on the street, I gathered my bearings and raced south toward the edge of Hyde Park and on to Buckingham

Palace. While I had lost time in checking with my brother, I also knew I could make it up with a faster pace than two girls on a leisurely stroll through the city. I bumped into more than one pedestrian as I tried to make my way through the crowded sidewalks and got a grumbled oath in response. Between those seeking to show off their spring finery and servants who were enjoying their half-holiday, the foot traffic was unusually magnified.

More than once, I would spot a foursome, only to discover they were complete strangers when I reached them. It took almost an hour for me to enter the park, where I found my search complicated because of the crowd of couples, families, and young people going every which way.

A church bell rang out five o'clock, and I still hadn't found them. I would have to leave soon to avoid raising my parents' concerns. With a sigh, I turned around to return home. At that point, I caught sight of a flash of red hair through the crowd. Promising myself this would be the last time I would approach a stranger to call out my friend's name, I pushed through the other visitors.

While the redheaded lady bobbed in and out of view, I could tell I was gaining on her and she wasn't alone. At the same time, the two men with the redheaded girl wore tall hats, not the caps of laborers—or others of Adeline's class. Unless…

Had Adeline identified them as her "brothers" as a ruse? To avoid Mrs. Simpson's suspicions?

A new and more urgent reason now pushed me ahead. When I finally was within earshot, I called out Constance's name. She turned around in response, and Adeline turned to see what had attracted Constance's attention. So did the two men—

THE ADVENTURE OF THE DECEASED SCHOLAR

Harcourt and Tennyson.

The whole world tilted. My apprehension for Constance's safety now blossomed into full-grown fear—not just for her but also for our whole household. My brother had humiliated Harcourt at *La Lampe et Le Chien,* and I'd beaten them and helped Rose escape from the basement when they were supposed to watch us. They had more on their minds than just a stroll with two young girls. On shaking legs, I stepped sideways, hiding behind a couple, and hoped the two men hadn't seen me.

When I heard no response to my call, I peeked around those in front of me and confirmed the four had resumed their walk. I swallowed hard and continued to work my way forward, keeping a close eye on the group in case I had to duck again if they turned around. At the park entrance, they joined the crowds crossing the Thames along the Victoria Bridge.

I did the same, all the time running various scenarios in my head. Would they return to our townhouse? What purpose did these two men have for the girls? I thought of the brief interview Mother had with Lizette from *La Lampe et Le Chien.* Harcourt had shared about bringing prostitutes from France to England. Did the trade flow the other way as well? Was this his plan for the two they were escorting today?

And could there be even more malevolence on their mind? If the two maids were convinced to let them in our townhouse...

Anger and fear charged through my body. Not only did I need to protect my friend Constance, but I also had to ensure the safety of my family as well.

While I considered somehow passing them to arrive at

the townhouse first, I dismissed the idea. What if they chose an objective other than our house? I wouldn't be aware of any detour. I held my breath as they reached the corner of Hyde Park. If they went right, they would head to our townhouse. Left would mean another destination. My heart picked up its beat again as they separated: the girls toward Grosvenor Square, the men back in my direction. For one heartbeat, I froze, deciding whom to follow.

Simms and Edmonds had orchestrated Lord Surminster's death and that of his father, but Harcourt and Tennyson were connected to those murders as well as Crandall's. Rose and *La Lampe et Le Chien* certainly tied several of the Edmonds with these two. Perhaps they were all investors in the trading of women between the two countries? My stomach squeezed as I remembered the studied review Nathan Edmonds had made of Constance that night we met him outside the opera house. Scotland Yard had caught the first two, but I now saw how the whole enterprise encompassed much more than them. And I wasn't going to let these two slip from me or the law.

I stepped into a side street to wait for my two kidnappers to pass as I continued my pursuit. Big Ben chimed out six o'clock. Fewer people filled the streets—probably to return home for the evening—and made it more difficult for me to hide. As I let the distance between us grow, they were barely within my sight most of the time. If they turned a corner, I might lose them for good.

After a half hour when they were several blocks ahead, two urchins stopped me, asking for a ha'penny for a hot cross bun. Both were the same grimy gray from head to foot, one perhaps a year or two older than I. Reaching into my pocket for the coins I'd been handing out earlier, I glanced

THE ADVENTURE OF THE DECEASED SCHOLAR

back up the street and realized the men were hard to distinguish in the evening light.

About to push the boys aside to continue my tracking, a stroke of inspiration hit me. Pulling out two coins, I said, "I'll give you a whole penny each, if you'll do something for me."

The older one studied me with a frown and asked, "Ain't nuthin' criminal, is it?"

"Nothing like that." I had to admire his caution. I supposed it was a little difficult for them to consider the police as on their side. They were more likely to be on the receiving end. "Just bring a policeman to me. You bring one here, and I'll give you each a penny."

"Why don't you goes and gets a copper yerself?" he said, pulling back his chin.

"Because I'm watching those two men in the top hats up there," I said, pointing to Harcourt and Tennyson's backs slipping even farther up the street. I turned my head to show the bruise and scrapes on my face. "They did this to me. The police are looking for them. All you have to do is find an officer and bring him here so he can arrest the two."

"Lors," he said, staring at my face, then at his companion, and then up the street. "They's already gettin' away." Turning to the other boy, he said, "Charlie, you goes and get the bobby, and brings him up this way. I gots me an idea of how to keep them here, but I'll need a few more pennies. You just hang back, mate, and waits for Charlie."

Both boys held out their hands, but I shook my head. "Not until the policeman arrives."

The older gave Charlie a nod. "Off you goes."

"Righto, Stevie," Charlie said with a little salute. "A copper for a copper."

As much as I appreciated his clever comment, I found it impossible to smile, let alone laugh. Time seemed to be slipping faster by the second. It wouldn't be long before these two would initiate their plan with Adeline and Constance, and most likely, against my family.

Charlie took off in one direction and Stevie in another. I continued to follow my quarry at a distance, but the rapidly thinning crowd made the task more difficult. Not to mention I feared my penny offer to the boys had been insufficient. While I wasn't too familiar with London, I recognized we were again approaching the river, but toward a different bridge than the one to Battersea Park. Just as Harcourt and Tennyson reached a corner and turned toward the side street, a group of urchins surrounded them, led by Stevie.

Intrigued, I stepped closer to the scene playing out in front of me. With the streets near empty, the boys' voices were clear in the evening air.

"Mister, you gots any *min*?" Stevie asked, using a term for money I'd learned from Constance.

Harcourt swatted at the group. "Out of my way, boy."

"Come on, mister," he said, stepping up to him. Two others blocked Tennyson's path. "Just a penny or two? It's Easter. Even Her Majesty gives out somethin' for the day. Aren't you better than the queen?"

"She gave out coins last week, you twit," Harcourt said. "Let me pass."

One of the other boys held out his hand. "Will for a penny."

As if on cue, all the boys held out their hands and chanted over and over, "A penny to pass."

Two or three of the braver ones even fished in the men's pockets to see what they could find. The two men were so unnerved by this group of ragamuffins, they seemed unable to fight off the grasping hands, pinning them to the same spot on the street.

In what was most likely a fit of frustration, Harcourt grabbed one of the street arabs by his shirt front and raised him up to eye level. "Leave me be, boy, or I'll thrash you within an inch of your life."

The boy let out a shriek that notified everyone in the surrounding area of something untoward happening. His shriek called a number of those in the area toward the man and him, and they created a second circle around the boys. The two men and the still-squirming boy remained in the center. Some of the adults shouted the urchins should be arrested. Others shouted at the men to leave the "poor boys" be. Soon, everyone was shouting at everyone else, blocking my captors in.

Before my two targets could extract themselves from the commotion, another set of shouts, pounding footsteps, and a high-pitched whistle came from behind me. Charlie raced past me with a police officer not far behind. I had no idea what Charlie had done, but I needed to redirect the policeman's attention to the true criminals before they got away. Without a second thought, I followed the policeman toward the corner.

Charlie pulled to a stop just in front of the crowd. The officer did the same, letting the whistle drop from his mouth. He remained dumbfounded for several seconds as he seemed to assess all the actors in this little scene. Those gathered were still throwing accusations at each other, and the officer's shouted questions were lost in the overall din.

In growing frustration, he let out one long, shrill blast on his whistle, and silence reigned. Surveying the group, he asked, "What, in blue blazes, is going on here?"

The adults, the boys, and my former captors resumed their hollering at each other and at the officer, creating such a clamor, nothing was intelligible. The bobby gave one more blast on his whistle, forcing everyone to cover their ears. I felt this was a good point for me to provide some clarity and stepped up to the policeman.

"Excuse me, officer," I said. "Please allow me to explain—"

Harcourt glared at me and stabbed a finger in my direction. "You. You're behind all this, aren't you?" He turned to the officer. "He beat my friend and me almost within an inch of our lives."

My mouth dropped open. This was too much. How could he accuse me of assault? By the time I understood his efforts to turn the tables on me and faced the officer, I'd lost my momentum in the overall argument. "Only because he was holding me in a basement until Simms could kill me. Just ask Inspector Harrison of Scotland Yard. He works with Inspector Roggens and came to our house yesterday."

Before he could respond to my suggestion, three more police officers appeared—most likely called by his whistle.

"What's going on, Wagner?" the one with more gold braid on his shoulders than the others asked.

Wagner studied the crowd before him and pointed to Charlie. "This one was harrassin' the people on the street. I chased 'im all the way here. And then I find an all-out brawl between these people,"—he swept his arm over the crowd and then pointed to Harcourt and Tennyson—"and these two—who this one says caged him in a basement."

Seeing the new one was obviously in command, I

addressed my next words to him. "If you please, sir, find Inspector Harrison of—"

"Bring 'em all in," the commander said. "We'll straighten it out at the station."

Wagner glanced about the assembled. "All of them, sir?"

"Yes. Well, no." He pointed at me, Charlie, and Harcourt and Tennyson. "They appear to be the ones at the center of it all."

As soon as the police had determined who was to be arrested, the rest of the crowd melted away without a word or glance to the four of us now in the hands of the law. I then knew the humiliation my poor brother had suffered when the nipper had been slipped around his wrist. My only consolation was Harcourt and Tennyson experienced the same.

We were told we had to wait for a wagon, and try as I might, I couldn't get anyone to pay attention to my requests to send word to my parents or Inspector Harrison.

"The copper wouldn't listen to me either," Charlie whispered after I slumped onto the road next to him. "That's when I came up with the idea of beggin' money from the dandies on the street. I gots me a ha'penny afore I gots his attention."

While I admired the boy's ingenuity, I could only muster a weak smile. If the police wouldn't listen to me because they viewed me a child, would they believe Harcourt and Tennyson because they were adults? If they slipped from me now, I'd not see them again until they carried out whatever they planned for revenge.

When we arrived at the police station, the officers removed the nippers and ordered us to sit on benches in some sort of waiting area behind what could best be described as a reception desk. Policemen came and went, along with various individuals I assumed had also been arrested. Each time someone passed, I glanced up in hopes of identifying a familiar face and each time, my spirits dropped lower. I was so far from Grosvenor Square, I doubted anyone from my family would ever discover my whereabouts. So deep in despair and my own thoughts of spending the night in a London gaol, I didn't even hear when someone first called my name. Charlie jabbed me in the ribs and said, "I think they're lookin' for you."

Raising my head, a policeman asked, "Are you Sherlock Holmes?"

A new dread knotted my stomach. I had observed enough of my own father's proceedings to know I was most likely being brought before a magistrate. With a gulp, I stood and followed the officer on trembling knees. They almost gave way when I saw my father on the other side of the reception desk.

With a glance back at my escort, who nodded his assent, I rushed forward, only to slow to a more refined speed when I caught sight of his frown. The officer at the desk asked, "This your boy?"

"Yes. Thank you," he said and then turned to me. "Let's go."

I hesitated. "Please, sir. We can't yet."

"Cheeky little mite, ain't he?" the officer asked.

Father's eyebrows drew into a V, warning me I'd passed beyond anything he would tolerate. "What do you mean, 'can't'?"

"I found Harcourt and Tennyson. They are in the back with me. The police wouldn't listen to me, but—"

Father raised his hand to stop me and faced the officer. "May I see your commander?"

IT WAS ALMOST midnight when the two of us finally arrived home. I'd managed to convince my father to arrange for Charlie's release, along with a reward for having assisted in the arrest of Harcourt and Tennyson. These last two were at last safely ensconced in gaol until their trial, and while I faced a reckoning with my parents, I had no doubt I'd be forgiven when everything came to light.

My mother and brother were waiting in the drawing room, and I could see Mrs. Simpson, Constance, and Adeline gathered in the back of the hallway, also anticipating our return. After a long embrace from my mother and a slap on the back from Mycroft, Mrs. Simpson and Constance came in with tea and sandwiches. Only then did I realize how hungry I was, and I stuffed two of the small triangles into my mouth at once.

"I have to know," Mycroft said, breaking the silence in the room. "How did you wind up in a police station?"

During the cab-ride to the townhouse, I'd developed a storyline to keep Constance and Adeline out of it as much as possible. My parents could forgive me, but Constance might not receive as much sympathy. I limited Constance and Adeline's role to leading me to Battersea Park where I'd seen Harcourt and Tennyson and followed them from there. With me safe at home and my kidnappers in gaol, my family was relaxed enough to laugh at the melee the boys created just before my arrest.

The mantel clock chimed half-past midnight when

Mother rose. "I can't believe tomorrow is Easter Monday," she said. "Sherlock, you have a week to recuperate, and part of that regimen is rest. It's high time we all retired."

"However," Father said and took Mother's arm, "there's something we must do tomorrow as a family."

CHAPTER SIXTEEN

After breakfast on Easter Monday, Mother, Father, and I made a special pilgrimage to the small hospital where Inspector Roggens lay recovering. To my surprise, we weren't the only ones at his bedside. Officer Douglas and Inspector Harrison were there as well.

The inspector had a private room with a wrought-iron bed and a small bedside table holding a pitcher and a glass. An open window let in a light breeze and sounds from those passing on the street. Several pillows propped him up to a sitting position. Although his face was pale and he needed a shave, he appeared in good spirits and didn't seem to be suffering too great a discomfort from his injury. His right arm was in a sling, tied close to his body.

"Squire and Mrs. Holmes, Sherlock," Roggens said in a rather rough voice, "how kind of you to come."

After we exchanged greetings with the other Scotland Yarder and the uniformed officer, Roggens assured us he was on the road to a complete recovery. We also passed around the basket of hot cross buns Cook had prepared for a gift.

"You were very fortunate," Mother said. "The bullet missed several bones and a major artery in the area. My son will also suffer little permanent damage, thank goodness."

"You were lucky Nathan Edmonds was the one who fired," I said.

Roggens peered at me. "You saw who fired the revolver?"

"No, sir. Percy pushed me to the ground. I didn't see anything but the street. But if Simms had been the one to shoot, he would have aimed to kill. He's a crack shot who can dispatch an animal with precision."

Harrison glanced at his two colleagues, and Roggens nodded at him before addressing us. "The inspector was bringing me up to date. I don't see why he can't continue. This family probably knows more about some of it than we do."

"Right," he said, after a sideways study of the convalescent. "As I was saying, Simms and Edmonds turned one on the other almost as soon as we arrested them. Simms has been skimming the trust for a number of years, and Edmonds made a very lucrative business of keeping the lawsuit going and charging his fees. Simms sold a piece of land to the estate for more than it was worth. Old Lord Surminster found out, and so's Simms poisoned him."

"Arsenic," I said.

Roggens faced me. "Right. Got it from the earl's workshop."

"And the recent Lord Surminster?" Mother asked. "Was he poisoned too?"

Harrison shook his head. "The gamesman Clement

THE ADVENTURE OF THE DECEASED SCHOLAR

overheard Simms and Edmonds arguing one day. Seems Simms wanted to do something similar again—selling more land, that is—and Edmonds was saying how the current Lord Surminster was asking questions about the lawsuit and trust, and he might get suspicious. Appears he'd checked into his grandfather, Lord Thanbury, and found out the man was at death's door. He'd gone to Edmonds to review the suit and asked about what would happen if the man died."

"Clement must have contacted Lord Surminster. That's why he stole the map. To compare the original with the one Edmonds had," Mother said quietly as if thinking out loud. "Simms and Edmonds somehow captured the two men, but"—she turned to Harrison—"why the noose? Who did that?"

"That'd be Simms. He and Edmonds tricked both Clement and Lord Surminster into coming to the same house where they held Master Sherlock. Maurice Edmonds, Crandall, and others use it for private parties. Bring in girls from *La Lampe et Le Chien*, play cards, drink—things they can't do at their clubs. Simms and Edmonds tried to drug the two men to find out what they knew, but they used too much and the men passed out. Simms said they couldn't let them go. He found Rose's hair pin and used it to keep from making a bloody mess."

"As I mentioned earlier," I said, "he prefers a clean kill."

The inspector studied me for a moment with obvious contempt for my commentary. "Yes. As I was saying, they decided the only way to avoid more investigations into their shenanigans was to put Lord Surminster's family under their power. If they made it appear as if he committed suicide by putting the noose around his neck, leaving the marked-up photo of a girl in his pocket, covering up the wound in his ear, and then throwing him in the river, Miss Phillips would be more likely to agree to marry Jared Edmonds. Changing the clothes and the Cambridge jacket—all that was to throw off identifying them so fast. Of course, they didn't check the pockets, and the putty washed out in the river. That's why Edmonds took the body—to hide it again."

"They might have gotten away with it if my wife hadn't become involved," Father said.

Another studied glance and "yes" from Harrison—only this time directed at my father. I would have liked to point out it was a joint effort between her, Mycroft, and me, but I let it slide. More than once, Father had made it clear the family needed to show a united front to outsiders. Besides, Harrison was probably showing similar support to his colleague.

"And Harcourt and Tennyson?" I asked. "What will you charge them with?"

"Accessory to attempted murder and kidnapping among others," the Inspector Harrison said. "We also went to *La Lampe et Le Chien* to see if we could find this Rose woman or any other witnesses. It was empty, cleaned out. Where they moved them to is anybody's guess at the moment."

While my parents and I absorbed this bit of information, I regretted knowing the women from the night-house were most likely still in the same predicament as before—only in a different establishment. No wonder Rose took flight the first chance presented to her, and I wished her well whatever her fate.

As I continued to consider what the inspector had shared, I grew annoyed. We'd done a great service to the

Yarders, including most likely saving Roggens' life. While our role might be difficult to acknowledge, surely a little gratitude could be shown.

As if he could read my mind, Roggens turned to my mother. "Mrs. Holmes, I will be forever in your debt. The surgeon said your ministrations when I was shot probably saved my life."

"And your quick thinking at the trial probably saved a family from losing all," she said with a small smile. "We shouldn't keep you longer. You need your rest. I do hope you will call once you are well. It would be nice to have you for an unofficial visit."

ON THE CARRIAGE ride back to our town house, I stared out the window, considering the events of the last week as well as my future back at Eton.

Mother must have noticed my pensive expression because she asked, "What's troubling you, Sherry dear?"

"Several things, but mostly the nun's chest," I said, turning my attention back to my parents. "I was certain everyone was searching for it."

"It did seem to be a logical explanation. And you did discover it." She nodded.

"Only it turned out not to be a treasure at all. At least what we would consider valuable."

"And it almost cost you your life," Father said, meeting my gaze. "And Mycroft's."

My stomach squeezed at his observation, and I regretted that third hot cross bun I'd eaten at breakfast.

"I think the lesson in this is to not jump to conclusions

until enough information is collected," Mother said. "Or at least not voice them until you have the data in hand."

"I suppose," I said, returning to the view out the window.

ONCE WE ARRIVED HOME, we shared with Mycroft what Inspectors Harrison and Roggens had said at the hospital, and Mother assured Mycroft if his convalescence continued on the right path, he would be able to return to Oxford for his studies within a few weeks.

"And, of course, I will provide you with some exercises to work the arm muscles," she said in conclusion.

He frowned. "Exercise? Seriously?"

"If you want complete recovery, you need to build up the strength in your arm. Having it lie still will weaken it. You do want to be able to hold a young woman's hand while dancing?"

Mycroft's eyes widened. "You're not suggesting I must again—"

He stopped when Mother chuckled at his outburst. "When you can be so caustic over the suggestion of a few social events, I know you're on the mend."

The three of us shared her amusement, and for the first time in days, the tension I'd felt in my neck relaxed.

The anxiety returned only minutes later, however, when we left Mycroft. Mother turned to me and said, "Sherry dear, will you please come to my sitting room for a moment?"

Constance was waiting on a stool by the fire and popped up when we stepped into the room. Instinctively, I moved next to her. Mother had brought us together for a reason, and I felt compelled to defend my friend.

After she shut the door, Mother paced in front of us for two circuits before turning to say, "I want to know the full truth of what occurred this week."

I peeked at Constance and shifted on my feet. With no idea of what Mother suspected, I was uncertain how best to respond without giving away anything she didn't already know.

When neither of us responded, she tapped her finger to her lips and said, "Let me tell you what I have observed and what it suggests. When I returned with Mr. Holmes from his dinner with Sires, Constance's face still held some marks of face powder, and my makeup and the pearls I used in my hair had been disturbed. In addition, Mrs. Simpson reported Constance had disappeared some time during the evening. Regardless of what you reported to Inspector Roggens, I concluded Constance was never in the library. And then you just happened upon Harcourt and Tennyson when you went to look for Constance and Adeline. I believe the odds against this being a coincidence are too great. No, Harcourt and Tennyson were the girls' escorts that afternoon—who Mrs. Simpson reported as being 'Adeline's brothers.' Now, tell me where I erred."

My friend had maintained a stoic face during this recitation but burst into tears when my mother concluded. "Please, ma'am, it was all on me. Sherlock didn't do nothin'."

"But he did," Mother said, her mouth now a thin line. "He lied for you. And he sought to protect you and got himself taken in by the police. At the same time, his quick actions probably saved this whole household—even you.

Did you truly believe two men of their standing had any good intentions when they stepped out with you and Adeline—two serving girls? I'm sorry, Constance, for putting it so bluntly. I should take you to meet the women at *La Lampe et Le Chien*. Hear their sad tales. Did they offer to take you to France? To sing there? My guess is they planned to sell you to a brothel. Where you'd be locked in forever."

This admonishment forced even deeper sobs from Constance. An urge to comfort her washed over me, but Mother continued, rooting me in place.

"You must learn not everyone sees the potential Sherlock and I see in you. They only see your current status and will abuse you because of it. Were they not planning to meet you later? Perhaps at a back entrance to this house? You two could be easily overpowered, and they could have harmed everyone in the house to exact revenge."

Constance was sobbing now as the full weight of her actions hit her. Her tears stemmed from a humiliation similar to my own. Some of her actions squarely fell on my own shoulders. I'd ignored her to some extent. Prior to arriving in London, I had plans to show her the city. Then again, I hadn't considered being involved in solving yet another murder. Without any direction from me, she'd followed her own desires.

Mother paced a bit more before stopping in front of us. I dropped my gaze to the carpet and could feel Constance cringe under her scrutiny. "I truly debated what I should do and say to you," she said. "Adeline will be dismissed. I'll give her a good reference, but I'll not tolerate such a simpleton in my house. You, Constance, I can forgive your naiveté about the city and its dangers. At the same time, you knew what

THE ADVENTURE OF THE DECEASED SCHOLAR

you did wasn't correct, or there would have been no need for deception on your part."

My friend sniffled. "Yes, ma'am. Should I pack now? I suppose you'll be sendin' me home directly."

I raised my head. Constance leaving? Was Mother dismissing her too? My heart squeezed in my chest. Losing her from the household seemed too much for me to bear. Before I could protest, make a plea for the girl, Mother shook her head.

"No. I'm not sending you back or dismissing you—at present. You are now under a new trial period. Perhaps I've been too tolerant of some of your behavior. We'll be returning to Underbyrne shortly. When we do, there will be a strict schedule for you to follow. If you truly wish to better yourself, you have much to learn. That includes French."

"Excuse me?" she asked.

I stared at my mother as well, unable to determine the connection between the language and Constance's studies—other than she thought learning the language would assist in her studying opera.

"It was going to be a surprise," Mother said, her voice calmer now. "I've been in contact with my family in Paris regarding some…affairs I must attend to this summer. It would be helpful if you were able to use at least some simple phrases while there."

My friend and I exchanged quick glances. Were her eyes as round as mine? Mother had discussed such a trip before, but I had no idea the plan had advanced to such a degree. In that moment, I promised myself to stand guard over my friend for the next week and in the trip to come. If London was considered dangerous, I saw Paris as being even more filled with temptations. My duty as a gentleman was to protect my friend, and I wouldn't shirk from it.

Mother's shoulders relaxed, but her mouth didn't lose its tight line. "I expect you two to be on your best behavior for the rest of the holiday. Paris will only be achieved if you apply yourselves as you should. For you, Sherry dear, that means completing your studies at Eton, and Constance, making the most of your lessons as well."

Constance bounced on her toes. "Oh, yes, ma'am."

"As for Mycroft"—a smile played on Mother's lips—"if the young ladies in London don't appeal to him, perhaps a young Parisienne will. As it did for my father."

Despite the scolding we'd just received, my mind filled with the images of Paris I'd seen in the paintings and sketches here and back at Underbyrne. I couldn't help but wonder what "The City of Light" would hold for us.

Thank you for reading *The Adventure of the Deceased Scholar*. I hope you love this young Sherlock Holmes and his family as much as I do. The next book in *The Early Case Files of Sherlock Holmes* series continues his story during a summer vacation in Paris. Sherlock must unravel the meaning behind a compromising sketch of his mother and its subsequent theft —coming later in 2021.

To find out about all my news on upcoming books and appearances, sign up for my newsletter. Or follow me on Bookbub. New subscribers on either get a special book exclusively available to those who sign up.

THE ADVENTURE OF THE DECEASED SCHOLAR

This series requires quite a bit of research on Victorian England as well as Sherlock Holmes. If you'd like to learn more about the era, read my essays on *The Life and Times of Sherlock Holmes*. These short articles cover a variety of subjects—from Sherlock's ancestry to jellyfish (one appears in one of the original cases).

Turn the page for an excerpt from *The Adventure of the Purloined Portrait*.

The Adventure of the Purloined Portrait
Excerpt

Mother had always been the family rock—the one that could withstand all life's vicissitudes—but even a rock had faults that could break it apart under extreme pressure. This thought caused the pit of my stomach to roil, and not from the churning waves against our ship.

"Do you have the feeling this trip may be a mistake?" I asked Mycroft.

While I continued to stare over the ship's railing, I caught him turn toward me in the corner of my eye. "The crossing is almost over. You'll feel better when you get on dry land, Sherlock."

Shifting my gaze to him, I gave him a hard stare. "You know what I mean. Mother hasn't been the same since Easter. Out of the blue, she announces we're going to Paris while you're still recovering from a gunshot wound. And she'd been distracted before that. We both noticed it."

My brother and I both inherited our Mother's composed nature. I had rarely seen her rattled, but during our Easter holiday in London, she appeared preoccupied by matters she never expressed to either of us. At the time, I had put it down to concern over my father's efforts to invest in a business venture with an old school chum as well as Mycroft's wounding at the hands of his kidnapper. Both, however, were now behind us. The investment had produced a modest return, and I saw no lingering problems related to Mycroft's injury. All the same, we barely arrived home from school before she had packed our trunks and shuffled us all off to Newhaven for the steamship ride to Dieppe.

"I do believe bringing the entire family is a ruse," he said after his own inspection of the sea.

"Including Uncle Ernest in the trip did surprise me." Her brother rarely left the estate or his workshop. "Perhaps she thinks it will do him some good. I understand they were happy growing up there."

His gaze drifted upward toward the trailing coal smoke from the steam engine powering the screw propelling the ship forward. "If she was so happy there, why doesn't she seem to show it? She may *say* she's excited, but I find it all a façade. What do you think is behind her sudden interest in the trip?"

I ran through all the scenarios—from something as benign as a sudden bout of nostalgia to a fatal illness calling her back to see her French relatives one last time—that would explain her urgency and shook my head. "Without more information, I would only be speculating. You yourself have said that can be counterproductive. Whatever the reason, it has truly unnerved her. I turned back to the ocean, seeking any indication of the coastline. "Whatever it is lies in Paris."

Footsteps behind us caused us both to turn around. My mother's maid Constance approached us. "Your mother asked me to let you know there's tea in the cabin—if you want some."

"I would," Mycroft said. He turned to me one last time before he headed inside. "I suppose we'll know your answers soon enough."

My stomach gave another turn, but I didn't voice the

concern that came with the sensation--that the answers I sought might not be one I wanted to learn.

Constance stepped to the rail next to me and leaned her forearms against the top rung. We'd become friends when I'd returned home after my mother had been accused of murder. She'd been a great help to me in various adventures, and Mother had taken her under her wing to develop both her singing voice as well as her education. She was traveling with us as her lady's maid.

I took a similar pose to hers against the rail, enjoying the ocean's scent and letting the wind whip the hair from my face. Licking my lips, I savored the salt spray that seasoned them.

Letting out a soft "ooh," she took in the white-foamed waves reaching as far as we could see under a clear, cerulean sky. I tried to see it from her point of view but couldn't shake the anxiety remaining in my core.

She turned to me and a loose tendril of her red hair whipped across her face. As much as the untidy strand annoyed me, I resisted the urge to tuck it behind her ear. Social etiquette dictated that a young man wasn't to have such contact with a young woman—especially one who was his mother's maid.

To my relief, she moved the hair herself. "How long until we can see France?"

"The trip is supposed to take three hours. I'm not sure how long before we can see the coast."

"Will it be as hot there as in England?"

"I hope not."

The weather had been oppressive for more than a month now—with no rain to offer even temporary relief. The fields around Underbyrne, our family estate, held only dried, withered stalks, and the beehives my father had added to one back field hummed with a multitude of tiny wings fanning the hive to keep it cool.

"I can't believe we're goin' to Paris," she said, a joyful smile playing on her lips. "The farthest I've been from home was that trip to London with your family. Now Paris. What's it like?"

I shrugged. "I've only seen pictures, but I think it will be a lot like London in some ways."

She shifted back around to face the ocean. "Well, I'm not goin' to waste a minute not enjoyin' it. Like this boat ride. I ain't—er, haven't—been on anything this big in my life. It's like a floatin' hotel. Goin' to get me some tea on a boat—"

"Ship." She squinted a question at me. "It's a ship. Don't let the crew hear you call it a boat. Ships are bigger."

"Well, I'm goin' to get me some tea on this *ship* so's I can tell my brothers and sisters I had me some."

She flounced off, leaving me to ponder exactly what lay ahead and hoping I would soon know.

Coming in 2021

ACKNOWLEDGMENTS

Many eyes viewed earlier versions of this manuscript, and I am grateful to all these readers' comments, remarks, and corrections. I would like to especially thank the following: Nancy Alvey, Janet Wildeboor, and Liz Lipperman. A special thanks to two Alicias: Alicia Dean for her editorial review and comments and Alicia at iProofread and More for her review and final editing. Any errors that remain are my own.

Shortly after reading the final draft of this book, Dr. Sally Sugarman passed quite unexpectedly. Although we never met in person (Covid prevented a planned meeting in the fall of 2020), her support and enjoyment of my works provided a special inspiration to me. She will be sorely missed by me and all those whose lives she touched.

ABOUT THE AUTHOR

Liese Sherwood-Fabre knew she was destined to write when she got an A+ in the second grade for her story about Dick, Jane, and Sally's ruined picnic. After obtaining her PhD from Indiana University, she joined the federal government and had the opportunity to work and live internationally for more than fifteen years. After returning to the states, she seriously pursued her writing career. She is currently a member of The Crew of the Barque Lone Star and the Studious Scarlets Society scions and contributes regularly to Sherlockian newsletters across the world.

You can follow her upcoming releases and other events by joining her newsletter at: www. liesesherwoodfabre.com

KEEP UP WITH THE LATEST NEWS FROM LIESE SHERWOOD-FABRE

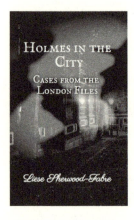

Follow Liese on Bookbub to receive automatic notices of future new releases and special promotions. Also receive a free short story collection of traditional Holmes mysteries set in London. Use the QRC code to find her Bookbub page and email her at liese@liesesherwoodfabre.com so that she can send you the book.

Visit liesesherwoodfabre.com to sign up for her newsletter and another free story. George Henley wants revenge on his ex-wife and ex-business partner. But is the hit man's price more than he bargained for?

THE NEW AUDIOBOOK FROM LIESE SHERWOOD-FABRE

Missing boys, an imposter husband, and a bizarre vampyre murder.

Sherlock Holmes ventures into the realm of the unnatural in these three cases: the disappearance of the Baker Street Irregulars, the true identity of a Great War veteran, and a vampyre's grisly death. Crossing into the worlds of the Grimm Brothers and Bram Stoker, he seeks the clues needed to unravel the mysteries confronting him. Can Holmes' conventional methods still function in the unconventional world?

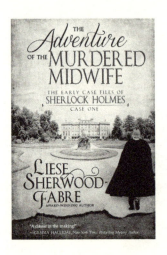

Only Sherlock Holmes can save his mother from the gallows

Violette Holmes has been accused of murdering the village midwife. The dead woman was found in the garden, a pitchfork in the back, after a public argument with Mrs. Holmes. After being called back from Eton because of the scandal surrounding the arrest, Violette tasks Sherlock with collecting the evidence needed to prove her innocence. The village constable will stop at nothing to convict her. Can Sherlock save her from hanging?

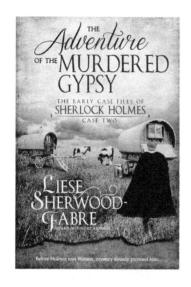

What's Christmas without surprises?

It's winter 1867 at Underbyrne, the Holmes family estate. The house is filled with family, relatives, and three unexpected arrivals—all ready to celebrate the holidays. That is, until another uninvited guest appears: dead in the stables.

The discovery marks the beginning of a series of bizarre occurrences: Sherlock's young cousin reports hearing footsteps outside the nursery, Mycroft suddenly falls head-over-heels in love, and the family learns more than one person under their roof harbors secrets.

Is someone in the household a murderer? Sherlock must discover the dead man's identity before another unwelcomed body materializes.

Made in the USA
Las Vegas, NV
20 September 2022